THE
PERFECT
CANDIDATE

THE PERFECT CANDIDATE

PETER STONE

SIMON & SCHUSTER BFYR

New York · London · Toronto · Sydney · New Delhi

SIMON & SCHUSTER BFYR
An imprint of Simon & Schuster Children's Publishing Division
1230 Avenue of the Americas, New York, New York 10020

For information about special discounts for bulk purchases, please contact Simon & Schuster Special Sales at 1-866-506-1949 or business@simonandschuster.com.
The Simon & Schuster Speakers Bureau can bring authors to your live event. For more information or to book an event, contact the Simon & Schuster Speakers Bureau at 1-866-248-3049 or visit our website at www.simonspeakers.com.
Jacket design by Greg Stadnyk
Interior design by Hilary Zarycky
The text for this book was set in Electra.
Manufactured in the United States of America
First Edition
10 9 8 7 6 5 4 3 2 1
Library of Congress Cataloging-in-Publication Data
Names: Stone, Peter (Media marketing consultant), author.
Title: The perfect candidate / Peter Stone.
Description: First edition. | New York : Simon & Shuster Books for Young Readers, [2018] | Summary: When Cameron Carter goes straight from high school in small-town California to a summer internship with a powerful U.S. Congressman he admires, he soon learns that not everything in Washington, D.C. is as it appears.
Identifiers: LCCN 2017040211 | ISBN 9781534422179 (hardcover) | ISBN 9721534422193 (eBook)
Subjects: | CYAC: Internship programs—Fiction. | Interpersonal relations—Fiction. | Legislators—Fiction. | Political corruption—Fiction. | Washington (D.C.)—Fiction. Classification: LCC PZ7.1.S7548 Per 2018 | DDC [Fic]—dc23
LC record available at https://lccn.loc.gov/2017040211

For X and T

"Washington is a very easy city for you to forget where you came from and why you got there in the first place."
—HARRY S. TRUMAN

"Everybody feels the evil, but no one has courage or energy enough to seek the cure."
—ALEXIS DE TOCQUEVILLE, *Democracy in America*

THE
PERFECT
CANDIDATE

Prologue—
The End of the Summer

You don't notice it at first.

Initially, you see our nation's next Speaker of the House, whose all-American grin is rivaled only by the *pick me!* smiles of the interns surrounding him. You see the gleaming, upright dome of the Capitol in the background—lodged into the building like some massive, neoclassical Fabergé egg. You see good, uncomfortable posture.

It *is* the official summer intern photo op we are looking at here. A glossy eight-by-ten, automatically sent by the Capitol photographer's office to summer interns' homes, a few weeks after they drain out of the city. It's the picture that will hit the proud local papers. The one that will stay on the refrigerator.

And in my case, some FBI file.

You don't notice it at first, but then you can't not see it.

It's the sweat pouring from my forehead, matting down my hair, and tickling the end of my nose. But I'm not sweating because it's hot.

It's the outline of two cell phones—one in each pocket of my khakis.

It's the smiles that aren't really smiles—at least not mine. How can you smile when someone is trying to kill you?

That summer was supposed to be my *Mr. Smith Goes to Washington*, the movie my high school government teacher had shown three times: at the beginning and end of the year and before winter break. He really should have just shown us the sequel: *Mr. Smith Goes to Washington, Where Secrets Get You Killed*. And the sequel to that: *Mr. Smith Goes to Hell*.

Forgive the strong language.

"Offensive speech" was forbidden in the intern manual they gave us on day one, after all. I just seemed to have some difficulty following the rules that summer. The first page listed guidelines of conduct for interns:

1. *No offensive speech*
2. *Don't talk to strangers (e.g., press!). Report suspicious individuals to intern supervisor*
3. *Do what you are asked*
4. *Be safe*

5. *Only enter the congressman's office when invited/accompanied*
6. *Ask questions!*
7. *Don't e-mail any sensitive documents that you wouldn't want to see plastered all over the political blogs within hours*
8. *Build our congressman's reputation!*
9. *You're not here to change the world*
10. *Have fun!*

I technically followed only one of them.

I asked questions.

Just not the ones they wanted to hear.

Oh, and I had a little fun, too.

1

The taxi was going eighty miles per hour. And we weren't even on the freeway yet.

When the driver made eye contact with me through the rearview mirror, I quickly hunched down in the back seat so that he wouldn't think I questioned his judgment.

"You think I'm going too fast," he taunted.

"No, no, it's fine." I shrugged with a brief smile, not quite grasping the courtesy I felt obliged to offer the man (I *was* paying him, after all).

As we left the Dulles airport, I saw a sign illuminated in the night sky: Virginia State Route 267.

We *were* moving too fast. Everything was moving too fast.

Three days before, I was graduating from high school, on a dusty and dry May night. The kind of heat that California's

Central Valley conjures up to warn you about the punishing summer ahead. Three nights ago, I was hugging and selfie-ing and lying to everyone that we would "totally keep in touch."

I guess they were *mostly* good people. Though among the graduating class were the guys who'd dipped me into a trash can, headfirst, as congratulations for winning the sixth-grade spelling bee. And the girls who pretended not to know me as they sat poolside and I mowed their parents' backyard lawns for my dad's landscaping business. And the vice principal who ratted out Ingrid Cuevas's family to the immigration authorities, which meant our student body president/softball team captain disappeared after spring break a couple months ago.

Okay, maybe they weren't mostly good people. But for some reason, three thousand miles away, hurtling toward an unknown city and a lesser-known summer internship, I missed home.

"It's late on a Sunday night—no traffic. We'll get to DC in no time," barked the driver, over the soft jazz station he'd tuned the radio to. "So where'd you fly in from?"

"Lagrima," I shouted back.

Pronounced *Luh-GRIME-uh*. My hometown was no exception to the grand tradition of California cities named after Spanish words with butchered pronunciations. The English translation of the word was chillingly accurate: tears. As in, *This town makes me cry*.

"La-what?" he shot back.

"It's basically San Francisco," I answered.

"Basically San Francisco": two hours inland, filled with tract homes past their prime and abandoned strip malls.

"So are you coming home or leaving home?" asked the driver, as progressive exit signs announced unfamiliar suburbs: Reston, Wolf Trap, Falls Church . . .

"Coming home," I lied. I'd be going to Lagrima Junior College in the fall, but one could dream. Or at least pretend.

"You work? In school?"

"I work for Congressman Billy Beck."

Summer intern, to be more precise.

I needed the internship because my mom met my dad while she worked for the Department of Agriculture in DC eighteen years ago. She got her start as a summer intern and then landed a full-time gig after graduating from the University of Virginia. Your parents show you your paths. And when your dad shoots horse manure pellets into rich people's lawns, and your mom once helped run the country—you choose your mom's path.

"Powerful man," observed the driver. "If the Dems take back the House in November, he'll be the new Speaker."

"You follow politics?" I was impressed.

"It's DC," he said. "Politics follow everyone."

Suddenly both talkative and surprisingly civic-minded, the

driver started ranting about none other than health care reform and if I could please do something about lower deductibles.

I nodded, but my thoughts were drifting.

To when my parents fell in love, or something like it, and I came along. And when my mom left the East Coast so she could get married and raise me. In that crap hole of a town. She went from senate hearings and lobbyist lunches to strip malls and cold cuts. I planned to do the reverse.

A semitruck started to merge into our lane, and the driver slammed the car horn and actually sped up.

"Think they own the road," he muttered as he coolly gulped coffee from a tall cup. "Sorry about the horn."

"No worries," I said.

"Even the name Affordable Care Act is a paradox, and they all know it . . . ," his rant continued.

Another distraction. A memory, maybe my first: a foggy December morning when my mom drove me to preschool. Someone had too many beers for breakfast and thought our lane was their lane. How do you explain a closed casket to a four-year-old? My dad did his best. Lagrima took my mom away from DC, and then it killed her. And Lagrima isn't going to kill two members of the Carter family.

"So are you in it for the long haul?" asked the driver. "On the Hill. You know, most folks only last a few years before they burn out. Working all the time, making less than me, even . . ."

"Oh yeah, definitely," I eagerly replied, naively certain of a career I hadn't begun. Though if you counted the grassroots committee for the last election, I guess I started a couple years ago. I led other high school students door to door, telling people to get out on Election Day. I even convinced some dude with an oil painting of Ronald Reagan in his living room to vote for Congressman Beck.

And I was hooked. Hooked on all of it. The policy, the possibilities, the campaign. I imagined the people at The Hill and Politico wondered who used that single Lagrima, CA, IP address that refreshed their sites day and night. It was me. My friends got on BuzzFeed to take quizzes that told them which celebrity child was their spirit animal. I read it because it's the best-kept secret of political news. And all I wanted was to be where that news—where history—was made.

I recognized the first city name on a freeway sign: Arlington. Getting closer. And then a sign for the Pentagon, like the opening act for the main event.

"Foggy Bottom, you said?" asked the driver.

"Yeah," I said, acknowledging my new neighborhood, which sounded more like the name of a garage band than the metro stop for George Washington University. I pulled out the orientation packet I'd received from the home office, to verify the apartment address. "Corner of New Hampshire Avenue NW and I Street NW."

I read through a few other details in the packet: I would be living with roommates "Zephaniah" and "Hillary" in an apartment just west of GWU. And I would take the blue line on the metro every day to the Capitol South stop. As in: the Capitol of the United States of America. My office for the summer. No big deal.

And then the leafy trees on either side of the freeway gave way to a view of that giant, gleaming Styrofoam cooler of a monument—the Lincoln Memorial. As we rounded the road surrounding Honest Abe's shrine, the piercing white Washington Monument appeared briefly in the distance. The driver banked to the left and headed through several clean, abandoned street blocks. We zoomed by a tiny brown sign that identified the hulking marble building behind it as the State Department, and if it was possible to be starstruck by an office building, I was.

The ride came to an end in front of a three-story brick building that looked like it was made of vomit-colored Legos. The driver's parting words were something about Hollywood fund-raisers, but I had long stopped paying attention. I stood in front of my summer residence, bags in hand. My jeans and long-sleeved shirt were suddenly oppressively hot in the thick East Coast air. The clumsy footsteps and bellowing laughter of some students echoed from the GWU dorms across the street. Though they were probably just a high school graduating class ahead of me, they seemed so much older. College students. Adults. Who lived in apartments with roommates instead of in a house with a dad. Like the apartment I was going to live in, starting in a few minutes. Like the adult I was about to become? An urgent desire to be back home at Taco Bell with my dad tiptoed toward the front of my mind, but it faded as I clunk-clunk-clunked my suitcase up the stairs.

I slipped in the locked front door as an oblivious resident walked out. That wish about Taco Bell kind of came true because the hallway smelled like a food court at three a.m.—all fried/sticky/industrial cleaner. Muted murmurings came from each doorway and floated through the stale air as I searched for my apartment—number 1F. I heard it (opera music) before I saw the apartment door. And that internship brief had not prepared me for the person on the other side.

2

"Hilly?!" I question-shouted—half shocked, half comforted by what I thought was a familiar face.

I caught a quick glimpse of Hilly Wallace's wide eyes—was it really her? The door slammed in front of me. A second later, it slowly opened again, and a newly controlled face and calm voice greeted me:

"Well, you're not Ingrid," she deduced. "Ingrid was supposed to be the intern."

"No—Ingrid was deported, which is insane but true. Hilly—it's me, Cameron. Didn't the local office tell you I was coming for the summer?"

"It's supposed to be the 'diversity' intern slot—you're not . . . 'diverse.'"

I suppose my contribution to "diversity" was being the

only intern who didn't get the gig by having rich campaign donor parents. I was diverse because my widowed father was a failing landscape architect.

She sighed. And some opera lady was getting *real* through the speakers.

"And why did you slam the door in my face?" I asked, though I thought I knew the answer. Hilly Wallace was in the class ahead of me at Lagrima High School. And not only did her family live in the nicest gated community in town; they owned the whole place. A combination of this fact plus her popularity at school apparently gave her and her girlfriends a license to spray me with a hose whenever I mowed her family's lawn. They called themselves the Chicas, even though they were as caucasian as the Volkswagen Jetta convertibles they drove and the spray-on suntans they liberally applied on each other.

I felt the undertow of introversion take over as I realized my new roommate didn't exactly offer a clean social slate.

"Two things," she spoke with a smart, new crispness, clearing her throat so the whole apartment could hear: "One, Zephaniah apparently did not share the roommate update with me. Two, my name is Hillary Wallace. Who attends the University of California at Berkeley and was the first Theta rush pick if you don't count Sheryl Sandberg's second cousin or something, who was technically picked before me, but only because of her Silicon Valley connections and marvelous Chloé handbag. And" — *finger quotes* — "'Hilly' is buried under a past of sad midnight orchard parties and embarrassing exes." A tremor of emotion invaded those last two whispered words. Composure reclaimed: "My name is *Hillary* Wallace, and I was named after Hillary Rodham Clinton."

"Ahhhh." This was all very new. As were her short dark hair and the preppy pink sweater tied over her shoulders. (Gone were the long blond locks and designer short-short shorts.)

I walked in to find a pretty basic living room that merged into a pretty basic kitchen. Four doors surrounded the walls of the living room — our three bedrooms plus the single, shared bathroom. The only closed door opened decisively as an African-American guy wearing a Stanford sweatshirt emerged. Before he could say anything, Hilly — I mean Hillary — declared: "This is Zephaniah Masters."

"My name is Zeph," he corrected. "And if you'll excuse me, I'm going to show our new roommate, Cameron, to his quarters."

Zeph opened the door to what was a completely empty room, save for a mattress on the floor and a cardboard microwave box next to it, with a tiny lamp on top.

"Nightstand." Zeph winked. "Why don't you get unpacked and we can tell you all about the wonderful world of BIB that awaits."

"BIB?" I asked.

"Oh man, I'm doing you a favor here. BIB. Office nickname for Congressman Billy Irman Beck—our boss for the summer."

He stepped out as I unzipped my suitcase and started to unpack into the chest of drawers that wasn't there. I lined the perimeter of the floor with my clothes and doubled up on the limited supply of hangers in the closet. With a few sheets on the bed and a towel-stuffed pillowcase, I was moved in in a matter of four minutes. The window afforded an exquisite view of the neighboring building, about two feet away. It all looked a little sad and spare, but I talked myself into thinking that this must be how college students live, right? College students and heroin addicts chronicled in highbrow photo essays.

I walked out into the living room to find Zeph and Hillary engaged in a vigorous exchange over trade sanctions. Naturally.

Hillary: "If abusive world leaders aren't humane enough to see the impact of their corruption on their people, then sanctions are the only way to wake them up."

Zeph: "I'm sorry, but the sanctions just make it worse for people who are already struggling. . . ."

Hillary: "I can't. I can't anymore with this one." She pointed to Zeph and spoke to the vacant air next to her.

They turned to realize that I was listening to their debate.

"So do we get to play angry cable news talking heads every night?" I asked.

Zeph chuckled. Hillary did not.

"Is this your girlfriend?" she asked as she held up a picture that had somehow slipped out of my things as I moved in. "She is so vintage. I love it."

I grabbed the photo from her and put it back in my wallet. "No. Not my girlfriend."

It was a photo of my mom, which my dad gave me before I got on the plane. It was her government ID head shot, a picture I'd never seen before, which he put in my hands like a good-luck charm.

"Awkward," Hillary singsonged. "Anyway, so, Cameron, please tell me you're not going to one of these faux–vy league colleges like Stanford and going to think your opinions are more valid than everyone else's. UC Berkeley may be a state school, but it's really hard to get into, and I got in. Where are you going in the fall?"

"Oh, I'll be at LJC," I said to Zeph's blank stare and Hillary's recoil in horror. "Lagrima Junior College," I clarified. "Just so I can help out my dad with the landscaping business, and get some of my generals out of the way before transferring. I'm thinking University of Virginia. . . ."

"That's really cool," said Zeph. I think it was his way of saying, *I have never used a lawn mower before, and I've never spoken to someone who went to a junior college.*

Clearly bored, Hillary changed the subject: "So, tomorrow is going to be a big day for you. We'll leave the apartment together at eight thirty and show you how to get to the office. Rayburn House Office Building 2292."

"And I have your access badge for the Hill," said Zeph. "It's red. Our very own personalized 'scarlet letters.' But at least they're all-access!"

I held it carefully—the official House of Representatives logo and fine print somehow made my laminated senior portrait inside appear . . . distinguished. Until you saw the all-caps INTERN right next to it.

They said good night, and just before Hillary closed her door, she added, "Welcome to Washington, Cameron Carter."

I went into my room and sat down on the low mattress, bent knees almost at the same level as my hunched shoulders. A frantic siren zoomed by outside, and an *oontz-oontz* beat from upstairs became increasingly intrusive. It was after midnight, around nine p.m. in Lagrima. So I was certain my dad was walking around the neighborhood, up and back along the perimeter of a nearby farm. We'd done that Sunday-night walk together every week for as long as I could remember. And then, tonight, we didn't. I thought of Humberto, my best friend since the fourth grade, who was probably having game night with his younger brothers. I always let them win at UNO; he never did. I felt the uneasy freedom of a new routine, a broken tradition. I probably should have called my dad or Berto, but I was worried I'd say something that sounded like homesickness.

Made it, I texted my dad. **Hitting the hay.**

I pulled out the wallet-size picture of my mom and leaned it against the base of the small lamp, when there was a knock at my door. I opened it to find Zeph handing me something.

"This is the second-most-important access card you'll have all summer." He smiled.

It was a driver's license from Alabama with my senior portrait laminated into it. A twenty-one-year-old, Alabaman version of myself—named Chester Arlington Vanhille III.

"But I didn't give this to you, okay?" Zeph's eyebrows were raised.

"Okay . . ." I examined the card cautiously. "That's a very elaborate name I've got."

"I pride myself on my work." Zeph laughed and closed the door.

My dad texted back and made me wonder if he'd somehow seen what had just happened: **Stay out of trouble.**

The jet lag was supposed to keep me up for another three hours, but I crashed hard. For years, I had dreamed about DC. But that night, I dreamed of Lagrima and the walk by the farm.

3

As I followed Zeph and Hillary that morning to the Foggy Bottom metro stop, at first it felt like some hazing ritual (make the new kid run!). But I soon realized that was how fast everyone moved in Washington.

Hillary provided unsolicited office gossip as we darted toward the metro. "So you're going to meet everyone. BIB himself, all of the LAs . . ."

"Legislative assistants," translated Zeph.

"And the staff asses . . ."

"Staff assistants," said Zeph.

"Well, 'staff ass' might actually be a more accurate title for Ariel Lancaster," said Hillary, tossing out a morsel of conversation bait.

"She runs the intern program," explained Zeph. "Also,

minor detail: daughter of junior congresswoman from Virginia Nani Lancaster."

Our hurried commuter numbers grew as we got closer to the futuristic awning that signaled the start of the escalators. I was relieved to stand on a moving panel for a second, but even that had a fast lane:

"Stand on the right, walk on the left!" some exasperated bureaucrat raged. At me.

Hillary grabbed me closer to her, opening a floodgate of disapproving commuters whom I had been holding up.

"Sorry," I said to each one. "I'm sorry! I'm new here."

Zeph laughed. "Amateur."

Hillary sighed and prattled on: "Okay, so most important, Ariel has been in the Fifty Hottest Staffers on Capitol Hill for two summers in a row, which almost never happens," said Hillary. "And this summer I plan to join her there."

"Wait a second." I finally got a word in. "Fifty Hottest Staffers on Capitol Hill?"

"It's this stupid list that HillZone puts together at the end of every summer—supposedly the best-looking staffers on Capitol Hill, and by that I mean anyone who will hook up with the editors of the blog," said Zeph.

"It's legitimate!" shouted Hillary.

We descended into the cavernous Foggy Bottom metro station, a gigantic oblong tube encased in a honeycomb-like design. Sleek silver trains shot in and out of the tunnels, the whirring sound of brakes preceding them and then peaking in intensity before the cars stopped. A friendly chime signaled the doors open, and a voice announced, "This is the blue line train, headed to Largo Town Center."

"This is our train," said Hillary. She grabbed my hand and we entered the packed tube of people.

I was riding to work on Space Mountain.

When the train arrived at the Capitol South stop, a mostly youthful crowd—sporting lanyards and badges similar to the one I had—lurched toward the doors as they opened. I kept thinking someone was going to call me out: *You're a landscaper from Lagrima. You're an impostor.* But they didn't. Maybe they were impostors too? In any case, I was one of them. Part of the army. If only for a summer.

As we emerged from the metro, I found my step quickening, the same way I'd walk faster to the Oakland A's games with my dad in the parking lot, even though it wasn't going to make the games start any earlier. I saw the tall marble walls of the Rayburn House Office Building a block away and bolted toward it, when Hillary shouted, "Slow down, cowboy!" The Capitol came into view, and I stopped to take a picture of the scene with my phone. I turned around to see Zeph and Hillary taking pictures of *me.*

"You're such a nerd," said Zeph. "You'll get used to it."

I wasn't so sure.

We entered a stream of Hill staffers walking through a metal detector and soon found ourselves in the lobby. I looked up and around, my mouth gradually opening in awe.

"Mouth-breather," said Hillary as she pushed my back with her hand. "Let's go to work!"

We took the elevator to the second floor and turned down a long, white hallway of doors, each one flanked by an American flag and the state flag of the representative whose office it signaled. Flowery leis adorned the entrance of a Hawaiian rep's office. Country music already blared from the office of a Texan congressman, at nine a.m. And the people inside a New Jersey congresswoman's office were really loud.

"I know, could it be any more cliché?" complained Hillary.

A trio of intense staffers zipped by, arguing about trade sanctions, which seemed to be a popular topic to debate. At that point, I realized Zeph and Hillary were no longer by my side and an angry set of footsteps stalked me from behind — each heel click a quick, nasty bullet into the hard floor. I turned to see the person, but instead I saw Zeph and Hillary urgently signaling me to get out of the way, which I did.

"Hello, intern," the woman behind me said, annoyed, as she stared and pecked away intently at her phone.

"That's Nadia Zyne!" whispered Hillary. "She's BIB's press secretary, aka bad cop. She does the dirty work, stuff he doesn't even know about, so BIB can be the hero. She wrecks people for fun. I heard she had a janitor fired once because they accidentally vacuumed up an Hermès scarf she left on the floor. It's awful. But she dresses really well." Followed by, "Oooh, she's rocking the DVF today."

We arrived at our office, announced by a plaque that read CONGRESSMAN WILLIAM "BILLY" IRMAN BECK, CALIFORNIA. HOUSE MINORITY LEADER. Aside from the obligatory flags, there were no distinguishing flowers or music or voices, which seemed about right for Lagrima. As we walked across the threshold, my foot hesitated for just a second. The internship, DC, Congressman Beck—it was all happening. I thought of my mom on the first day of her internship at the USDA. She wouldn't have hesitated. And so I wouldn't either. I took a deep breath and walked inside the office.

It was a large room, with tall, ornate ceilings, yet it felt cramped with desks and meeting tables and percussive office sounds. Just inside the door, I saw Nadia's lithe figure deliberately slip around a mess of mail and papers that another woman leaned down to collect. Hillary followed Nadia's steps, entranced. Zeph and I knelt down to help, recovering the spilled letters and files spread across the floor. The woman looked up at me.

"Happy Monday, I guess." She smiled and reached out her hand to me. "I'm Katie Campbell, chief of staff."

"Hi, I'm Cameron. I'm the new intern," I said, holding some letters in my left hand and a Sharpie pen wrapped in paper in my right hand.

Katie urgently snapped the pen out of my hand at the same moment I realized it wasn't a Sharpie pen wrapped in paper; it was an unused tampon.

"Oh my Lord," she said, her voice cracking and her cheeks lighting up red. She stuffed my discovery deep into her briefcase.

Zeph put his hands in the air and walked away, his pained laughter barely suppressed.

"Oh my gosh, I'm so sorry," I said to Katie, instinctively stepping away from the scene.

"No need to be sorry; we're just gonna move on here," she blurted out, now haphazardly cramming everything into her briefcase.

"I mean, I guess you just don't recognize certain things when you don't grow up with any sisters. . . ."

"And *that's* where you're going to stop talking, okay, Cameron?" She stormed away to her office, both arms straining to hold the spilled materials and a few sheets of paper seesawing their way to the floor anyway.

"Ugh, tragic," moaned Hillary as she watched Katie scramble to the other side of the office. "A pushing-thirty workaholic who thinks her Ann Taylor Outlet blazers can hide her muffin top. All those Bikram Yoga sessions can't save you from your genes, honey," she added, eyelids flittering to the vacant air.

Zeph rolled his eyes. "You're just jealous she was made chief of staff in her twenties and you never will be."

"Hi!" A girl wearing a yellow blouse and billowy linen pants had approached us. "I'm Ariel, the summer intern coordinator."

"Hi, I'm Lagrima—I mean I'm Cameron, and I'm from Lagrima," I stumbled, her dirty blond shoulder-length hair and smattering of freckles effectively halting my ability to say my name. "And I'm a summer intern here for the summer. Interning."

"I figured that." She chuckled. "So, are you ready to get to know all of the good constituents of the fifty-seventh congressional district of California?"

"Yes, I would love to do that," I replied, like an idiot.

"Good." She started to walk toward the mailroom. "Your friend Zeph here knows the ropes, but basically you'll start each day opening all of the mail. Anything from VIPs"—she pointed to a list of names on a sign marked VIPS—"goes in this pile. Regular names, you'll process them in the system on the computer. You have access to all of BIB's people's contact information in here, so no identity theft, okay?"

"Of course not!" I blurted out. "I will treat it all with the utmost confidentiality. When I was on the campaign back in Lagrima, I managed the donor lists, and—"

"Oh man, calm down. So formal," she said. "Very cute."

The feeling's mutual.

"Well, I can see that you're a fast learner," she remarked. "This is good."

She continued to show me around the office: the kitchen, the reception desk, and the phone system. All the while, I was able to verify every inch of her consecutive years of eligibility for the Fifty Hottest Staffers on Capitol Hill. She was better-looking than any of the girls in Lagrima. Her eyes were light green with tiny slivers of yellow barely peeking through. And the rasp of her voice somehow made a phrase like "tour guide manual" sound like a two p.m. breakfast.

Ariel continued the orientation with introductions to the legislative assistants—four fidgety thirtysomethings who all wore glasses and, with remarkable uniformity, each clutched a coffee in one hand and a smartphone in the other. The whole orientation felt like the opening credits of an old-school TV show—each person giving a brief wave and an even briefer smile before turning away. The senior staffers popped in and out of their own rooms, which surrounded the chaotic main floor. And a set of closed dark brown double doors proclaimed the most senior office of all.

I recognized the conspicuously stylish young man who walked in the door, though his perfectly manicured goatee was new.

"Jigar Shah, nice of you to come to work this morning," announced Ariel. "This is our new intern . . ."

"I know." He patted me on the back. "I interviewed this guy when I was visiting the home office!"

And by "interviewed," he meant talking to me from a bank of urinals as he scanned e-mails on his phone. "Sorry, no time; if you want an interview, the interview's in here," he had told me as he'd walked through the bathroom door.

He was scanning e-mails on his phone this morning as well. Ariel snapped her fingers so he'd actually look at me, but he spoke without making eye contact: "How are you doing, buddy? You're looking sharp. Sebastian, right?"

"His name is Cameron Carter," corrected Ariel.

"Of course it is! Welcome to DC, bud!" He proceeded through the office, oblivious.

Jigar walked into the office of his boss, Nadia Zyne, the one person to whom Ariel did not make a personal introduction.

"That's Nadia Zyne," she said, pointing to the slightly ajar door.

"The one I'm supposed to stay away from?" I asked with a smile.

"Well, I won't confirm nor deny that, but I will say that you are a quick study, Mr. Carter," she said. She walked me to her desk. We sat down and she continued, "I just want you to know that I'm here for any questions you may have. I know it's tough to be away from home for the first time."

It was, though I'd never acknowledge it to her.

"Well, I do kind of feel like an outsider here," I admitted.

"Maybe that's not such a bad thing," she responded. "Outsiders see things we insiders don't notice anymore, you know?"

"Yeah, I get it," I responded. "It's like this one time I went to a farm and all of these cows were running around, and I was like, 'Hey, guys, get off the tractor because the cows . . .'"

A heavy *click* sounded from the double doors and Ariel's eyes immediately darted in that direction, though her head didn't move. I was actually grateful for the interruption to my word vomit.

"Sure," she said, not listening, as Congressman Billy Beck opened the doors and emerged from his office. Most everyone else seemed to share the same reverence I had for the moment, but Ariel looked down at her desk and shuffled some papers.

A couple voices sang out, "Good morning, Mr. Congressman," but they were outnumbered by those who said, "Hey, BIB!" And suddenly, the man, the acronym, was standing in front of me, reaching out his hand.

"Billy Beck," he introduced himself. And before I could reply: "And you are Cameron Carter." His bright blue eyes locked on mine from about six inches above, and his long fingers firmly wrapped around my right hand in a hearty, seismic jolt. Like my track coach's congratulations after a good meet. An honorable mention in the form of a handshake.

"You're a great guesser!" I exclaimed, which is basically the exact opposite of the first four words I intended to say when I met the congressman. In fairness to me, I wasn't expecting him to know my name, and it threw me off a bit.

"And you're going to be a great intern, I can tell," Beck retorted. His expression looked exactly like it did in those ads I passed out all over town—a smile that curved up to one side, with wrinkly, almond-grower eyes. The fluorescent lights of the office bounced off the signature American flag pin fastened to the lapel of his navy-blue suit. "Your dad has that big landscaping business, doesn't he? Real salt-of-the-earth guy—that's what I love about the people of our district. . . ."

"Yeah, he's doing really well," I said, though BIB clearly hadn't heard that my dad had lost out on some major contracts in the past few months.

"That's great." Katie smiled as she gently tugged at BIB's elbow. And then, to him: "You're going to be late for the vote."

He slowly lifted his hand to Katie and continued looking at me. "So . . . Lagrima High, I assume?"

"Yes, sir," I said, a little surprised that he was taking time for small talk with the most junior person on his staff.

"Bolander is still the football coach?"

"He's retiring next year," I said, incredulous. "How do you know him?"

"He was the assistant when I started for the team," he explained.

"BIB . . . ," interjected Katie with a sharp, quick smile.

"Great man," he mused. He then leaned in toward me and said, as if a secret, "So please tell me the teenagers are still breaking into the Del Lago golf course at night and ice blocking down the hills?"

My eyes widened as I realized he'd once taken part in a time-honored but unspoken activity among Lagrima's youth — buying huge chunks of ice at a convenience store and riding them down the green hills of the golf course, destroying the fairways in the process. I had done it two nights ago with Berto.

"Not sure how to answer that one." I laughed nervously.

"Well, we always used to say it's only a crime if you're stupid enough to get caught," he whispered in my ear.

By that point, most of the staff watched our interaction, surprised and maybe a little jealous at the face time I was getting.

"Look," said Katie, "you guys are clearly hitting it off, but you're going to have to continue the nostalgia session later."

"Okay, okay," said BIB, like a teenager being picked up from a party by his mom. "But one last thing. Most important advice you'll get all summer . . ."

I noticed the rest of the staffers were watching intently, hoping to glean any wise tips from their boss.

"The best food on the Hill is on the Senate side, Dirksen cafeteria, to be exact. And Cups for coffee." He laughed. "Don't even bother going to the place they have in the basement here. Rayburn's the worst. Can I say that?" He glanced at Katie, who was texting someone on her phone. "I like this kid," he concluded, sizing me up.

Katie looked up and said, "Yes, he is going to be a great intern. He's already proven very proactive." She playfully raised an eyebrow. "And now, Mr. Congressman, we need to get you to the floor for a vote and prevent those Republicans from scaring more senior citizens."

"Subtle," Beck reflected.

"Those grandpas and grandmas will be going to the voting booth in five months; I don't care what you call it," instructed Katie as she guided Beck out the door.

As lunchtime neared, I waited for Ariel, who told me she would host a welcome meal for me, with Hillary and Zeph joining as well. However, she apologized for having to cancel twenty minutes into the lunch hour. She repeated this rain-checking for the next few days. Always canceling at the last minute. *Something's come up*, she'd say. *We'll do it tomorrow.* Always with a concerned, distracted look on her face.

• • •

The week passed quickly, and though she bailed on lunch, Ariel had taken an interest in me. Or at least, my ability to compensate for struggling staffers. She pulled me off filing duty and asked me to help Marcus with a report on literacy statistics. Marcus, education LA and office Cheetos hoarder, "could use the help," she said. It was true.

I typed a note to Ariel on MessageNow, the instant message app on our computers: **So is this whole thing a joke and I'm supposed to find out that Marcus is the literacy statistic? He spends most of the day watching sneaker unboxing videos on YouTube.**

He hasn't done anything for the report, has he? she replied.

That thing is all me. I finished it this morning, I typed back. **Just sent it to him so he can take credit for it. So . . . what's next? You aren't going to send me back to letter-opening duty, are you?**

No, she responded and paused. I looked at her across the room, her eyes barely above the computer screen on her desk. She continued, **We never had that welcome lunch, did we?**

Correct. You bailed on us on Monday, I replied.

Rayburn cafeteria, today? she typed back. **11:15 a.m. See you there.**

I looked up and made eye contact with her, surprised by the early hour and somewhat confused given BIB's negative review of the eating establishment. Then my eyes pointed toward Hillary, who was showing Zeph the correct way to store reams of paper in the supply closet. Ariel shook her head back at me: *Just us.*

She left for the basement at eleven, signaling that we were to walk there separately for some reason. As I walked out of the front door alone, I told Zeph and Hillary that I had to make a phone call to my dad. I was following Ariel's lead; this lunch was off the record.

The Rayburn cafeteria provided just the right number of people to make Ariel and me anonymous, unnoticed. Two congressmen sat in the middle of the place, and they seemed to draw the attention of any onlookers. Ariel's table selection (two-top behind a refrigerator filled with preprepared food) added to our privacy. The whir of the machine's motor masked our conversation to anyone farther than five feet away.

"I hope you like Caesar salad," she said and pushed a plate of wilted, soggy lettuce toward me. I sat down across from her.

"Oh, the famous Rayburn Caesar!" I feigned enthusiasm. "Lunch of choice for secretive Capitol Hill encounters."

"It's not a secret," she defended herself. Her eyes darted to the left as she said it, which confirmed that it was at least kind of a secret. "I just . . . can't stand that intern girl with the weird voice thing."

"You mean, 'thing-*ah*'?" I asked, doing my best Hillary

imitation. Ariel nodded and laughed. And I realized that I'd made her laugh. As in, intentionally. She smiled back at me. The bottom of my lungs did that weightless thing for a second, before I told myself to *get a grip and play it cool.*

"So you ran circles around Marcus on that project?" she asked.

"Well, he gave me his Congressional Quarterly login name and password, so I didn't do *everything*," I explained.

"You don't have to be modest," she said. "You're smarter than he is."

"He's an LA," I reminded her. "I just graduated high school."

"I know, I know," she said. "But I can already tell. You're quick. You're going to do well here."

The refrigerator motor machine grumbled to life. I could feel the warm exhaust from the vent blow on my ankles.

"So do you mind telling me why we're eating lunch at the worst cafeteria on Capitol Hill, sitting in the corner next to a dying fridge?"

She laughed again and spun a piece of lettuce around with her fork. "So Sasser from the district office told me that you submitted your résumé like seven times or something," she said.

"What?" I exclaimed. "That's crazy. It was just three times." A pause begged further explanation: "There was a temp one time, and I was pretty sure she didn't know who to give it to . . ."

"You're persistent," she said. "You're resourceful."

"And you're not answering my question," I replied. "Anyway, I'm not hating on the people back home, but if you lived in Lagrima, you'd understand about the multiple-résumé-submission thing."

"No offense," she said, "but I didn't expect a high school grad from Lagrima to seem so at home here. You fit in, but you're still normal."

I fit in. Best thing I'd heard anyone say all week. I wanted to stand up and tell the sparsely populated cafeteria that *I fit in!* but then I realized that would be counterproductive.

"Oh, I have family in the area, so . . ." I was referring to my mom, eighteen years ago. Close enough.

"'Normal' is a secret weapon in this town, you know," she told me.

"A weapon against what?" I asked.

I could tell she had something to say. Or she just needed someone to listen.

She inhaled a bit and then smiled and said, "DC changes people. Power . . . it facilitates things. It's like BIB, you know? He's not a big name yet. But he knows everyone. He's tight with the maître d' at Old Ebbitt Grill—can get the private room there, just by showing up. He can make tax audits happen, get protesters arrested . . ."

It was her turn for the word vomit.

"What?" I blurted out. My question stopped her increasingly whispered stream of thought. "What are you talking about? How do you know he did that?"

"Anyway," she deflected, "it's better to be in the background with a bunch of people owing you favors, I guess. And the biggest favor they owe him is voting him in as Speaker of the House in the fall."

"Okay," I told her. "Our boss got the IRS to look a certain way and put some people in jail? You can't take that back. You said it yourself: I'm persistent."

She scanned the room and her eyes unmistakably said, *Shhh*. She looked less cute all of a sudden. More vulnerable, worried even. She sat back and folded her arms, her body language telling that she wouldn't say more.

And then she did.

She leaned forward and said, "BIB's buddy in the IRS initiated an audit of the chief fund-raiser for his competitor a few cycles ago. And the protesters? BIB got them arrested in the same phone call he set up a fishing trip with the DC chief of police. The same trip he invited my mom on." She paused and then explained to me, "Nani Lancaster, junior congresswoman from Virginia Beach . . ."

"I know who your mom is," I told her.

"Anyway, she hates the outdoors. But ever since she got

elected, she'll tag along wherever BIB goes. Like I said, DC changes people. . . ."

I tried to reconcile her model-next-door looks with the increasing severity of her words. Cute girls back at home could be cryptic—but nothing like this. The conversation made me feel uncomfortable—guilty. But it also made me want to learn more.

"Why are you telling me this, Ariel? These stories about BIB, your mom's extreme political makeover . . . this isn't exactly intern orientation material. Also kind of hard to believe."

"I'm telling you because I might need your help with another project, Cameron," she answered, "and there isn't much time."

I had barely celebrated my apparent promotion from the copy machine when a surprise guest showed up at the table.

"Well, what are you two doing hiding down here? It's not even lunchtime yet." Katie Campbell appeared out of nowhere and opened the frostbitten refrigerator door. Ariel cleared her throat and then smiled a very convincing smile. As she pulled out a small cup of yogurt from the shelf, Katie said, "Word to the wise: This is the best yogurt parfait on the Hill. I find myself down here basically seven times a day. Which is why Ariel's so skinny, and I'm . . ." Her voice trailed off as she examined Ariel's toned upper arm.

"I was just giving Cameron an orientation—a little bit about the office, the people . . . ," said Ariel, suddenly all business.

"Oh, she's telling you where all the bodies are buried?" Katie asked me.

"No," I quickly answered. *Nothing to see here.* "No, she's just . . . I'm learning a lot already."

"It's a figure of speech, Cameron." Katie smiled warmly. "See you back at the ranch, you two," she said, before walking toward the cash register, both hands clasping her snack.

We followed her to the office a few minutes later. As we got on the elevator, Ariel said, "Look, Cameron. I'm afraid that was a rather serious lunch. And I do have something in mind for you to work on. Just need another day or so to get things ready. And anyway, you shouldn't forget to have fun this summer either."

We walked down the second-floor hallway, back to BIB's office, where we bumped into Zeph and Hillary, who were on their way to grab a bite to eat.

"I see you found time for lunch." Hillary broke her silence to Ariel. "With *some* of us."

"I was just telling Cameron about a little fun we're going to have tonight," said Ariel, ignoring Hillary's jab. "And you're all invited. A few of us from the staff get together at Capitol Sinny on Thursday nights. Little place in Adams Morgan.

Nothing official. And by that I mean, you should bring the twenty-one-year-old versions of yourselves."

"Our fake IDs?" said Hillary, in an attempt to clarify.

Zeph laugh-shushed Hillary's rookie move.

"I have no idea what you're talking about." Ariel winked.

4

After having dinner from a curbside hot dog vendor and a balmy evening walk along the Mall, Zeph, Hillary, and I took the metro to Dupont Circle. Even riding the escalator, it took forever to emerge from the extraordinarily deep subway depot below. Once we reached the street level, buzzing cars ringed around the otherwise abandoned roundabout.

Zeph led us down one of the spokes that shot north from the circular road, and we dodged our way through an oncoming wolf pack of frat bros. The sidewalks became saturated with raucous staffers, annoyed locals trying to walk their dogs, and "business casual" clones clumsily downing cheap and greasy pizza by the slice. Walking past the successive skinny buildings was like rapidly changing the radio dial—from smooth jazz to bad karaoke to EDM and back to bad karaoke. DC after dark. Interns gone wild.

"Almost there," said Zeph, as he pointed to a narrow, four-story structure, the top three stories of which were exposed because the adjoining building was only one story high. The bare wall was a vast canvas for a gigantic portrait of George Washington—with spray painted devil horns and red eyes. Passersby jumped to slap a hanging, swinging sign out in front: CAPITOL SINNY.

As we walked up to the door, I reached for my fake ID and hesitantly offered it to the bouncer. He scanned the card, and I prepared to be arrested. My screaming conscience made me feel like a drug smuggling, tax-evading serial killer. Fortunately, the bouncer thought otherwise, and let us through.

"You're welcome, kid." Zeph winked as I put the Alabama driver's license back in my pocket.

We entered the cramped first floor. The decoration was the interior design equivalent of Lewis Carroll's and Slipknot's love child. One wall was covered in bendy mirrors, while a corner of the ceiling featured a goth mannequin lady riding a tricycle and brandishing—what else?—a chain saw. The air was thick with the booming vocals of an overweight rocker lady on stage, the stinging vapor of beer, and the pungent memory of cigarettes that were probably banned last year. Decades of booze and sweat on the floor clung to my shoes with each footstep. Guys with glazed eyes yelled into the ears of goofily smiling girls, while green-faced coeds made frantic beelines for

41

the bathrooms. There seemed to be no in-between at Capitol Sinny. These peoples' evenings were either going to end very well or very badly.

I didn't tell Zeph and Hillary that this was my first time in a bar. Most of the parties in Lagrima took place in foggy orchards, until the owner started pumping his shotgun or a passing cop shined the lights. This was a whole new level. Four levels, to be precise.

We made our way up a narrow, winding staircase in the back to the second story. Aside from the residual din, this area looked nothing like the craziness below. It was also where we saw our first familiar faces: a welcoming Katie Campbell and a demure Ariel Lancaster, who was surrounded by four guys in khakis and blue button-up shirts. In DC, this apparently doubled as both office wear and party attire. They all looked very interested in what Ariel was saying. She wore a light yellow dress, and one of the guys was tugging at the cap sleeve. She didn't seem to mind.

"I see Ariel's found her dude-tourage," said Hillary.

"So glad you guys could make it," greeted Katie. "And you survived the first floor! This area is much more hospitable. And sanitary."

Three pool tables dominated the floor, with plush red velvet couches lining the walls. A waitress came by and offered me a drink. I declined.

"Good answer," said Zeph. "You don't want the boss's number two thinking you're underage—"

"No, really, I don't drink," I clarified.

Alcohol meant car crashes. Well, not always. But it did for some dude who hit my mom. And that was enough for me to have never given it a try.

"Boring," Hillary declared.

I took in a shallow breath and started to explain, before stopping myself.

"Weird," she said as she walked away.

She wasn't worth the explanation.

"Well, we can be designated partiers together," Katie told me. "I don't imbibe either. *Someone* needs to get these people home safely."

She offered me a Diet Coke and we clinked glasses.

A tall, tan guy with a loosened tie was the self-appointed manager of the pool tables. "*This guy* looks like he's up next," he loudly announced to the room while pointing at a guy who was apparently going to play pool next. "*These ladies* need a drink," he declared to a group of giggling girls.

"You'll find that every party has a mayor here," commented Katie. "You know, the guy who decides that everyone else needs someone to be in charge and tell them what to drink and do."

I watched as Mr. Mayor bought a tray of shots and then

pushed one of the tiny glass cups in the face of an underling, who was unsuccessfully saying no.

"This town is filled with big fish from small ponds, and some of them don't realize that they're actually little fish now. And you and I have the pleasure of dealing with them," said Katie.

"Speak for yourself," I told her. "Are you calling me a little fish?"

"I'm calling you one of the good ones, Cameron. I can already tell you have potential."

"I may have gotten into this establishment under false pretenses. Do you still feel that way?" I replied.

"I'm strategically looking the other way." Katie laughed. "It's actually a good career tip for this town."

This town. She'd said it with equal parts admiration and disdain. Like a bad relationship you don't want to quit. Or can't.

"Cameron, get over here!" shouted Ariel from across the room. She was holding court on the couch, and the guys surrounding her were not pleased with the increased guy-to-Ariel ratio that I created.

"Save me from these savages," she said to me. One "savage" in particular had his arm firmly placed around her neck and a *don't even think about it* smile on his face. She was slightly tipsy but sincere as she introduced me to her admirers. "So,

I've only known this kid for a week, but he is a really cool guy."

"Ariel, you don't have to . . . ," I said.

"No, no, no, no, no. You're normal, like we were talking about. The good normal, like under the radar. I'm sick of all these silver-spoon Bush relatives everywhere. This kid and I share . . . humble beginnings." Her words were sloppy but adamant. "I've decided we are going to be friends. And now my friends are your friends. Right, guys?"

They nodded in grudging agreement. They didn't really have a choice.

Ariel grabbed my hand and pulled me down so that her mouth was a tiny beer-breath cloud away from my ear. "My friends are your friends. You need to meet all of them—especially Caitlin." Her eyes watered, and I couldn't tell if it was emotion in her face or a clumsy, drunk pout. "We need to talk before you leave tonight, okay? It's that thing, that project from lunch—our lunch. Just you and me. Just talk with me before you leave. . . ."

Zeph suddenly put his arm around my shoulder and apologized to Ariel. "Excuse us. Jigar Shah is reportedly smashed out of his mind and singing karaoke Disney songs on the third floor. This is a historic moment, and I cannot let our Cameron miss out."

"Have fun tonight, gentlemen," Katie said from across the room. "I'm heading out. Too old for this."

As we scaled another circular staircase upward, she called out, "It's not historic, by the way. Happens all too often. Tell Jigar I'm requesting 'Feed the Birds (Tuppence a Bag)'!"

The third floor was yet another scene change—a dramatically lit, disco ball karaoke stage where Jigar Shah himself was belting "Let It Go" without any need for the scrolling lyrics on the screen in front of him. The song clearly hit an emotional nerve, as his eyes were watering and strings of saliva spanned his warbling open mouth. Half the crowd was booing while the other half sang along (including most of the LAs from our office).

Jigar was just one squeaky chorus into the song when the homesickness hit me. Like a late-August downpour ruining a barbecue, my dad and Lagrima and the smell of freshly pulled weeds filled my mind. I felt guilty that I wasn't there helping him. Guilty that I didn't want to be. I wondered what my mom thought when she first came to this city. My dad made her leave, but what kept her there in the first place?

"Dude!" shouted Zeph. "This song getting to you or something? You look like you're feeling it."

"Yes," I said with an instinctive, masking smile, "Jigar cuts to the core."

As much as it felt wrong or disloyal to leave Lagrima behind, I had already taken the first step. This summer *had* to work, because I had to move on. Big fish or little fish—I didn't care. I just needed to get out of the pond and into the ocean.

"Hide me." Hillary appeared out of nowhere and burrowed herself between Zeph and me. "Unwanted middle-aged lobbyist alert. Can't keep their hands off me."

Zeph and I scanned the crowd and found no such suspects in the vicinity.

"Oh, I guess they left? Anyway, speaking of leaving: Can we?" She pivoted. We excused ourselves from Jigar's one-man musical and headed downstairs.

The second floor was abandoned—no sign of Ariel and her man harem. Everyone, it seemed, had descended upon the jam-packed dungeon of a first floor. Between us and the entrance, about 120 bodies pressed up against one another. Zeph assuredly guided us through the kitchen while various cooks and servers told us to "get the hell out." We did as they said and exited through the back.

"Express route," he proudly informed us.

I learned that the subways ran far less frequently late at night, with eighteen- and fourteen-minute waits for the red- and blue-line legs of the journey back to our place. It was just after one a.m. when we got back to the apartment, realizing that a walk probably would have been faster.

"Amateurs," I declared us.

"Speak for yourself." Hillary yawned as she dramatically dragged her feet to her room.

The last thing I thought before blacking out (in a nonalcoholic way) was Ariel's drunken command for me to talk with her before I left the bar. And a name: Caitlin.

First thing in the morning, I groggily thought to myself.

5

I dreamed that a crazed intruder was banging on my bedroom
door, only to realize that it wasn't a dream and it wasn't an
intruder.

Zeph urgently knocked on the hollow door. He kept saying something, but the morning stupor prevented me from
comprehending it. I reached for my phone to see that it was
6:22 a.m. I threw on a shirt and slowly opened the door.

And Zeph's words became totally clear.

"Ariel Lancaster is dead."

"No . . ." was all I could reply.

"I got a text from Nadia just now—Ariel Lancaster died,
and we're not supposed to talk to any press on the way to the
office this morning," reported Zeph.

Hillary came out of her room and turned on the TV. Zeph

and I joined her on the flattened couch cushions to watch. In our pajamas in the blue morning light, we looked like friends having some sort of horror-movie marathon. Except we were supporting characters in the story. TV reporters' words formed a kind of mental nightmare collage with the images on the screen and our own stunned comments.

"... *confirm that one of the victims is the daughter of Representative Nani Lancaster, junior congresswoman from Virginia* ..."

The images flashed between a helicopter's view of stopped cars on a road and that of a handheld camera on the ground, angling to see what was behind the gleaming red rubies of emergency vehicle lights.

"This can't be happening," said Hillary.

"*Ms. Lancaster was a passenger in the vehicle with an unidentified male who also died in the crash. . . .*"

"That guy," said Zeph. "That guy from the bar . . ."

Back to the helicopter view, which now revealed a mangled red mash of metal that had skidded from the road down to . . .

"... *just after midnight* . . . *a bank of the Potomac River, where the car appears to have struck a tree and ricocheted into a pedestrian fence and nearly fallen into the water* . . ."

The cameraman on the ground finally got his money shot: the twisted sedan bursting through a low-lying fence by the river, precariously balancing on the edge above the water. A tow truck dragged the car away from the brink.

Hillary made a mucousy sniffle as I felt my stomach drop.

It was a lot like the scene my mom's accident must have looked like. My dad kept the pictures from me (along with the vast majority of his feelings about that day), and the archived online news coverage of the crash was scant. But we returned to that spot near the orchard every year on the anniversary of her death. And my miraculous survival. "You're my miracle," my dad would say. It was the only day of the year that he allowed himself to be emotional.

Zeph scanned his Twitter feed and said, "Everything here is saying it was drunk driving. . . ."

". . . lost control at speeds of up to ninety miles per hour in a twenty-five-mile-per-hour zone. Again, we are looking at Rock Creek Parkway, just north of the Kennedy Center, where Ariel Lancaster, a staffer for House Minority Leader Billy Beck and daughter of first-term congresswoman Nani Lancaster, has died in a car accident."

Two photos suddenly filled the screen—on the left, the official House portrait of a patriotic-looking Representative Lancaster, and on the right, a pixelated shot of a smiling Ariel, wearing a tank top, her arms around another person who was cropped out. That same smiling Ariel who'd celebrated a random Thursday night with us just seven hours prior.

The helicopter camera panned out to reveal an overhead

shot of two hulking, crescent-shaped buildings near the scene of the accident.

"Watergate," said Hillary.

"Commuters are advised to avoid the area, as crews will be on site for cleanup and forensics through the morning. . . ."

Workers wheeled a covered body away from the crash. A bunch of yellow fabric gently flapped alongside the gurney.

"That's the dress she was wearing," I said—more to my disbelieving self than to Zeph or Hillary.

"It's too much." Hillary snapped off the TV with the remote.

Zeph continued the news report from his phone. "It's a Georgetown Law School student—'James Clayton, twenty-six, was driving the vehicle with Ariel Lancaster, twenty-three, in the passenger seat. Both were last reported to be seen at the Capitol Sinny bar in Adams Morgan, just before midnight.' Tested high for alcohol, car spun out before rolling over a couple times. This is insane. . . ."

For a few minutes, we all got lost in our phones, searching for more details. Zeph called Nadia, Jigar, Katie—only to hear coldly perky voice-mail greetings. One by one, we silently got up from the crumpled couch and went to our rooms. Ariel's death took up most of my mind. The rest of my mind throbbed with the memory of the last words I heard her say: "Just talk with me before you leave." *What was she going to tell me?* It was hard to think of anything else—even unbuttoning my shirt from a hanger.

We walked outside together to find a morning that felt like the end of a hard-lost kids' soccer game—listless and already sweaty. The unwelcoming gray sky seemed to coax us back into the air-conditioned apartment—to quit before things could get worse.

As we stepped off the escalators at the Capitol South station, Zeph broke the quiet only to remind us to avoid any reporters. Nadia Zyne's warning would prove unnecessary, though. There was no press gathered outside Rayburn. Just curious heads and can't-look-away eyes in the hallway near our office. Wondering what mourning a congressional staffer looks like.

Mourning looked like a closed door.

We entered an empty office to find the belongings of the permanent staff strewn about their desks. Everyone was holed up behind BIB's thick wooden doors. For a while, we pretended to log in to our computers while actually trying to understand the muffled words coming from BIB's office. I couldn't make anything out, but the tones were unmistakable. Urgent instructions from Nadia. Lots of *me too*–ing from Jigar. The occasional question from BIB. An emotional Katie. It sounded like a strategy session more than a memorial. Suddenly, the doors clanked open, and the three of us did our best to look like we weren't eavesdropping. The staff milled out of the office—everyone but Nadia—and filled their desks.

A puffy-eyed Katie came over to our corner of the big room. "How are you guys holding up?"

"Just really hard to believe . . . ," I said.

"I know. It's horrible," replied Katie.

"How is her mom doing?" asked Zeph.

"BIB's in there with Nadia, talking with Representative Lancaster right now," said Katie. "Really rough. Ariel was her only child."

"Does anyone know that other guy who was driving?" asked Hillary.

"It was one of those guys from the bar last night. Law school student. First time anyone had seen him. I guess he offered her a ride home . . . ," said Katie as her eyes watered anew. She sniffed away the emotion and cleared her throat. "Anyway, this is a really crummy way to start your summer, but I want you to know that I'm here for anything."

"Thanks, Katie," I said as we made eye contact.

She continued, looking at me: "We will get through this togeth—"

"Okay, everyone." Nadia Zyne emerged from BIB's office, commanding our attention. "Interns," she said as she acknowledged our presence with a quick look and fluttering eyes.

"Ariel's accident this morning is a tragedy. We will miss her positive attitude and resourceful nature in this office. Hers is a life cut short by a national plague. A monster that has touched nearly everyone in this nation, and today it touched each of us. I am talking about drunk driving. And as a result of one young man's careless decision, Ariel is gone."

Nadia wasted no time moving from tragedy to PR triage.

Jigar stepped next to Nadia and said, "As a result of today's tragedy, Representative Beck and Representative Lancaster will be leading a commission together to study the psychology behind drunk driving and how we can promote responsible drinking, one driver at a time. We are all just devastated at this news."

This was not entirely convincing, given the impromptu legislative session we were apparently having.

Jigar continued, "Every year, thousands of people die in drunk-driving accidents."

Nadia had had enough of her number two's words: "Ten thousand people. Twenty-eight each day."

I could almost detect a smile. Her strange satisfaction in one-upping a subordinate. The triumph of a nastier statistic.

"We'll be coordinating with Representative Lancaster's office in the coming days and expect each of you to devote your time and energies to this cause," said Nadia. "This is how we halt more tragedies. Our work. This is how we honor Ariel."

Zeph, Hillary, and I gave the same look to each other: *Is this weird?*

"Will we be honoring Ariel with a funeral, too?" One of the LAs asked the obvious.

Nadia looked oddly irked that the conversation had been changed from her legislative crusade back to our colleague who had perished hours prior. She began to respond when a hunched-over BIB emerged from his office.

"There will be a memorial for Ariel next Friday in Virginia Beach," reported a gravelly BIB. "May our prayers be with her parents. And all parents across this nation who get a horrible phone call like the one Representative Lancaster received early this morning."

"Thank you, Representative Beck," said Nadia with a Dignified Look on her face. She patted him on the back.

Good boy.

"Everyone, let's really try to be there for one another this week. I'm around for any questions," said Nadia, just before firmly shutting her office door.

A phone rang and Hillary's greeting to the caller broke an awkward pall. "Congressman Beck's office! How can I direct you . . ."

Someone opened the refrigerator. The copy machine made its sonic gulp to life. And the staggered waves of keystrokes began to fill the office.

Just another Friday.

Honoring Ariel.

I spent most of the day online, where there were lots of stories about Ariel Lancaster. There was a photo gallery of her life—a childhood ski trip with her parents. College graduation. Standing next to her mom at her congressional swearing-in ceremony. On the steps of the Capitol, BIB sandwiched between her and her mom. His arms around both. And the same head shot that all news outlets seemed to be using—a higher resolution of that pixelated image I saw early in the morning. Bright-eyed, tank-topped Ariel. Cropped out of a group photo, like she had been cropped out of the office.

By the late afternoon, however, most of the stories focused on the perils of drunk driving. All of the major outlets touted similar headlines. They declared BIB's study on the "national plague" and insistence that "we must act on behalf of all of the parents in the country." And nearly each article featured Nadia's statistic: twenty-eight people die in drunk-driving accidents each day.

After lunch, I got a text from my dad. **Was that girl from your office? Are you okay?**

Yes and yes. Weird day, I texted back. What I really wanted to say wouldn't really make sense to my dad: that I was feeling a little dizzy from what I think was my first up-close dose of political spin.

I started texting again, **And it made me think about Mom. . . .**

I deleted the text before sending it. It was another thing I wanted to say but couldn't. Or shouldn't. No sense in upsetting him.

I texted Berto instead: **So this girl dies and everyone's basically ignoring it and talking about drunk driving?! Messed up.**

His immediate reply: **Most exciting thing that happened to me so far today was getting to tackle a shoplifter. It was sweet. Straight-up MMA. I dominated.**

Then, my dad texted back a picture of little Rogelito revving up my lawn mower—he was my substitute for the summer. Supposedly sixteen, though he looked more like twelve—his light green shirt was already blackened by sweat in the oven-like Central Valley morning. **Rogelito might be stealing your gig.**

Don't let him get too comfortable. I lied. I put my phone away and joined Zeph, who was sorting a mound of letters.

By the end of the day, Ariel's story and head shot had been reduced to a thumbnail photo buried below other articles about Middle Eastern refugees, some Hollywood star's appearance at a congressional panel about global warming, and yes, our new legislative priority: the "national plague" of drunk driving. One opinion piece conjectured: "Calling attention to a social ill. Something good coming from something so tragic.

It's what the kind of girl like Ariel would want."

What Ariel wanted was to talk with me before I left the bar. She had something to say. Another "project." And I wasn't there for her.

As Zeph, Hillary, and I packed up our things to leave, Jigar informed us that Nadia wanted to have a word. The three of us crammed into her compact and startlingly fragrant office, where we found her plugging her nose as she gulped down a bottle of clumpy orange liquid. She placed the bottle on her desk, where I could read the label of her late-afternoon treat, written in a big superhero font: "Find your SUNRISE: Carrot/ Cayenne/Cauliflower." Delicious.

She locked eyes with each of us in a more severe way than before. "A lot of people have worked very hard to get Representative Beck where he is today. A lot of people have sacrificed. Yes?"

We nodded.

"Good. And you'll learn that when a person is as successful and respected as BIB has become, there will be others who try to bring them down, to tarnish their reputation in some way. In the coming days, you may hear things about BIB that are surprising to you. I just want you to know that this is natural and expected for someone who has given their life to the public sphere."

"Yeah, we know," concurred Zeph. "Congressman Beck is one of the best representatives in —"

"And you must never engage with any reporters, any individuals, who may contact you trying to prove otherwise," interrupted Nadia. "So. If anyone reaches out to you, asking about Ms. Lancaster or BIB, will you let me know?"

I guess it was technically a question, but it sounded more like a commandment.

"Sure."

"Yes."

"No worries."

We fumbled over one another's replies, mostly so we could get out of there. The forceful, flowery smell of her scented candle started to make the back of my mouth feel like an impending sore throat, and I wasn't sure how much longer I'd last. Given that Ariel had been dead for less than twenty-four hours and all Nadia was worried about was how it all looked for BIB, I couldn't decide if her comments were completely heartless or simply pragmatic. Maybe for press secretaries, the terms weren't mutually exclusive.

Nadia flashed a smile. At once she looked both very beautiful and somewhat disturbing. "Wonderful. Much appreciated. So glad you'll be with us this summer. I'm glad you're all clear on that."

The last sentence was the only one that sounded real.

"Have a good night," I said as we exited the claustrophobic space. "We'll be sure to be careful."

"Cameron." She sliced into the air. "I'm not telling you what or what not to say, and I don't appreciate your intimating that I am. I'm not in charge of you, thank God. You can say whatever you want."

Instead of pointing out that she had just directly contradicted herself, I figured a simple "Thank you" would provide the fastest escape.

"You're welcome," she snapped as I walked out of the office and Jigar closed the door behind me.

"Smart," whispered one of the LAs nearby, who winked.

I joined Zeph and Hillary as we walked down the hallway, down the elevator, and to the exit of the frigid Rayburn building.

"Yikes," said Zeph. "Passive-aggressive much? Hillary, do you still have a crush on her?"

"I will forgive a lot for a good sense of style, but that was over-the-top," replied Hillary.

"Warning us about things that might come out about BIB. Like she's been hiding stuff all along or something?" I asked.

"The only thing Nadia hides is her plastic surgery history," said Hillary. "Which must be extensive. I can *always* see the scars."

"Disgusting," Zeph dismissed. "Anyway. Seriously, was that chat with Nadia weird? That was . . . suspicious."

"Ugh. Conspiracy theorists, can we please make this day

go away with bad reception food?" replied Hillary.

"You're right," said Zeph. "We *have* to eat. And we haven't yet introduced our friend Cameron to the fine art of intern reception crashing."

Hillary explained, "Every night, there are at least ten free buffets, happy hours, or receptions for interns and young staffers. It's like soup kitchens, but in fancy buildings and with partially defrosted crab cakes and generic lime sodas."

"And you're welcome, because I am on the Hungry Intern distro list," Zeph said. "It's a daily e-mail that rates that day's receptions across town. The K Street ones are the most popular."

"And stay away from anything Cabinet-related," warned Hillary. "They are cheap and gross. I heard some girl got a parasite from a pork skewer at the Department of Health and Human Services mixer. Health and Human Services!"

"Friday nights are spotty," said Zeph, as he scanned the his e-mail. "Looks like our best bet tonight is a reception at the National Press Club."

"Who's speaking?" I asked.

Hillary simultaneously clamored: "When is the food?"

Zeph chose to answer my question: "A bunch of former ambassadors to Japan talking about Japanese-American trade relations over the years."

Hillary made a snoring noise.

We opened the front door of the Rayburn building and felt a welcome blast of balmy evening air. They ran ahead as I looked back—and up—at the five stories of graying white that towered above me. The evening shadows started their crawl across the glistening blocks of marble. I walked backward, and the structure appeared to get bigger with each step. Like it was puffing its chest or something. Threatening that it could crush me with just one of its clean, sharp chunks of stone.

6

Though the name sounds impressive, the interior of the National Press Club building was not all that different from the ball-room of the Lagrima Red Lion Inn, where I attended Brett Bergsman's bar mitzvah party five years earlier. Fluorescent lights shone down from ceiling panels overhead. And a polka-dot carpet spread across three adjacent conference rooms whose adjustable walls had been removed for the evening's event to form one giant forum space. A group of five men relaxed in plush chairs on an elevated platform as a line of eager young Washingtonians chirped paragraph-long questions into a microphone.

My eyes were immediately drawn to a girl in a yellow dress. . . .

"Dude," Zeph nudged me. "You're thinking about Ariel.

I can see it. I know it's a shock, but just try to take your mind off it. I can guarantee you half the office is getting smashed at some happy hour right now. We can enjoy a civil intern reception."

"You're right, I know," I said. Zeph didn't know that I had an outstanding message from Ariel. Something she needed to tell me. But he was right about moving on from the shock. And the regret.

Per Hillary's insistence, we had arrived late—just in time to hear the last few questions of the Q&A, though it was clear that she had no intention of listening. Upon entering the standing-room-only space, she was scanning the crowd.

"She's looking for trophy friends," Zeph confided. "Out here in the wild, she likes to collect high-profile people and then call them her friends to everyone else. Ambassadors' kids, rich junior lobbyists, and pretty much anyone with the last name 'Kennedy.'"

"*Juliette!*" whisper-shouted Hillary, in an accent that desperately wanted to be French, and to no apparent reciprocation from anyone in our proximity. She scampered off to the other side of the conference room as applause signaled that the Q&A was over.

Though he called out Hillary, Zeph also seemed to size up the room, his squinted eyes asking: *Who should I know here?* "Let's meet up a little later," he said as he proceeded to join a large group that surrounded one of the speakers in the front. The conversation in the room got louder—punctuated by explosions of laughter and intense pats on backs.

It all happened around me, in spite of me, and I wasn't quite sure how to dive in. Kind of like when you show up to a high school dance with a hundred people to talk to, and you opt for the table of stale sugar cookies and the radioactively bright red punch instead. So, naturally, I worked my way to the food. A long table covered with a faded blue tablecloth featured trays of Japanese hors d'oeuvres. The extent of my experience with Japanese food in Lagrima was this restaurant where a bunch of Salvadoran ladies dressed up in kimonos and cooked shrimp on a big stove in front of your table. This sophisticated array of options was new and a little intimidating. Neat rows of sushi were flanked by crinkly dumplings. A kettle of soup steamed in the corner. The most familiar option seemed to be a bowl of big shiny green beans—I picked one up and chewed on the surprisingly slimy and increasingly fibrous bean sheath. With, oddly, no beans inside. I gulped it down and popped in a few more of this unusual food. As I munched away, I noticed a girl put a strand of the same food into the bowl that I had taken mine from. When her friend did the same thing, I realized that I wasn't eating what was intended to be eaten. I had eaten what was left behind. A separate bowl of smooth, bulging green beans was situated nearby the "trash bowl," and it became clear to me that you were supposed to eat the beans and then throw away the rest. I discreetly spit out the bean refuse into my napkin-covered hand as I looked around and hoped that no one had been paying attention. I locked eyes with a black-haired girl who was shaking her head as she walked toward me.

"Well, you're either extremely waste-conscious, or you just really happen to like eating other people's edamame husks. Which one is it?" she inquired, with slight effort applied to each word that revealed her to be a native Spanish speaker.

So *that's* what edamame was.

"The real answer is that I'm not from around here." I shrugged.

"Well, neither am I," she said. "And I think edamame is kind of weird. But just the husks, however . . ."

"I don't recommend them either," I assured her.

"Ahh, good to know." She laughed. "I'm Lena." She reached out her hand.

"I'm Cameron." We shook.

Lena's dark hair was wrapped up in a bun, and her light brown eyes hid behind a pair of horn-rimmed glasses. She wore a black skirt and a tight buttoned-up blue shirt, with a colorful necklace made of small porcelain tiles. Before I could read her name tag, she covered it with her crossed arms and Moleskine notebook. Her smile revealed that one of her front teeth was slightly crooked, but it just kind of looked perfect to me. She looked like she could be eighteen or twenty-eight. I hoped for eighteen.

"What brings you here, Cameron?" she asked.

I pointed to Hillary, who was double-kiss greeting a row of people who weren't double-kissing her back. "Her," I said. "And him," I added, gesturing to Zeph, who sported his best fake-captivated facial expression while talking with some old man. "They're my roommates. We're interning for the same congressman, and they said this is where you can get a free dinner. And network."

"Looks like you're enjoying the dinner and they are enjoying the networking. So mission accomplished," she dryly observed.

"Uhhhhm." I just looked straight into her eyes with a dumb smile.

She smiled back.

"Okay, well, it sounds like you're new in town and could use a little explanation of the social map." She cleared her throat. "This is a National Press Club Q&A and reception, which is slightly more prestigious than your average DC happy hour, hence the slightly more prestigious crowd." She began to signal around the room: "Here you have the congressional interns, like yourself. Usually first-timers in town, affluent and adequately connected in their home districts, which is why they got the gig . . ."

"Affluent. Well, actually," I began to correct her when she carried on.

She pointed to a group of slightly better-dressed twenty-somethings. "And here are the senate interns. They think they are superior to the congressional interns, as you can see by the way they dress. I suppose this reflects how senators think of congressmen generally."

She directed my attention to the front of the room, which was packed with hyper kids talking over one another and trying to get the attention of anyone who looked prestigious. "These are the think tank interns. They probably applied to intern on the Hill, but got rejected, so they tell everyone that they actually prefer to have"—*finger-quote gesture*—"'a more academic experience.'

"You can see that we have a few White House interns in our midst," she continued, pointing to a guy and girl who both looked very sophisticated and proud. "They have found the Holy Grail of all internships, and they like to think it's because of their résumés and leadership abilities, but in reality it's because their parents' super PACs favored the president."

"Is that legal?" I asked.

"People ask that question all the time in this town. I guess the answer is 'legal enough.'" She shrugged. "Anyway, moving on, you have the congressional pages. They are like the . . . the *elfos* . . . how do you say that?"

"Elves?" I asked.

"Yes, of course, the elves. They are the little elves of the city. Vulnerable sixteen-year-olds by themselves, but an elusive army of privilege as a group . . ."

Who is this girl and how does she know about everyone in the room?

"And finally"—she pointed to a group of girls in noticeably short skirts—"the Skinterns. Girls who mistake their internships for a fashion show, and in some cases, a day at the beach. Easy to spot for both the obvious reasons as well as for their subconscious Monica Lewinsky kinship."

"Good to know," I said.

"You'll note that most conversation revolves around who people are working for and, well, gossiping about one another. In whispers," she added. "You know no one ever whispers a compliment. So who are you working for, anyway?"

"Congressman Billy Beck—fifty-seventh congressional district of California," I said.

"House minority leader," she observed. "And probably the next Speaker of the House, if all goes well in November."

"Well, I guess he is kind of a celebrity in town," I said, surprised by her instant recognition. "So what brings you to Washington?"

"Well, you know what they say about DC. It's Hollywood for ugly people," she mused, not answering my question.

"Yeah, I guess that's kind of true," I said. "Except for you."

If I were back at the high school dance, I would have walked away and wished I hadn't said those last three words for the rest of the night. But not with her. Something about her made me feel like it was okay to say them. Something about her made me want her to know that's how I felt.

She wasn't wearing much makeup, which made her slight blushing clearly perceptible. "Listen, I've gotta run, but I'll see you around, okay? Probably another Q&A/reception plus food?" she suggested. "Ciao." And she headed out, apparently alone.

Not four seconds had passed when Hillary grabbed my shoulders and said, "OMG, do you know who you were just talking with?"

"Lena," I said.

"That was Marielena Cruz, the Mexican ambassador's daughter! She's been living in Washington for eight years with her parents and just graduated high school. Early admit to Princeton in the fall. And if I read the room right—I'm really good at doing that—she totally has a crush on you."

7

You would never have thought there was a death in the office
the next week, had it not been for Jigar's mass e-mail about
Ariel's memorial service details (Friday evening in Virginia
Beach, plus some charming fine print: "Invitation limited to
full-time staff," aka no interns, aka *Classy, Nadia*). There was
barely any mention of our fallen coworker. Katie rushed BIB
out the door for votes. Nadia and Jigar did whatever PR voodoo
they did behind closed doors. LAs did their best to calm down
Very Concerned constituents with conversations ranging from
farming subsidies to *my neighbor's a meth cook*. Zeph and
Hillary conducted tours of the Capitol for eager tourists from
home, reminding me that someday soon I'd be able to lead a
tour group. And I stuffed envelopes with fund-raising flyers,
while practicing my forgery of BIB's signature. (Sorry, district:

That personalized letter you got from him was actually signed by a kid barely out of high school.)

In an unexpected turn of events, I got upgraded from the card table that was halfway lodged into a closet. My new desk was Ariel's old one, and as I sat down in her chair for the first time, it felt like moving into a house where someone had died. As if her apparition would visit me regularly or something. I opened one of the desk drawers, which was still filled with Ariel's things. There was a faded Post-it note with an all-caps reminder to "SEND RENT." A stack of ripped movie theater tickets, which revealed an eclectic fondness for both science fiction and art house. And a framed picture of a teenage Ariel, arm around a girlfriend and smiling like you only can during a high school summer. The same picture that had been cropped for the news reports. It all started to feel a bit voyeuristic, so I closed the drawer, even as I wished Ariel could have made good on her promise for us to be friends. Or at least to work on that project she had mentioned.

On Friday, most of the permanent staff cleared out of the office for the memorial service. It was a pretty quiet day—Zeph read every page of every national newspaper, while Hillary changed the reception desk TV channel from C-SPAN to a reality show about rival social media stars, with the volume so low she thought we couldn't hear. And I, of course, was diligently typing away and researching public school funding for Marcus. And by that I mean: I was chatting with Lena, the secretive and very resourceful Mexican ambassador's daughter who had somehow tracked down my MessageNow account. It was a welcome distraction. Aside from a couple questions about Ariel's memorial service, we mostly just IMed about nothing: emojis and links to photo galleries of unflattering pictures of politicians eating. And bad jokes.

LENA: **How many interns does it take to screw in a light-bulb?**

ME: **Ummm . . .**

LENA: **It doesn't matter, you'll have to do it again anyway.**

ME: **That is hurtful. I could totally screw in the lightbulb right.**

LENA: **Is that a euphemism?**

ME: **You are disgusting.**

LENA: **And you are spending your whole Friday on Message Now with me. Is this what you meant by all that "hard work" you said you were going to do this summer in your interview?**

ME: **Well, I'd be able to get something done if a certain stalker would leave me alone.**

LENA: **I wouldn't say stalker. More like guardian who doesn't think you're ready for an hordurves table, let alone a big city. And a little bit of a stalker.**

ME: **It's hors d'oeuvres, Miss Princeton. I guess you missed that one on the TOEFL.**

LENA: **How did you know I'm going to Princeton?**

Caught. Hillary's intel. I'd let it slip. My face burned and my heart thumped quietly and quickly.

But I was quite proud of my comeback: **You're not the only one who is allowed to be a stalker.**

LENA: **Touché. So if you are like most interns on their second week in DC, you still have nothing to do tonight, right?**

ME: **I have a very fulfilling night of Scandal binge watching ahead with the roommates. Hillary claims the show is educational. "A second internship."**

LENA: **Okay. Well, I can't handle another night of my dad's nerdy diplomat friends. And that is why you and I are going to meet at Kramerbooks.**

ME: **I wonder if that place has anything to do with books.**

LENA: **It's only the best bookstore in the city and probably this country and maybe the universe. They have books AND pies.**

ME: **Well, then I guess we have to go.**

Bonus: Pie was about all I could afford for a Friday night out. It would be a nice break from my alternating schedule of PB&Js and Top Ramen. I thought I might even be able to pay for her slice. . . .

LENA: **7:30 p.m.**

When I told Hillary I wanted to check out a bookstore that night instead of watching *Scandal* with her and Zeph, she replied, "Just know that I will not be rewatching any episodes with you. And I cannot keep myself from revealing spoilers. Remember that this is your choice."

I gladly accepted her verbal waiver, and we parted ways at six p.m. And I headed to what I think was my first date of the summer.

I found myself emerging once again from the Dupont Circle metro station—exactly eight days after the first time I came out of that extremely deep hole. As I watched the cars chase each other on the roundabout, I wondered if Ariel and that guy passed through here on their way to their appointment with a tree and a guardrail. If maybe I could have prevented the doomed ride had I just talked with her that night like she'd wanted. When you're one of the last people someone talks to before they die, you're linked to that person. You're connected. There's a little groove in your brain that they nestle into and never leave. I knew this because of my mom. And I was already feeling it again with Ariel.

Kramerbooks was just off the Circle, on Connecticut. An odd crowd of hipsters and grandparents and hipster grandparents hovered around the entrance. In an outdoor dining area, at least two girls' nights out leaned into small tables dressed with picked-over paninis and already-drained wine glasses. I entered and smelled a combination of that dull, sawdusty old book smell and perfectly cooked chicken, with a whiff of melting chocolate and coffee. A man in a suit and tie tuned a violin on a stage in the corner, apparently having come straight from work to play a gig. The distant cacophony of a busy restaurant kitchen competed with some soft European techno music.

"We're both early!"

I turned to see that Lena and I had walked into the same cramped corridor of books. Books about sex positions.

"I think this is a sign," said Lena.

"Yes, all of these guidebooks will come in handy tonight," I replied in an ironic creeper voice that came off as a legit creeper voice.

"Pervert."

"Wait up, you can't call me a pervert when you start off saying that it's a sign, and then—"

"Enough about books," she interrupted. "It's time for pie." As she walked to the restaurant part of the store, she looked back at me. "By the way, nice to see you, Cameron."

"Nice to see you, Lena."

She wore a long blue dress made out of T-shirt fabric, cinched at the waist with a wide brown belt. Plus some scuffed-up Vans that look like they were white four summers ago. Earlier this week, she'd looked cute. But tonight, somehow this simple getup made her look beautiful. We sat down, ordered (apple crumble for me, vegan pecan for her, $17.50

total—*sheesh, we're not at Marie Callender's anymore*), and promptly had nothing to talk about. We made eye contact and simultaneously raised our eyebrows like you do when you have run out of things to talk about at the end of a date. Except this was the beginning of a date.

"So. Your dad's diplomat nerd friends . . . ," I said, as she asked at the same time, "How was the second week of work?"

"You first," we both said to each other.

I obliged. "It was exactly what I was expecting, which is weird," I said. "It felt like a normal week, but it shouldn't have been normal. I mean, Ariel died, and then everyone's all 'business as usual.'"

"Yeah, that is horrible. Any word from the memorial service?"

"It's happening right now," I replied. "Whole office headed down there, except for the interns."

I told her about Nadia's harsh warning and Zeph's OCD system for folding letters. I told her about Marcus the Cheetos hoarder and my heroic educational research. About when I delivered a folder of select constituent mail to BIB so he could read them—a single act that instantly made me feel cooler than my entire high school graduating class.

"So basically, I'm going to be running the country by the end of the summer," I said. "And by the way, Congressman Beck is awesome. We grew up in the same hometown, and he always likes to talk about it with me. He's going to be the next Speaker of the House, and he treats me like I've been around for years."

"Impressive, but you know that's what politicians do—right?" She laughed as the waiter promptly served up two heaping plates of pie, into which we both promptly dug. It was my preferred ratio of crumble to apple, which is precisely three to two.

"What do you mean?" I asked.

"You know how everyone who met Bill Clinton said that it was like they were the only people in the world in that moment? That guy seduced . . . okay, maybe 'seduced' isn't the best word choice . . . he mesmerized everyone, from granny voters to heads of state. But spoiler alert: They weren't the only people in the world. He was just the only one who could make them feel that way."

"So you're saying I'm not special," I concluded.

"No, Cameron, I think you're special," she said. "But not because a career politician makes you have a crush on him." She smiled as she lightly bit her fork and chewed on a mouthful of chocolaty pecans. "Anyway . . . you can't find this at a stupid intern reception."

"Well, I'm still gonna believe that Beck and I have something special." I laughed, but I was partly serious. "And now it's your turn."

"Oh." She nodded. "My dad and the diplomats. Well, I

guess if we are going to be friends this summer, I should be up front with you. I am the daughter of the president of Mexico, and I have escaped my bodyguards to be with you tonight, but we can only stay together until they find me."

"Excuse me?" I asked.

"Actually, that is the plot of some Disney Channel movie I watched as a kid." She laughed, her slight Spanish accent creeping into her speech.

"I think I saw that movie too. Didn't Miley Cyrus play the part of you in this scenario?"

"No way, gross," she quickly dismissed. "So actually, my dad is the Mexican ambassador to the US. . . ."

Okay, finally some truth here.

". . . and I've been living in DC since junior high. And I like it a lot more than Mexico City. And sometimes I feel guilty about that. Hi, my name is Marielena, and I'm an expat."

"Wow, so did you go to high school with the president's son?" I asked.

"Yes, I had the pleasure of knowing Timothy *and* his various body odors in sophomore year chemistry at the Sidwell Friends School. Goooo Quakers!" she added with a sarcastic fist in the air.

"Yeah, he looks like he would stink." I tried to relate. Somehow.

She continued, "But honestly, the best part about high

school is that it's over. And I can't decide who is more obnoxious: the kids here in DC who tag along at state dinners by night and smoke pot by day, or my friends back in Mexico who fly in their parents' G650s to Miami for weekend shopping trips and drive Hummers to school."

"The plight of the privileged," I commented.

"And my dad thinks it's better for public impressions that I go to university in Mexico, but I secretly applied to Princeton and he is not happy that I'm going there. So I'm trying to spend this summer as far away from him and the Beltway brats as I can. Which is why I spend my time hiding at the Press Club and Kramerbooks. And you're my accomplice."

"Well, I've never been to a state dinner nor flown to Miami, so you're in luck," I offered.

Seriously—being high at a state dinner and weekend shopping trips to Miami? She wasn't just out of my league. She *ran* her own league. She was the president of a league far, far away.

"Aaaand I've officially overshared, so now you get to tell me too much. But first, you're not eating the raisins," she observed. I wasn't. Because raisins are disgusting. "And you're out of ice cream already. Proper ice cream management is key when one eats pie, you know?"

"Very observant," I said.

"Anyway, okay, back to you. Tell me about yourself. What's your family like? What does your dad do?"

I coughed on a bite of pie as I realized my dad's occupation didn't exactly compete with "ambassador."

"He's the CEO of a landscaping corporation," I said, teeth clenched with technical honesty.

"Wow, that's cool," said Lena. She was clearly just trying to make conversation, but I was trying to make an impression.

"Yeah, he runs the thing," I added. "Like a hundred people work for him, I guess?" I squinted my eyes and looked up as if I were counting his extensive payroll. All I could see in my mind were him and Rogelito in sweat-stained T-shirts.

"What's Lagrima like?" she asked.

I hesitated, then asked the question that would explain it all: "Have you heard of cow tipping?"

She cocked her head with a concerned look. "You mean, like, cows?" Her arms gestured wide as to indicate an ambiguously large thing. Somehow, in the privileged circles of the Mexican and political elite, this concept had eluded her.

"On my way over here, I saw a Facebook photo of some guys from my high school. They had pushed over a cow on its side."

"Like, to the ground? That's awful!" exclaimed Lena.

"That's Lagrima. You see, all throughout high school, everyone talked about going cow tipping, but I don't think anyone actually did it. It was like an urban legend. Or a suburban legend, whatever. Not physically possible. So I guess these guys decided to actually make it happen last night. Twelve of them cornered some poor cow and pushed it over. And then took pictures with it."

"These guys are your . . . friends?" she asked. Her forehead crinkled slightly and her eyes grew bigger, intrigued. Confused cute.

"Well, we were pretty tight in elementary school. But paths seem to diverge halfway through the seventh grade, you know? That's when everyone puts you in your place and doesn't let you out until high school's over. Or actually, in Lagrima, they don't let you out until you get out of town," I said.

"Is that what you're doing here in DC?" she asked. "Finding your new 'place'?"

The answer was "yes," but it somehow felt traitorous to say it out loud—to my city, my family. I guess she had experience trying to shed some adolescent skin. She could relate, a little. But would she think I was disrespectful—or worse, pathetic, a poser?

Apparently, it took a little too long for me to answer, because she said, "I'm sorry. I'm asking too much. I guess it's not fair of me to avoid your questions and then go full-on therapist with you." She looked down and cut the remains of her pie into neat cubes. A thick strand of hair fell down her right shoulder. She quickly tucked it behind her ear. And shot a quick smile at me. Even though I'd only known her for a week,

Lena was easy to talk to. And even though she flew on private jets and went to school with the president's son, she felt more like home than anyone I'd met in DC. Since Ariel.

"No, no, you're not asking too many questions," I said. "You're just . . ." *Beautiful*, I thought. ". . . really good at asking them. I guess I *am* realizing that I don't want to grow old in the place where I grew up. My high school graduation was a few weeks ago, and it already feels like it was a year ago. Other than my buddy Berto, I haven't talked with any of those classmates since. And I'm okay with the distance. And the not cow tipping."

"I am too," Lena's eyebrows raised.

The server dropped the little black check envelope at our table. I quickly pulled out the only twenty from my wallet and placed it inside like it was nothing. Except it was approximately three to four lunches I would have to scrounge for somehow. She was worth it.

"You don't have to pay, Cameron!" she exclaimed. "Coming here was my idea."

"I guess manners are one of the *good* things about growing up in a small town like Lagrima," I answered and handed the check back to the server.

As we finished our pie, Lena told me more about the magical bookstore restaurant we were in. Like how it was open twenty-four hours on Fridays and Saturdays. And how in 1998, they refused to comply with a subpoena to disclose the purchase records of a frequent customer, one Monica Lewinsky. And they won.

"This is like if a bookstore was Kurt Cobain, but also Stephen Colbert. With baked goods."

"Exactly," Lena confirmed.

Two tables away, I noticed a lady scanning her phone and saying to her friend, "That poor girl . . . and her *mom*. I love her mom." I instinctively knew they were reading about Ariel, and I told Lena we should see if there was any more news about the memorial. We both whipped out our phones.

REPRESENTATIVE BECK CONSOLES FORMER STAFFER'S FAMILY, said one headline.

Lena pulled up a picture of the funeral—a stoic Nani Lancaster flanked by her husband on one side and BIB on the other.

We each searched for more info.

"Some local newspaper has posted a photo gallery," said Lena. She showed me a picture of a jam-packed high school gymnasium, with Ariel's picture projected onto a large screen in the middle of the basketball court.

I skimmed an article: "'Lancaster's office has released a statement—she hopes Ariel's passing can be a warning to all Americans, about the dangers of drunk driving, and the need to hold our loved ones close because—'"

"Wait," Lena put down the phone. She covered her mouth with one hand and shook the other hand like it had just touched something unbearably hot. "No way."

She refreshed her phone again.

"What?!" she said again, as if something she'd hoped would disappear had come back, even stronger.

"What's up?" I asked.

Lena pushed her phone across the table to me. I turned it around so I could read the words.

Words that screamed off the small, gently glowing screen.

DEAD STAFFER AND REP BECK—SEX ON CAPITOL HILL.

8

BIB's alleged indiscretions with his now-dead staffer were suddenly the only thing people talked about. Including us.

And it's a shame, because the whole Kramerbooks *are we
flirting or not?* thing with Lena was actually kind of great. We
got on the metro, taking the red line to the blue line. Throughout the trip, we heard fragments of Very Opinionated people's
conversations:

"Someone that high up . . . Can't these guys keep it in
their pants?!"

"Wouldn't be summer without a sex scandal . . . but she's
dead now too!"

The conversation with Lena became more serious as we
thought about the increasingly complicated dynamic at my

office. Despite the tantalizing subject matter, news of a possible sex scandal had sure killed the mood.

"A little weird, don't you think?" she asked.

"What do you mean?" I replied.

"This girl dies, and within a week, the press is jumping all over allegations of an affair she had," she said.

". . . it's worse now that she died in that accident . . . ," some lady loud-talked from a few rows behind us.

"And he works with that girl's mom on the Hill! How awkward . . . ," said the woman next to her.

"Like she died because . . ." I realized my own voice was louder than normal too, to compensate for the shrieking steel of the metro. I spoke more quietly, in case anyone else was listening to me. "Like she died because they were . . . *doing it*? She was having an affair with BIB. That's crazy."

Lena's station was next: Farragut West, just one stop before Foggy Bottom. As the train vroomed to a halt, she stood up and shrugged her shoulders. "I don't know. But see, you're doing it too. Talking about an affair. Not her death anymore. An affair. Everyone on this train is, apparently. And in this town, what everyone is talking about is usually not an accident."

Eight years in DC had either made her really cynical or really smart.

Suddenly less pensive, she said a quick, "Had fun tonight. Thank you, Cameron," as the hydraulic train doors hissed open.

"Me too," I said, walking toward her to give her a hug. She stepped off the train before she saw my outreached arms. By the time she turned around to wave good-bye, I tightly folded my arms around myself, as if my standing self-hug were totally intentional. As the train jolted to life, I resisted the urge to see if anyone noticed the unreturned embrace. Less awkward for all of us if I didn't make eye contact.

I walked in our apartment door to hear a salacious salutation from Hillary: "It says she was sleeping with a whole fraternity at American University!" She and Zeph were in full-on news junkie mode—news blaring, laptops glowing, and phones jumping from headline to headline. "I can kind of see that."

"Nice, Hill," said Zeph. "Hi, Cam. You can see we have officially moved on from the bereaved-ex-colleagues phase."

"No, I'm serious. It sounds like Ariel was quite, um, prolific," reported Hillary.

"According to some desperate blogger who just wants to grab the attention for a few minutes," clarified Zeph. "Can we please just listen to some truth from my man Anderson Cooper?"

"I'm sure he'd LIKE to be your man," said Hillary, straining for a laugh.

Neither Zeph nor Anderson seemed to care about Hillary's unfortunate nonjoke as Mr. Cooper's nasal voice droned on the

TV: "... *detailed in pages from Ms. Lancaster's diary, which has been obtained by the website DistrictDaily—who first broke the story earlier this evening. No word yet from Congressman Beck, who was attending the former staffer's funeral—and sitting next to the girl's mother, Congresswoman Nani Lancaster—when the news hit. ...*"

"Awkward . . ." was Hillary's astute observation.

"You always know how to say the right thing, Hillary Wallace," said Zeph.

I continued to third-wheel my way through the weekend as the news cycle cranked out more sources and rumors and questions—and Zeph and Hillary provided their own commentary.

We were all speechless, though, when BIB himself appeared on *The Week with Sterling Steele*, a Sunday morning news show whose anchor was three decades too old for the job but did have a spectacular name. BIB and his wife sat before the octogenarian host, who asked about their relationship with Ariel Lancaster. It was a familiar sight—the accused politician, the supportive and modestly dressed spouse, and the barely contained glee of a reporter who had them cornered.

"Ms. Lancaster was a hard worker, but more important, a daughter and a friend to many. She joined thousands of her peers in wanting to make our country a better place by working on Capitol Hill. And I join those fellow staffers, as well as

Congresswoman Lancaster and her husband, Jim, in mourning her life cut short, but also in honoring her."

Katherine Beck resolutely nodded along with every sentence.

"And by having sex with her?" strained Steele.

Mrs. Beck's head nodding lingered for a fraction of a second after the bold question was asked.

"Did anyone else see that?" I asked.

"That man is senile—how did Nadia let BIB get in that chair?" yelled Zeph, not noticing what I had noticed.

Hillary screamed with horror and voyeuristic delight.

"Sterling," BIB said, his voice suddenly peppered with resentment, "if you are going to speak plainly, then so will I. These stories about a relationship between Ms. Lancaster and I are totally inappropriate and totally false. And in the wake of Ms. Lancaster's accident last week, we should be better than to entertain such garbage. *You* should be better than such garbage."

"There's this diary of hers that says you did it with her on top of the copy machine. How exactly does that work?" Steele was apparently not better than "such garbage" as he plowed on.

Mrs. Beck, ever voiceless and slightly uncertain, looked to her husband with incongruous pride.

"Dirty old man!" shouted Hillary at the TV.

"Sterling, you have been at this since you revealed the recipe for Mamie Eisenhower's fudge on national radio, and you've been a fine reporter and a fine friend. But this is not reporting. This is . . ." He hesitated. "Katherine and I have been married and devoted to each other for twenty-eight years, and what has sustained us is our faithfulness to each other and our faith in God."

"But where there's smoke, there's fire," suggested Steele.

"Where there's smoke, there's smoke," BIB stated firmly. "And I hope we can all clear the air now so we can focus on the Lancaster family's tragic loss."

Someone behind the camera mercifully played *The Week*'s patriotic, flute-based theme, as an overacted commercial for night-driving glasses appeared.

"Well, that was a disaster," said Hillary. "Let's see if Nadia still has a job on Monday."

"Or was that perfect?" I asked. I tried out the lens of Lena's recent suspicion as a way to think about the situation. "Use the doddering old man to discredit the accusations. Remind viewers that this guy was around for some cooking show on the radio in the 1950s. Keep the message on the family in mourning. The wife, the faith in God . . . and our man BIB gets bullied by a misinformed old man . . ."

"You're saying this was intentional," Hillary said, shaking her head.

"I'm saying I think Nadia knows what she's doing. Give that interview to a reporter who knows what a blog is, and BIB would have walked out of there with some bruises."

"Our little boy is growing up to be such a cynic—and an ageist!" cracked Zeph.

BIB and Mrs. Beck did not return after the commercial break, but the news stories paraded on: There were interviews with Ariel's teachers and more than one former boyfriend from Virginia Beach. Minibiographies of BIB followed—detailing his almond-growing roots, philanthropic efforts, service in Congress, as well as this new disgraceful asterisk that would now disfigure an otherwise pristine profile. A particularly desperate reporter probed a barista from a coffee shop near Ariel's apartment: "What did she order every morning?" One blogger celebrated that "the slow news of spring" had finally come to an end.

I guessed the news landscape *had* been a little dry. For weeks, the media had been testing the limits of a jet plane disappearance in Indonesia. Our very own Ariel had lit a spark in the middle of a thirsty forest of readers and reporters—who got fire instead of water, and eagerly spread the flames. And my chat with Lena at the end of the night made me wonder if the dramatic headlines were real or arson—lit by hack bloggers eager to watch the story burn brighter.

The PR firefighters came in the form of Nadia Zyne and

Jigar Shah—who looked uncharacteristically exhausted when we showed up at the office on Monday. Throughout that week, Jigar's stubble and Nadia's wrinkled blouses denoted multiple all-nighters, as they worked to salvage the boss's suddenly sullied name. And BIB's resolute manner, reverence for Ariel's loss, and focus on work gave everyone confidence that he was right; the rumors had to be garbage. The affair news didn't add up for me, either. I hadn't gotten to know Ariel very well, but if anything, she was wary of BIB, not attracted to him.

In an apparent victory for either the truth or good PR, the week yielded multiple stories about how Sterling Steele was better suited as the emcee for an old folks' home talent show than for the serious news show he once confidently helmed. How the writing in the diary didn't necessarily match Ariel's. How the dates of the alleged encounters corresponded to times when BIB and Ariel were on opposite sides of the country. The carelessness and desperation of online journalism. The need to focus on one girl's brilliant life, and not on ugly rumors. It was as if the talking heads looked back on the earth they had scorched over the week and now pointed fingers at one another for the destruction that had been caused. Their own hastiness became a whole new story. The show's over. Nothing to see here.

And then we were back to stories about that lost Indonesian plane.

Through it all, I thought about Lena and her skeptical response to the news. But mostly, I wanted to hang out with her again. Tuesday felt about right for following up—I didn't want her to think I was too into her and freak her out. Wait until Wednesday, and I'm a dick. But Tuesday—Tuesday is just close enough to aloof dickness while still being a good guy. I sent her a note on MessageNow: **Are there more exceptional bookstores you're going to take me to?**

It took her fifty-seven minutes to reply: **Ha! No, K-books is the only one.**

Well, then, my turn to pick a venue, I replied. **But mine's going to be more obvious: Washington Monument this week?**

I'm not above touristy stuff, but unfort I'm traveling with my dad in Mexico until Sunday. He's put me to work—embassy event planner for the summer. :(

I was trying to be hard to get, but she had turned the tables. I had to wait almost a week to see her again?!

Okay, I replied. **You, me, and the obelisk. Next week.**

That sounds vaguely risqué, but, um, sure. She abruptly logged off before I could assure her that my reference to the phallic monument was mainly innocent.

On Friday afternoon, one brief televised statement seemed to shut everyone up for good. As the evening shadows grew—and families across America settled in for a weekend together—the staff gathered around the multiple TVs in the office for "a statement by Congresswoman Nani Lancaster." I found myself standing next to Nadia as the screen cut to a plush DC apartment living room.

Representative Lancaster sat on a couch, flanked by her frowning husband and framed by an array of family pictures featuring the various stages of her dead daughter's life. Though she had passed through horrible events in the past weeks, Nani looked sharp and intense and ready. She took a deep breath, and then said, "My fellow Americans. My fellow mothers, and sisters, and friends. One week ago, I was discussing the menu for my daughter's funeral dinner. Everyone told me to stay out of those details, but I couldn't. All of the moms listening will relate: that's what we're supposed to do. You care even when it's almost impossible. And Jim and I have felt a similar kind of care from all of you. Thank all of you for your words of comfort, the letters, and even some wonderful pictures your children sent us." Nani smiled as she held up a Crayola masterpiece of a blond girl floating up to the clouds. Her angel. Her Ariel.

"Since our baby's funeral, there have been unfortunate statements bandied about in the media. I am here to tell you that these stories are untrue. Congressman Billy Beck is an upstanding and moral man and faithful husband, who I am lucky to call a friend. I assure you that you can call him that as well. And I think the American people want to talk about more substantive things."

As the sentence ended, I glanced over to see Nadia subconsciously mouth every word. Her words. Her speech. Representative Lancaster's statement, as heartfelt as it sounded, was not her own. I snapped my head back as I felt Nadia's gaze shift toward me. Representative Lancaster ended the statement with the obligatory "God bless America" as Nadia grabbed Jigar and her tall leather purse and walked out of the office.

"BIB, are you there?" she spoke into her phone as the front door closed behind her.

"Am I the only person who thinks that every time politicians say 'God bless America,' it sounds like they really mean 'God bless me'?" Zeph mused to himself.

"Zephaniah! The woman lost her daughter," scolded Hillary with sudden moral superiority.

"And God bless Friday!" shouted Marcus. He declared an impromptu office party at Tortilla Coast. "It's the best bad Mexican food you'll ever have, right by the Capitol South metro stop. No excuses!" He pointed at Katie.

Based on the way he singled her out, it appeared that she usually had an excuse.

"Marcus," she said, "if you must know, I'm going on a date tonight." Though Katie was technically senior to Marcus, they were all pretty close in age. The long hours and intensity of their jobs seemed to foster an informal, family-like dynamic.

"Good for you," he said. Not letting Katie kill the party

recruitment momentum, he added, "Last one there picks up the first round of 'ritas!" announced Marcus as he rushed out the door with a few others in tow.

"I feel sorry for him," said Hillary. "We should at least make an appearance."

"That is so sweet of you," observed Katie, as she headed out the door. "With all the help he's getting from you with his social life, Hillary, and from Cam on all that research—I don't know what the poor guy is going to do after you guys leave here."

We followed her out the door soon after, and I briefly thought that instead of helping Marcus with "all that research" I could have been working with Ariel on whatever it was she'd urgently wanted to tell me.

9

My Alabaman alter ego came in handy yet again, since a guard checked my ID as we entered the packed doors of Tortilla Coast. Clearly, Marcus was not alone in his surrender to the cheap and convenient draw of this restaurant—so close to the Capitol complex, it might as well have been named after a famous lawmaker. Manic Spanish guitar blared through the speakers—and although this music choice wasn't exactly culturally accurate for a Mexican restaurant, I was willing to forgive the oversight because the chips and salsa were actually quite good. Though I lost Zeph and Hillary to the throbbing Friday-night crowd pretty quickly, Marcus appeared out of nowhere and frantically offered me a half-eaten enchilada before disappearing again.

"Thanks?" I asked.

The anxious guitar, the constant bumping into strangers, the decomposing mound of cheese and tortilla, the more confident guys hitting on the girls who only saw straight through me—it was a lot to take in, and I wasn't sure I wanted to anymore. So I texted Berto: **Que pasa, Humbertonius?**

He wrote back immediately: **TV reruns with the old lady. Can life get any better?**

I answered, **Yes, it can. It gets better in DC.** Then I stretched the truth a little. Okay, a lot. I needed to prove to him that DC was the right decision, and for Berto, that meant simply texting: **I am at a party and there are so many hot girls here.**

Get some! he replied.

I texted back an ambiguously confident **Yup**, when some random guy asked me, "Are you going to eat that?"

"All yours," I told him as I pushed Marcus's plate his way. That's pretty much what I told the whole restaurant, too, as I Irish-good-byed my way out the front door.

The breezy core of the Capitol South station was deserted as I stepped on the Franconia-Springfield train just as the doors were closing. A few lonely stops later, I got off at Foggy Bottom and emerged to the sidewalk. The humidity that was so punishing during the day felt like a comforting blanket in the dark, late-June evening. And partly because it was a nice night, but mostly because only losers get home before nine p.m. on a Friday, I walked in the direction opposite my apartment—south, to the Lincoln Memorial.

I shared Honest Abe with a number of tourists that night— shuffling back and forth from reading the second inaugural address, etched into the interior wall, to fulfilling requests for family photos. The marble cavern glowed with a gentle golden light. Though visitors' talking bounced off the walls, there was a reverence befitting the Greek temple structure that enclosed the massive seated statue of the "Savior of the Union." I turned my back to Mr. Lincoln to see the adjacent pool and the distant, towering Washington Monument reflected there. I weaved my way down the stairs between a few seated couples and a group of fiftysomething men dressed in military fatigues, who must have been veterans.

The ghostly, underlit figures of the Korean War Veterans Memorial beckoned me from the right as I continued my solitary, improvised tour. About twenty statues of servicemen—wearing helmets and ponchos and weary looks on their faces treaded through a triangular patch of fenced-off grass. A woman and what appeared to be her grown children clustered and hugged one another in the far corner of the monument area. In my US History class, we spent three weeks on the Vietnam War, and like half of a period on the Korean War—and I wondered how these guys standing before me and that family in the corner would feel about that.

I followed signs toward the Franklin Delano Roosevelt Memorial. Was it too nerdy of me to be excited about this historical scavenger hunt I'd found myself on? It was the first time I'd come face-to-bronze/marble-face with these monuments. At the entrance of the FDR Memorial, I looked out across the large body of water—a sign identified it as the Tidal Basin— and saw the gleaming Jefferson Memorial around the bend of the tree-lined water. For a moment, I wasn't thinking about Ariel's death or the affair gossip—and how my time in BIB's office so far had featured about 100 percent more tragedy/ scandal than I'd been expecting back home. If only for a few seconds, it was the stately, grand place I had always imagined.

Out of the corner of my eye, I noticed a whip of hair of a person seated on a bench by the water. The kind of "whip of hair" that results from someone who has seen you and doesn't want to be seen back. Unsuccessfully. Because I immediately knew who she was.

Katie Campbell turned and made eye contact with me just long enough to prompt the requisite "Hello"/acknowledgment that *Wow! What a coincidence we're both in the same place at the same time.* She sat on a green bench at the edge of the Tidal Basin—slightly hunched over and looking rather timid, even apologetic. Nothing like the preppy, crazed, and authoritative chief of staff who ran the office each day. Her date had apparently stepped away, because she was alone on the bench. I noticed that she was engaged in a rather elaborate textile project, hands clasped around knitting needles and frozen, as if this was a secret hobby and she had been caught.

"Hi, Cameron." She lifted her right hand for a quick wave.

"Hey, sorry, you don't have to talk to me," I said and started to walk away. "Don't mean to interrupt your date."

Her face hesitated for a moment before she replied, "No, no, don't worry. Come over here."

I walked closer to her as she moved across the bench to make room for me. I sat down next to her and asked, "So, where's the guy?"

"He's over there," Katie motioned behind us, toward a cluster of Asian tourists who admired the towering statue of a seated FDR—green from the oxidization of its copper material.

"You're dating a middle-aged Japanese man," I said.

"No such luck," she mused. "I'm with him." I realized she was pointing at the statue, not a person.

"You're on a date with Franklin Delano Roosevelt?"

"Yes, yes, I am. Standing date. Every Friday night, this bench. We talk about the evolution of the welfare system, Scottish terriers, and you should hear the juicy stuff he's told me about Eleanor. Let's just say that she was a very complex lady. But you have to keep our relationship a secret, okay?"

"Sure." I shrugged my shoulders.

"Because I need to keep my legitimate excuse for not schmoozing every weekend," she continued. "And I wouldn't want to disappoint the other men."

"Others?" I asked.

"Yeah. Abraham, Thomas, George, and George," she said as she pointed at the distant monuments that surrounded us.

"Not just one, but two Georges!?" I asked.

"We'll get to that in a minute. Let's go over to TJ," she said as she motioned toward the shining white dome of the Jefferson Monument. We stood up and headed in that direction when she asked, "Why don't you tell me about your internship so far?"

"Well, Ariel was kind of the only nonintern in the office who really talked to me during my first week," I said. "She showed me around, got me started on a project with Marcus, and—"

"Cameron."

"Yeah?"

"I asked you about the internship, and you're talking about Ariel."

"Oh, wow. Sorry. I thought you asked about her. Or maybe I was just thinking about her."

"She's on your mind; it's fine," she assured me. "She's on all our minds."

"I just really appreciated how she saw me as capable of being more than just an intern," I said. "I'm not above opening and sorting mail, but she had me doing research on my second day. . . ."

"You're ambitious," she said.

"I'm just finishing week three of the most important summer of my life. I guess you could call it ambition. Maybe a bit of desperation," I answered. "If you were from Lagrima, you'd be the same."

"You're desperate," she said.

"No, not exactly," I replied. "Desperation" was a bit dramatic. Or maybe a bit too true. "I just want this summer to mean something—to be the start of a new direction, a career."

"I hear you; I know," she said. "I've been there."

"How did you get your start?" I asked.

"Well, unlike a lot of my fellow staff here on the Hill, I did not start out at Andover, Exeter, or Phillips. . . ."

"Where?" I asked.

Katie laughed to herself. "Oh, bless your heart. Please never know what those places are. Please never change."

I shot her a querying smile.

"I'm a single-mom-raised public-school girl from Philadelphia. I was smart and I think I filled part of the 'poverty' quota, so UPenn let me in. Poli sci. Even though Philly is technically a big city, DC was always The City for me. So I guess that was always the next step, you know?"

"Yeah." I could relate to poverty quotas. "I know."

"So I spent a couple summers in my local congressman's office, and then got a full-time gig on the Ways and Means Committee, where I met BIB, who ran the committee and was on the rise. . . ."

"Six years ago," I said.

"Are you trying to tell me I'm old?" she asked, clearing her throat. "So anyway, BIB took a chance on me, and I didn't burn out like everyone else does, and now I'm his chief of staff. Younger than some of our LAs, which makes them die inside. But it's all because BIB saw something in me."

"That's amazing," I said as I calculated a potential similar fate for myself—in twelve years. "Working on the Hill—trusted advisor to congressional leadership. Seriously, *anything* to congressional leadership. That's kind of my dream. How'd you do it?"

"Well, I'm not going to say that I haven't done my share of all-nighters or hyperventilated by blowing up too many balloons for campaign events—but it really comes down to having a mentor—someone who believed in me. BIB. Look, you don't want to be this guy's enemy. . . ."

Like the protesters or that opponent's fund-raiser chief who Ariel told me about, I thought and nearly spoke out loud. Katie's allegiance to the man stopped me from speaking the words.

". . . but if you're his friend—if you demonstrate commitment—he is loyal. He can *make* you."

As we neared the towering temple to our third president, I kept walking toward it, while Katie diverged down a stairway to a poorly lit granite grotto.

"No TJ?" I asked.

"The second George," she said and pointed to a small pond and a plain cement bench where an iron statue of a slightly larger than life-size colonial man was casually seated. Flanked by his cane, hat, and a stack of books, he pensively and eternally stared right through us. As if we had interrupted his reading, his right index finger held his place in a book on his lap.

"Cameron," Katie announced, "meet George Mason."

"Who?"

"Exactly," she said. "Founding father, originator of the Bill of Rights, and one of the first founders to think that maybe the whole 'slavery' thing was a problem. And yet he's hidden down here. Those giant tour buses are parked a hundred yards away to check out Jefferson and the cherry blossoms in the spring. And they don't even know he's over here."

"Well, nice to meet you, Second George," I said as I sat next to his large frame and strained to put my arm around his shoulder. "I apologize. I should have known you, but I blame my culture for only focusing on the celebrity founding fathers. You should have had a more elaborate autograph. . . ."

"See!" Katie said. "You get it. It's the presidents, the Hancocks, the loud ones who get noticed. No one pays attention to the people in the background."

She sat down on the bench, on the other side of the statue. We leaned forward to see each other's faces around the hulking mass.

"Wait." I stopped her. "Are we talking about you now?"

Katie answered, "I'm talking about anyone who works on the Hill for eight years. Yeah, I guess I'm talking about me."

When she was in DC, my mom was in the background. Like Second George. My mom could have been a chief of staff like Katie. She would have loved it. She would have been great. And now I needed to be great for her, in her place.

Katie continued, "Not that I'm complaining. I don't want to fly across the country every weekend to see the district. I don't want to have to answer the nasty questions from the press. I'm the person who's slightly out of focus in the pictures online, standing just behind BIB. I make last-minute changes to his speeches—the lines that turn into sound bites every time. I get to do the real work. Trust me, it's better than the political kabuki. I leave that to him."

The "real work." I wanted it, too. Maybe it was the mind-softening humidity—or maybe it was hearing about Katie's career trajectory and thinking I could do the same. Or maybe the city was already changing me, empowering me. But something made me say the words that Lagrima Cameron would never have said: "Will you do that for me?"

"What do you mean?" she asked.

"Show me the ropes. Help me make the summer mean something."

She laughed to herself and said, "Well, you're something between ambitious and desperate, yes, you are!"

I looked down and realized that I had overasked. Daydreaming tends to be the most vivid late at night.

"Of course I'll look out for you," she said. I looked up at her, grateful and incredulous. "You're basically me, when I first started out! This environment can be tricky, and you can always come to me with questions, or if something seems off."

"Like how Nadia was acting after Ariel's accident . . ." I stopped myself as I didn't want Katie to think I was criticizing her peer.

"Ah yes, so you've experienced Nadia," she said. "Well, since I'm your mentor or whatever now, I'll tell you something that a chief of staff probably shouldn't say to an intern, but it's for your own good. It's better to stay away from her. I've seen her torture enough interns. Just be careful what you tell her, because she'll use it against you."

"Yeah, I get that vibe," I said, nodding, not fully understanding what that last phrase meant but wanting to appear in the know. It was comforting to hear Katie's advice—like getting a map of a minefield that pinpoints where each unexploded ordinance lies.

"Here," she said, pulling her phone out of her leather purse and typing a text. "My contact info. In case you need anything or want to reach out. I already have your number in my contacts. Ariel gave it to us. . . ."

Her voice trailed as a "Katie Campbell" contact popped up on my phone. I opened the text to find her phone number and an address.

"My apartment. You probably didn't need that. Anyway, that and the Nadia stuff is as much TMI as you're going to get from me tonight." She sighed, standing up. I joined her and we walked away from both TJ and Second George, across another bridge. Thousands of crickets chanted as the summer came into better focus. Ariel's memory and her promises of more work—more experience—had started to fade as I realized that Katie—*the chief of staff!*—believed in me.

We approached the bright white shaft of the Washington Monument, which shone starkly against the inky blue sky. First George.

"That's my stop. . . ." Katie pointed toward the distant light of the Smithsonian metro station. "I hope you keep secrets as well as the monuments do. Remember—I was on a date tonight."

"I wouldn't dare disclose your relationship with FDR," I

assured her. "I mean, mostly out of respect to Eleanor."

With that, I stepped onto the deserted Mall and back toward the now-distant Lincoln Memorial, and she briskly walked toward the metro station. As my feet hit the gravel of the walkway, I pulled out my phone to find a bunch of text messages from Lena, which started with **Save me from my father's bureaucratic dinner from hell**, and then a few **Where are you?**s. Followed by, **Have I been replaced by someone else?** And then, **Don't tell me you're sleeping with Beck too?!**

I stopped in the moonlit summer air that had somehow grown thicker and warmer as the night went on—thinking about how to respond.

No, just hanging out with Abe, Franklin, George, and George, I texted back.

I put my phone in my pocket and continued the long trek back to the apartment, and thought to myself, *And the chief of staff of the office. Who sees herself in me and wants me to succeed and confided in me and finally, yes, this is the DC I've been hearing about my whole life.*

10

With Zeph and Hillary checking out New York City for a couple days (they invited me, but my wallet said "no") and Lena still in Mexico City with her dad, I was friendless in DC for the weekend. Flying solo in the apartment was cool, but mostly and surprisingly lonely. I filled the void with a visit to the National Air and Space Museum because 1) free and 2) obviously. I tried to remember why the flimsy-looking frame of the *Spirit of St. Louis* looked so familiar. Then I remembered a photo of my mom and dad standing in front of the ancient plane. I asked a stranger to take a picture of me in the same place where they'd stood. Family photo. Kind of. I sent the picture to my dad with the caption, **Look familiar?**

My phone had collected a number of selfie texts from Lena in packed hotel ballrooms, each expression more bored out of her mind than the one before. I sent her a bunch of selfies in front of airplane exhibits.

I also talked with my dad, who apologized for not being able to share any updates from home that competed with a congressional sex scandal. And he confirmed that my picture in the National Air and Space Museum did, in fact, look familiar—but, predictably, not much more about my mom. I caught Berto between a couple of his shifts at work. He talked about going to this waterslide park near Lagrima late at night. One of our friends was a lifeguard there, and got us in after hours. I had forgotten that this was one of my favorite parts of summer back home—and tried to convince myself that I didn't miss it. I did. I found myself strangely looking forward to Monday—to the order and "lots of people around" of a busy office.

As I emptied a bag of constituent mail onto the long sorting table Monday morning, Zeph and Hillary informed me that I would be joining them on a guided tour of the Capitol building. Though most summer visitors stand in line for the official visitor's center tour, the smart tourists know that they can get a private, front-of-the-line pass, courtesy of their congressman. It was Hillary's turn to do the honors.

"You're in good hands, Cam. I give a much more interesting tour than Zeph does," said Hillary.

"Oh, really?" I asked.

"And by that she means that she drops every US Capitol urban legend in the book on these poor people who don't know any better," informed Zeph.

"I just enhance things a bit, and they love it. What they don't know just makes them have more fun!"

"Every congressman's office has a tour script, and over the years some of the stories have gotten a bit exaggerated. All of a sudden you get the ghosts of Civil War soldiers terrorizing janitors at night," said Zeph.

"That is awesome!" I said.

"Watch and learn," affirmed Hillary. "I just better not get one of those Dan Brown fans who wants to know where the eternal flame under the crypt is, or how they can dig under the Washington Monument to find a Bible. So *obno* . . ."

On Hillary's handy abbreviation for "obnoxious," a cluster of baseball caps, jean shorts, and white tennis shoes with shin-high socks entered BIB's office. "You must be the Ferbers!" she exclaimed, her arms outstretched and her voice an enthusiastic octave higher.

"Yes, ma'am," said the apparent patriarch of the family. "I'm Bert, and this is my wife and our kids." He gestured to a staircase of descending heights: boy, girl, boy, girl. And then he acknowledged the short, white-haired, track-suited seventh wheel of the family vacation, "And this is my mother-in-law, Rihanna."

"Rihanna?" I burst out, incredulous.

"Yes," said Bert, unamused. "It used to be an Irish name."

"I don't do stairs," interrupted Rihanna.

"We'll be just fine," comforted Hillary as she confidently guided the group out the door and down the hallway. "So, Mr. Ferber, what is your line of work?"

"I've been a US history teacher for thirty-three years," he replied.

"Well, you'll have to keep us all in check, then!" I said, mostly looking at Hillary's stunned face.

"I don't know the real tour," whispered Hillary in desperation to Zeph, his laughter barely contained. He gleefully gestured back to her, *All yours.*

Hillary guided the group to the basement of the Rayburn building, where we boarded the Capitol subway. It was a 1960s-looking train with no cover, which started to make the tour feel like Disneyland. The operator whisked us through the tunnel, as Hillary explained in her best Megyn Kelly, "The foundation stone of the Capitol was laid in 1793 by—"

"George Washington!" shouted Bert above the noise of the ride, providing further evidence that no one else in his family spoke.

"Oh wow, we've got a live one. This should be fun," she said under her breath to Zeph and me, while sending a veiled SOS signal through her eyes.

After the thirty-second ride, we got off the train and headed up an escalator to the first floor of the Capitol building. Our first stop was the Crypt, a vast basement of columns holding up the building above. Hillary then guided the group down a hallway to a room that resembled a colonial courtroom, which is exactly what it was.

"Hey, guys," said Hillary in a more colloquial tone that was likely created in a plea for goodwill. "So, this is where the Supreme Court met for most of the eighteen hundreds—deciding cases like Marbury v. Madison and Dred Scott v. Stanford."

"Sandford." Bert cleared his throat.

"Lovely." Hillary nodded. "And if you take look at that clock, you'll notice that it's five minutes fast! That's because an old chief justice insisted that everyone be five minutes early to everything, and wouldn't let anyone in after! And to this day, the US Supreme Court operates five minutes earlier than the rest of us!"

I noticed a red-jacketed Capitol docent by the door shaking her head. Zeph just smiled. Bert drew his children closer to him, as if to protect them from an unpredictable stray dog.

As Hillary walked us toward the elevator that would take us to the Rotunda, I heard Bert whisper to his kids, "She doesn't know what she's talking about."

Due to the tight squeeze of the group in the elevator, Zeph

let us go first and then followed in the subsequent ride. Once he joined us, we single-filed our way down the hallway. Inside the Capitol Rotunda floor, the walls somehow commanded everyone to *Look up!* It was the kind of upward view that gave you vertigo, even though your feet were planted firmly on the ground. The giant domed room overwhelmed the eyes and somehow appeared to be much larger from the inside than it did from the outside view of the building.

Hillary proudly declared, "Welcome to the Rotunda," as if she were welcoming the Ferber family to her home. "The ceiling is over two hundred feet tall. You'll see at the very top a fresco painting by Constantino Brumidi," she said, her accent suddenly fluently Italian.

"That's her favorite part," Zeph whispered to me.

Hillary continued to describe the frieze that wrapped around the base of the dome. I turned around in a circle to take in countless families like the Ferbers, and a group of junior high school students wearing matching neon blue shirts. Every camera I could see pointed upward as well— except for one. Out of the corner of my eye, I could see a man wearing a khaki fishing vest, who aimed his camera directly at me. I turned to look more closely, but he disappeared into the shifting crowd.

"Where's Reagan?" blurted out Bert.

"I'm glad you asked that," replied Hillary as she walked

us over to a bronze statue of the Gipper. "Ronald Reagan is one of two statues that represents the state of California in the Capitol. The other is in the Statuary Hall, or what used to be the House of Representatives. Right this way. . . ."

We walked out of the Rotunda and into an adjacent room lined with large statues.

"Our second statue is over here." She pointed toward the wall. "Father Junipero Serra."

At the base of the dignified monk with a cross in his hand stood Khaki Fishing Vest, casually taking pictures—with no wife or tag-along kids in sight.

"And now for the highlight of the tour," declared Hillary.

"We already had that; it was President Reagan," responded Bert.

"Well, why don't you all just come over here and listen— to the floor!" She pointed to a gold plaque on the ground as she walked about twenty steps away.

We heard her voice—sugary, like toddler storytime at a public library: "I hope you enjoyed your tour!"

Rihanna gasped as Hillary came back to the group. "You are standing where Representative John Adams sat before he was President. Adams would often keep his head in his hands, and everyone thought he was sleeping. But he was actually listening to the sound of his political opponents, whose voices carried throughout the House floor!"

Bert gleefully pounced. "I don't think so. First of all, everyone knew there were crappy acoustics in this room, so Adams couldn't have fooled anyone. And second, they filled this place with drapes and carpet because the reverberations drove everyone crazy."

Hillary started to charge at Bert, her rage barely contained. I held her back, shrugged my shoulders, and did my best at diplomacy, saying, "You learn something every day, Mr. Ferber!"

"If you'll just follow me back to the elevator so we can return to the congressman's office," Hillary said, composure regained. The group followed her to the elevator. This time, I was the last one to enter the cramped space, so I waved them along and waited alone for the next car. I felt someone behind me waiting as well, and when the doors opened, we both walked into the elevator. I turned to see that it was Khaki Fishing Vest, who had a casual and calm look on his face. He was balding and looked Hispanic.

The second the elevator doors closed, he pulled the stop button out and an alarm began to sound. He looked at me directly with his dark brown eyes and said, "Cameron Carter, we have exactly forty seconds."

"Excuse me?" I said and reached to press the button back in. He stopped me. The old-fashioned school bell screamed on. "Who are you? Let me out of here."

"Listen to me," he commanded in an intense but some-how trustworthy way. "The Ariel Lancaster affair is not the story people should be paying attention to. It's her murder."

"Murder? She died in a car accident," I said. "What's happening here? What about the diary?"

"I don't care who wrote that diary—but it wasn't Ariel. Fake news. And it doesn't matter anyway." He spoke deliberately and very fast while looking at his watch. He looked back up to me, his eyes both harsh and imploring. "What you should be asking yourself is why Nani Lancaster isn't pushing this story. And there is a story, and there is a cover-up. But we can't let it stop with a junior congresswoman who doesn't know better."

We.

I resisted the conspiratorial overtures as the grating alarm finally stopped and the elevator continued down. "You're a crazy person." I pushed the door open button even though the cart still lurched downward.

But there was something about him that was definitely not crazy. There was something about him that was sure.

"Wade Branson," he said to me as he handed me a small card. "Look him up, and tell me who's the dangerous one."

A tinny tone announced our imminent arrival on the ground floor.

"Sunlight kills mold," he said, as the doors finally opened and suddenly he started panting and darting his head around. Acting.

"What the hell happened in there?" he breathlessly asked the Capitol Hill security that greeted us at the opened elevator door.

"Everything okay?" one guard asked.

"I guess so. It was so small and so dark in there!" he whined and whimpered.

Zeph grabbed my arm, as I flinched and almost hit his face.

"Whoooaa, there, buddy. It's just an elevator," Zeph said. "We need to catch up with that family!"

"Did you see . . . ?" I turned to where the crazy but sure man had just stood. He was gone. I started to tell Zeph what had happened, but I stopped short. I didn't know who else should know what I had heard. Or who already knew about it.

"Dude, calm down and follow me. I'm supposed to worry about losing the constituents in here, not you," Zeph said as he put his arm around me and led me to the exit and the subway. I turned my head back, only to see that same sea of neon blue T-shirts that had been upstairs in the Rotunda clustered in the hallway. Khaki Fishing Vest and his casual photography were nowhere in sight.

A rush of wind from the approaching subway ripped the card from my slackened grasp. The white paper flailed in the air and then sharply down toward the subway track. For a moment, I wanted to let it fall, to run over and erase that surreal conversation from the elevator. But something inside me darted for the card, and I grabbed it just as the subway came rolling in.

Hillary let out a small scream as Zeph pulled me back. "What's your problem, man? Do you not see a train coming to run you over?"

"Who *are* these kids?" burbled Rihanna to her daughter.

We boarded the subway back to the Rayburn building. I sat alone in one of the cars. As the operator whooshed us back toward the House side, I unfolded the rescued, crumpled card in my hand. There was an unusual e-mail address: guanaco49@1x7y4f9. com. And, again, those three words, scrawled as if written at the last minute: *Sunlight kills mold.*

11

By that afternoon, I had almost convinced myself that the conversation in the elevator hadn't actually occurred. After all, who corners a congressional intern in the Capitol and goes off about forged diaries and mysterious deaths and some stupid mantra about a fungus? On the way back to the office, I planned to talk with Nadia about what happened during the tour, given her over-the-top speech about communicating any unusual interactions. But I remembered Katie's warning not to trust her. And if I told Katie, she'd probably think the whole *and then he trapped me in the elevator and talked about a cover-up!* thing was a little melodramatic. Not exactly chief of staff–in-training material.

As I glanced down at the corner of the card, peeking out from my clenched fist, I felt an odd sense of duty. Like when you see an old lady struggling to load groceries in her car, and you kind of wish you hadn't seen her so you don't have to go over and help her and hear about her grandkids for ten minutes. And even though I wish I hadn't, I *had* seen an old lady, and the old lady was a crazy-talking but sure-sounding man who just asked me to look up a person named Wade Branson. Was there any harm in that? A quick search to see if there was a *there* there? I didn't want to alarm Katie, especially after she'd expressed so much confidence in me. I'd do a little research—*people seemed to think I was good at it*—and then decide later. Keeping my elevator encounter confidential made me feel instantly relieved. My tour time smile returned as I felt my forehead relax and we returned to the office.

Any Wade Branson research I could have surreptitiously conducted that afternoon was halted by Zeph's recruiting me to do multiple runs to the congressional supply office. In between loading and unloading reams of paper and copy machine toner, I traded texts with a distressed Lena.

Washington Monument tonight? I texted.

I thought you'd never ask, she replied. **But . . .** There was a long pause before any other message appeared.

Oh, great. "But." Good things rarely follow "but."

There's this reception tonight at the embassy that my dad wants me to help set up and attend.

Your dad figures prominently in your social calendar.

I know, it's weird. He says he likes to show me off to his diplomat friends. He likes me to start conversations and make people feel comfortable. The good news, she continued, **is that I have a plus-one.**

I'm sorry, I answered. **I'm all booked up with events at the Albanian and South Korean embassies tonight. I am very popular with the embassies. Another time?** I replied.

Okay, you'd better not be serious, because it's something about green tech and I can't handle these events anymore. Por favorrrrrrr.

I waited a few minutes. A guy can't make himself too available.

She roared back with another text that was apparently and oddly a continuation of the previous one: **rrrrrrrrrrrr.**

Okay, but only if I get a Tesla, I wrote.

I will personally arrange for it, she instantly responded.

Conveniently just down Pennsylvania Avenue from the ghetto of GWU student apartments, the Mexican embassy looked like someone had plopped a boring brown office building on top of and around two colonial row houses—to form a single, architecturally schizophrenic structure. As I approached the entrance, I saw Lena, who was chatting with the formally dressed security guards.

"*Bienvenido a la cárcel.*" She smiled as the guards laughed. *Welcome to the jail.*

She opened the door for me as I caught a peek at the massive security infrastructure in the guards' area—dozens of screens revealed live camera footage surrounding the building.

"This is the warden and his assistants." She gestured to the security guards, who said some Mexican slang back at her, which seemed to intimate that she had a boyfriend. "Aka my only true friends in this city," she muttered to me.

"*Gusto de conocerles,*" I said. *Nice to meet you.* I picked up a little Spanish from Berto's mother back home, but it only seemed to intensify their teasing.

Lena snapped back with a sibling-like "*Cállate.*" *Shut up.*

She took me to a conference room that had been converted to a stately dining hall, where a handful of men in suits surrounded a chicly dressed couple who looked more like Lena's older brother and sister than her parents. I did not get much more than a head nod from the ambassador, but Lena's mom promptly glided over to greet us as we entered the room.

"*Un gusto*"—*a pleasure*—she said as she confidently double-kissed me and I unconfidently watched it happen. She then grabbed a guest and introduced him to Lena and me.

"This is my daughter, Lena," she explained. "She's going to Princeton in the fall. And this is her friend." She gestured to me. "Where are you going to college, Cameron?"

I figured this crowd would not be familiar with Lagrima Junior College and hesitated for a second. *Getting my generals out of the way* just didn't have the same ring as Ivy League. In this social circle, it felt like Lagrima was best left unspoken.

"Cameron's interning for the next Speaker of the House," Lena intervened. "It's a very big deal."

"I'm sure it is." Her mom smiled as her eyes scanned the room for other conversations to spur on.

Lena began chatting up the guest about wind turbines, as a bow-tied server offered a tray of the most carefully arranged gourmet nacho plates I'd ever seen. Lena reached for one of the chips from my plate and said, "These are my favorite." I noticed Lena's formal posture and attentive facial expression as the Spanglish conversation plowed forward, and I did my best to imitate her. But ultimately, talk of energy conservation lost out to throbbing thoughts of that name: Wade Branson. As Lena continued to schmooze, I slipped out my phone and typed the name into the search field.

A Wikipedia page came up first, followed by websites touting *THE SUICIDE OF WADE BRANSON* and *PHARMA KING FOUND DEAD IN WOODS*. I clicked on the Wikipedia entry and my eyes drank in the words fast, unavoidably— like accidentally gulping down pool water and you instinctively gasp to breathe again, but the water's still there.

Suicide.

Found Dead in Woods.

My eyes darted around the page to find that Branson had been the CEO of Livitas Pharmaceuticals for fourteen years. Billionaire and philanthropist. Thativan controversy. Shot himself in the head. Wife currently residing in a mental inst . . .

Without looking at me and as she continued her conversation, Lena grabbed my phone and placed it between her hand and her left side.

I'm not sure whether it was an odd form of retaliation or just instinct, but I grabbed her hand and held it. She held mine in return. At least she would have no excuses about a boring reception anymore. My hand inconveniently started to sweat, and I felt the little pockets of air between our fingers heat up. Did she notice? Was her hand sweating too, now?

The reception continued as a revolving door of diplomats, lobbyists, and a telenovela star spoke with Lena and me. Spanish wasn't the only second language I heard. They spoke of long weekend trips, gallery openings, "summer camp ten-year reunions," and, of course, clean energy. One of these things was not like the other, and that was me. The only thing that prevented me from graciously making a trip to the restroom (from which I would never return because my "trip to the restroom" would really be a trip back to my apartment) was Lena's gentle grasp of my hand. So I stayed. She thought I could handle this crowd, so I thought maybe I had it in me.

Even though I ate more nachos than I spoke words.

The ambassador announced the start of dinner, as Lena whispered to me, "Ugh, finally. Let's get out of here. And . . ." She held up my phone and looked at the Wade Branson page — the last thing I was looking at before she took it from me. I grabbed it from her, thinking it was best for her not to think I read about suicidal CEOs in the middle of a cocktail hour.

"Whoa, whoa." She smiled. "I was just going to snoop on your phone before giving it back to you."

We left the embassy, heading down Pennsylvania Avenue before turning south on a quiet Seventeenth Street toward the White House. Even though it was the western perimeter of the most famous residence in the country, the street was abandoned, except for a few late-night deliveries to some cafés and businesses along the way.

As we walked closer to it, the gleaming white pillar of the Washington Monument grew larger, and Lena asked, "You guys still talk about Ariel Lancaster in the office?"

If by "you guys," you mean the guy from the elevator and me, then yes. Yes, we do. We talk about Ariel and a six-year-old suicide and how they are somehow linked. . . .

"Yeah, sometimes. You know I got her desk?" I answered, trying to keep the conspiracy on mute. "It's a little weird."

My mind raced, trying to think of a connection — any connection — between Ariel and Branson.

"Well, it's probably a better desk, right? That's good," she answered.

But I didn't really listen. What I really wanted to do was read more about Branson on my phone. But I couldn't exactly share details of my Capitol encounter with her. And I didn't want her to think I wasn't interested.

"Are you okay?" she asked.

Too late.

"Because you're, like, very clearly thinking about something else," she continued. "What's up?"

"Sorry, I just want to make sure we get to the monument before it closes," I lied. But it would be nine p.m. in a few minutes, so at least it was a plausible answer. I tried to wipe away the thoughts of Branson from my mind. Reaching for Lena's hand helped. She talked about a birthday party for the president's son, which she'd attended at the White House once. I talked about how I had gone to a birthday party at a city park where a territorial homeless lady made most of the kids cry. Our drastically different upbringings seemed to be a frequent topic of conversation.

We approached the base of the Washington Monument, from which the tower looked like a vast, windowless building. I initially thought the lack of crowds was a good thing—no line! But when I saw the closed door, I realized we were too late.

"Bummer," I said. "I hear the view is even cooler at night."

She went to reach for the door handle.

"It's closed," I said.

"I hear the view is even cooler when it's just us," she replied as she knocked on the door.

A security guard opened it, and motioned us in. Like it was a secret. A personal favor. The heavy door slammed shut behind us.

"Thank you, Raymond," she said to a smiling guard, her voice echoing in the marble lobby.

Lena pressed the elevator button as my eyes and slightly dropped jaw correctly conveyed my amazement.

Raymond the guard joined us for the ride up. It was my second-most-exciting elevator experience of the day.

Lena explained, "You get to know people when you live in DC for eight years. And forget the schmooze-fests: Guards at the embassy have the most interesting connections. They somehow know all of the kind monument security folks like Raymond. A good man who sticks around for a few extra minutes so that my friend who is new in town can check out the top of the Washington Monument . . ."

I felt my ears slightly pop as the air pressure changed, and the elevator dinged our arrival at the observation floor. Still in surprise at the after-hours access, I nodded at Raymond.

"Only one stop on this elevator," he announced.

"We won't be long," she said to the guard, as we walked

together toward the small square windows that looked out over the city. The fluorescent lights of the floor were dimmed.

"And I thought my *intern badge* gave me behind-the-scenes access . . . ," I mused.

"We make a good team," she answered.

We peered out the window that looked down on the Capitol building, and then walked around a pathway to look down at the White House. The massive buildings looked tiny from our five-hundred-foot perch. The absence of city lights marked the long grass strip of the Mall and the Tidal Basin near the Jefferson Memorial. The quiet, the distance, the perspective—it was exhilarating and grounding at the same time. As I looked out the thick window, my nose nearly pressed against the glass, I turned back to see Lena, who was clearly amused by my childlike wonder.

"So, Cameron, I've been going to these stupid receptions my whole life, you know?"

"Thrilling," I said as I put my back to the window and looked at her.

"No, seriously, it's awful. But when I was a little girl, there was this boy, Javier, who was also at the dinners. And when we were bored, we'd both crawl under the table, weaving in and out of the guests' legs—climbing over the shined shoes, carefully crossing the bright high heels—until we found each other. . . ."

"Does this story end with Javier being an imaginary friend?" I asked.

Lena playfully hit my arm. "No! I'm serious. Anyway, we'd be down there, playing games and pretending to have our own adult dinner together. For hours, sometimes. Like the people's legs under the table would disappear, the party would be over, and we wouldn't want it to end. Just hidden there under the tablecloth. Our own little safe world."

She continued, "So anyway, I guess what I'm saying is that for the first time since Javier . . . for the first time since I was six, I'm feeling that same feeling . . ."

"*Abajo del mesa,*" I replied, trying to foment some sort of mood. *Below the table.*

Lena laughed. "It's just '*bajo la mesa,*' but nice try."

"*Bajo la mesa,*" I said. We started to lean into each other as I brushed her hair behind her ear. And while I didn't spend my childhood crawling under diplomats' dinner tables, I did know what it meant to feel safe with someone.

"Lena," I said, "I wasn't totally honest with you. My dad doesn't own a landscaping firm with hundreds of employees. He's a landscaper, and barely hanging on, at that."

She moved her head back slightly. And while it felt good to tell the truth, my stomach dropped in anticipation of her response. "I'm not . . . like you," I admitted to her.

"And that's exactly why you are wonderful," she answered.

"Why did you feel like you had to tell me that about your dad?"

"Because you go to birthday parties at the White House with the president's son. Because your dad represents a whole *country*. Because guy code is telling me to act too cool for you, but what I'm really thinking is that you are—in actuality and not in a snobby way, it's just who you are and there's nothing you can do about it—too cool for me."

"Nonsense," she answered. "You are different, Cameron. Different is refreshing, good. You see things differently."

"Well, all I saw tonight was nacho chips, apparently," I answered. "They were delicious, but it was probably rude of me."

She laughed and stepped closer to me, looking out the window over my shoulder. I kept looking at her. She was suddenly more captivating than the view of the city.

"Do we have to go back down to the ground?" she asked.

"Yes," I answered.

And then I felt the thrilling *I'm going to kiss this girl* pit in my stomach. Like when you know you're going to eventually barf, but it's kissing someone instead of throwing up. Just as nauseating, but in a good way.

"But we'll be different when we get there," I added.

"What do you mean?" she asked, her eyes shifting toward mine.

"Because I will have kissed you," I said, as I leaned slightly forward and put my lips on hers. Nothing fancy and nothing saliva-y. Just a simple, perfect kiss. I pulled back to see her eyebrows slightly raised. She wasn't the only one with a surprise in store that night.

A few seconds passed before Raymond appeared around the corner. "You know I love you, Lena, but I'm not getting overtime for this."

She instinctively took a couple steps back away from me. *Nothing to see here.* "Yes, of course. We'll come with you, Raymond."

As the three of us we went down the elevator, I was so excited that I felt like it was still going up. But the only sound in the elevator was the awkward silence that follows a kiss that was maybe eavesdropped on by a security guard.

As Raymond locked the doors, we stepped away from the entrance, and I said, "So next time we kiss we can talk about how we had nothing to talk about after the first time we kissed," I said. "Okay?"

"Deal," she answered, in earnest.

We said good night to Raymond, and he told Lena that he'd called the embassy for her. As we walked toward the nearby street, I wasn't quite sure what he meant until I saw a black SUV by the curb.

"That's my ride," she said. "When it's late, the driver comes to pick me up."

"Of course he does." I shrugged.

"Thanks, Cameron," she said. "And I mean it. You belong here. I'm glad you're here."

Conscious of the driver's gaze, we gave each other a chaste hug, and she got in the car.

As the heavy black car drove away, I started toward the apartment, heading up Virginia Avenue toward GWU. The street grew oddly vacant as I walked closer to the university zone. Lena shot me another **Thank you** via text.

You still owe me a Tesla, I replied.

What about lots of leftover nachos instead? she retorted. **I hear you're a fan.**

I smiled, as the brakes of a car screamed at me and I found myself in the middle of an intersection with headlights just a few feet away. A very angry woman at the wheel shouted some very angry words that amounted to "Don't text and walk!" plus the gerund forms of some swear words thrown in for emphasis. I ran across the rest of the street and stopped on the sidewalk—feeling that rush of adrenaline that comes after you do something really stupid but don't get hurt.

Another text lit up the screen of my phone. I was eager to see what else Lena would say.

So I hear you had a very interesting tour of the Capitol today.

The text was from Katie.

I stopped on the deserted street corner. Did she know

about the fishing vest guy?! Partially purged thoughts of that name—Wade Branson—crept back into my mind. *Suicide. Found dead in the woods.*

I was halfway through typing, **Did you see the guy in the elevator too?** when she followed up with, **I hear Hillary met her match.**

I erased my text.

I typed back a less revealing **Yes, I guess sometimes the best way to learn is by seeing what not to do.**

How very diplomatic of you, Katie replied.

I'm learning from the best, I texted back.

And then I realized that I didn't need to tell her about my conversation in the elevator in order to learn more about Wade Branson. She *had* offered to help me with any questions. Maybe Katie could save me some research time. Mostly I was hoping she'd say something to make me realize he wasn't worth thinking about after all. Because I didn't want to go to bed with his name and grim Wikipedia entry ringing in my head.

So I abruptly typed and sent: **Do you know who Wade Branson is?**

A minute or two passed with no response, though I could see the dancing ellipsis indicate that she was typing. Then not. Then typing again. With every passing second, I regretted asking the question. She was thinking about her answer, which meant it wasn't an easy answer.

I continued walking down I Street as the lights of a large grocery store shut off. Every few steps, I looked back at my phone to see if she had responded.

Katie's reply eventually came. **Yes, old friend of BIB's. Tragic loss.**

Did you know him? I responded immediately.

Another long pause and another round of wavy dot-dot-dots.

Finally: **Not a very popular topic in the office. Hits close to home.**

Okay . . . , I typed back. And waited for a response that did not come.

At that moment, I didn't see a single other person around. A thick summer wind sloppily yanked at the long tree branches above me. The street was zombie apocalypse abandoned. And despite the incredible evening with Lena—for the first time that summer, DC felt fallible. Unreliable. Maybe it was the lonely street or maybe it was the echoing regret for having sent that text, for having shown too many cards. But the city suddenly felt like a hastily chosen New Best Friend who suddenly says something or does something that makes you wish you hadn't gone all in so quickly, so willingly. I walked faster with each empty block back to the apartment. Like I was being chased.

12

The next morning in my bedroom, I stared at an empty e-mail on my creaky laptop from home. I filled out the "To" field: guanaco49@1x7y4f9.com.

I hadn't done anything wrong by googling "Wade Branson." Anyone could do that. Thousands probably did. But sending an e-mail to this weird address felt like exposure at best and betrayal at worst.

What do you want? I typed, then erased.

I'm sorry, I can't help you out, I typed, then erased.

But if you need anyone to mow your lawn, I'm your guy, I typed, then erased.

Hillary knocked on my bedroom door. "Later, skater." I slammed my laptop shut and joined her and Zeph on the way to work. When we got to the Rayburn entrance, I told them to go ahead inside as I called my dad. It was just after sunrise in Lagrima. I knew I shouldn't tell him about my extracurricular research (he would either overreact and call the Lagrima Police or tell me I was wasting my time and should stay out of it). But just being on the phone with him and knowing that I *could* would be a nice shot of familiarity in the midst of an increasingly complicated summer.

He picked up the phone, and I could hear Rogelito in the background singing along to "Heaven," by Los Lonely Boys, which is easily one of the worst songs in the history of songs. My Dad *shhh*ed him. "It's Cameron!" he announced. "How are things on the Hill?" he asked me.

"Great!" I enthused. "Just about to head into work."

"Us too! New office park we're working in. First day," he said.

"That's awesome, Dad." *Almost makes you forget about losing CVSU*, I thought to say. But I didn't. The last thing he needed was a reminder about losing the biggest landscaping gig at the Central Valley's new state university.

"Everything okay?" he asked.

A fresh wave of commuting staffers approached the Rayburn entrance. I stepped out of the way of the stampede and stood alone by the base of the stairs.

"Yes, it's really fun! I'm learning a lot, and Congressman Beck is great. All that crazy scandal stuff has pretty much died down," I said.

See? I *was* learning. How to spin.

The radio suddenly blared loudly through the phone as the sing-along picked back up. My dad reprimanded his companion for interrupting the call, even as he laughed his deep laugh.

"Well, listen, son, that's great. We're just pulling up here, and we might lose cell recept—"

The call died. I called him back and a robot lady told me to leave a voice mail. I didn't have confidence in my dad's cell phone proficiency, so I decided not to leave a message.

Thinking of Lena's confident posture, I put my shoulders back, stood tall, and walked into the building. As I neared BIB's office, I bumped into Katie in the hallway. My immediate instinct was to look away, embarrassed that I had asked her about Branson the night before. But I tried to appear confident ("Of course it's fair game to ask about a dead friend of the boss!") and shot her a quick "Hi."

"Sorry I didn't text back; my phone died last night," she said.

She clearly didn't realize that my generation was way past that kind of excuse, but I forgave it anyway. "Oh, no worries." I shrugged.

"I was just a little surprised at the question," she added.

"Yeah, I know it kind of came out of nowhere," I said. "You know how you get into those Internet rabbit holes where you're buying a book online and then you're watching YouTube videos of evil teens paintballing homeless people and then you're reading about CEOs who commit suicide . . . ?"

"Well, in my case the sequence is usually high heels, political gossip sites, and vintage Richard Simmons motivational videos, but yes, I am familiar with the concept of Internet rabbit holes," she replied.

"Well, anyway, that's where the question came from. But don't worry, I know it's off-limits here," I said as we walked into the office.

Katie got swept up in some committee preparation as I sat at my desk and tried not to think about Wade Branson. And waited for a decent hour to text Berto back home. When it was ten fifteen a.m. (seven fifteen a.m. his time), I decided he should be awake.

I texted, **Good morning, sunshine.**

About a minute passed when he replied, **Dude, you woke me up! You suck, but I love you anyway. Qué pasa?**

I replied, **Can't really text now, but all of that scandal stuff is getting more interesting.**

Oh, really???? he responded.

If you knew that knowing something or finding something out could help someone, but it would also be dangerous, would you still want to know?

Hell yes. Don't be scared. Soldier for truth LOL haha, he wrote back.

Easy for him to say.

Look, guerito, he added, **don't go all Watergate on me, but why not do a little digging?**

Okay, I have some research to do, I typed back.

Just remember to give your boy Berto a shout-out when you're testifying in court, he taunted.

Thinking of that nightmare scenario nearly made me stop the Wade Branson querying altogether, but I searched for the name anyway. I kept one window on my laptop open to some literacy nonprofit home page—and another window open for research about Branson. Whenever anyone neared my computer, I flipped over to the literacy nonprofit, and when they left, it was back to Unsolved Mysteries with Wade Branson. This was a common intern trick, established by most to concurrently check social media and instant messaging while working; I was doing it to research a suicidal CEO.

Over the next few days, I must have read every Internet site that mentioned Wade Branson. Most of the articles focused on his death—that Wade Branson, CEO of Livitas Pharmaceuticals, shot himself in the head in Boston, six years ago. His body was found under the Kingsley Park entry bridge near the company's headquarters in the Fresh Pond neighborhood. The photo that every article seemed to feature was a distant view of the death scene, with a tieless set of railroad rails that led under a bridge. A bright yellow tarp covered the mass of

Branson's body, which lay on the tracks—just under the small overpass. And an angry policeman approached the photographer and was frozen in a hand-waving *get out of here* gesture.

Branson's death coincided with reports that one of Livitas's blockbuster drugs had fatal side effects in a small group of patients. Thativan was a celebrated depression drug—known for its swirling rainbow logo and ubiquitous marketing campaign which featured parents and kids, couples, and even people with pets— all reunited because they had finally found a way to manage their depression. No more side effects like nausea, tremors, headaches, and the brutal brain "crackling" many patients reported in association with their previous depression medications. Thativan changed the pharmaceutical game as the depression drug market exploded and less desirable competitors were crushed. Patients were happy again. Almost as happy as the millionaire execs at Livitas.

They just didn't realize that their miracle drug also made people brain-dead.

Though it eliminated the common side effects of depression medication in most patients, a trend emerged among Thativan patients. First it was a junior high teacher in Appleton, Wisconsin, who had a really bad headache one day and was in a coma the next. Then a high school quarterback in Baton Rouge who collapsed on the practice field and an accountant in Dallas who called in sick one day and never showed up to work again. A growing list of victims had one thing in common: They were all Thativan patients. I didn't really understand the multiple clinical essays that explained the reaction, but it seemed that in a small group of users, the drug destroyed key brain synapses and thus full mental function. Thativan killed their brains.

And when Branson realized he was responsible for these pharma-induced plagues, he killed himself.

My breaks from the bleak investigation were lunches with Lena in the various cafeterias of Capitol Hill. She told me about her upcoming Princeton class schedule and her end-of-summer trip to Mexico City. And I did my best to not mention the mysterious suicide that was filling my days. Being uncomplicated, noncontroversial—different from the intrigue and the gossip of her city—these were my selling points with her. And so I was happy to critique the different lunch menus with her. And scandalize her with tales of thirty-five-plus student class sizes in my public schools back home. And kiss her a couple times in between. We both knew the summer would end—and with it, probably any semblance of a sustainable romantic relationship. It wasn't her fault that Princeton girls didn't have boyfriends from junior colleges; that's just how it was. But there was something about the transience and brevity of the summer that made our time more easy, more fun.

I returned to the office after lunch one day to hear Marcus tell me that he had jumped on my laptop to get the anemic list of new literacy statistics I had been assembling while not researching Branson.

"I hope you don't mind, bro!" He shrugged. "You found a ton of stuff in there! It's great." I clearly should have set lower standards for myself, given that he was overjoyed with about 15 percent of my effort.

My face flushed red, and I bolted to my open laptop. No signs of Wade Branson were readily apparent, but it made me wonder who else could have accessed my computer, and the websites I'd visited. It was a careless mistake, and from then on, I wiped my search history every time I looked up anything about Branson.

One of the final items I found about his suicide seemed to confirm his death as such—it was a suicide note tucked into his jacket pocket and found by an examiner. A couple websites had pictures of the brief and neatly typed message, which read:

> Please forgive me. I drove my company to release
> a drug that saved thousands but destroyed a sliver
> of users. This is a tragic trade-off, and I will spend
> eternity living with my conscience.
> I made mistakes due to avarice and scientific zeal.
> I misled my partners and best friends, who have no
> responsibility for nor knowledge of my indiscretion.

After causing the death of a few bright lives, the same conclusion only seems fair for my toxic one.

–WB

If suicide could be generous, his was. Generous and nicely written. Absolving his associates of any knowledge of his wrong-doing, he took the fall—fully and unquestionably. But the man from the elevator had questions anyway. Questions that were starting to be my questions too: *What did Branson's death have to do with Ariel? What did Ariel's death have to do with me?*

Livitas was sued into oblivion in the following months, and those blameless "partners and best friends" quickly condemned Branson. Among them were colleagues, scientists, lifelong friends, and one early investor in Livitas: congressman and burgeoning political power Billy Beck.

Those words from the interrupted Capitol tour echoed in my mind:

"Look him up, and tell me who's the dangerous one."

"Sunlight kills mold."

I opened the desk drawer—Ariel's desk drawer—just far enough to see that unclaimed, framed picture of her and her arm around a friend. And though I was veering closer to Watergate territory than Berto had cautioned, I typed a quick message and hit send:

"Let's talk about mold."

13

The man responded within minutes: Saturday, 10 a.m., Ben's Chili Bowl. The daytime hour and public restaurant setting were comforting. Maybe he'd save a spooky subterranean parking garage for later.

And when I stepped out of the U Street metro station that quiet weekend morning, I found a neighborhood in transition. Fluorescently lit drugstores cozied up to crumbling Victorian row houses, utilitarian office buildings next to shiny new high-rise condos. It was as if these buildings were playing musical chairs with each other and rushed to land wherever they could when the music stopped. Our meeting place, Ben's Chili Bowl, claimed a prime spot across the street from the metro station. I stepped through the colorful exterior and found a simple diner atmosphere and sparse, prelunch crowd inside.

An epic, smoky smell of chili hung in the air and seemed to say *Since 1958* louder than the sign on the wall.

Next to that sign sat the only familiar face in the restaurant. It was the man from the Capitol, though he had lost the fishing vest in favor of decidedly nondescript jeans and a flannel button-up shirt. He casually motioned for me to join him. As I walked over to him, I noticed two sloppy cardboard boats of hot dogs and french fries on the table.

"Thanks for meeting me here," he said. He was relaxed but matter-of-fact. This was a business meeting, after all. "Have you ever heard of a half smoke before?"

"Why am I here?" I demanded.

"I hear that both Bush Two and Gore ordered this when they came here," he said, showing me his half-mutilated, chili-soaked hot dog. "One thing they could agree on was a good chili dog."

"What is this about?" I continued.

"Some people say ten a.m. is too early for a half smoke, but I say it's all of the deliciousness with none of the crowds," he said.

"This place is about to get even less crowded if you don't tell me what's going on." I did my best to sound bolder than I felt. I was literally taking my lead from watching crime shows on TV with my dad. Though if this were a TV show, the person playing me would start to look around the restaurant and realize that he'd been set up, outnumbered, and was not getting out alive. However, as I scanned the restaurant and saw a group of senior citizens at one table and a gregarious busboy passing by, I figured I was okay. For the moment.

"Tell me what you know about Wade Branson and Ariel Lancaster," he said. He spoke in an efficient, clipped manner. He scanned the restaurant, inside and out—not in a nervous way, but the way a father scopes out a park where his child is playing.

"No connection," I said. "Branson is some greedy CEO who killed himself six years ago. Ariel died in a drunk-driving accident. That's it."

"So you researched Branson," the man said.

"Yes," I responded. "He sounds like a monster."

"Branson's not the monster," he said.

I sat down. "Well, then who is?"

"Cameron," he said. "The answer to that question could put you in danger, but we need your help."

"Come on, man, just tell me or don't." I took a bite of the unwieldy hot dog, and it was ridiculously delicious. But this guy's runaround was getting annoying, and I didn't want to give him the credit for introducing me to the greatest chili dog I'd ever tasted. So I placed it down with an indifferent shrug.

"A little over three weeks ago, I had lunch—" he said.

"I get it, you like meetings over meals," I interrupted.

"I had lunch with Ariel Lancaster the week that she died," he added.

I moved my plate of food to the side and leaned in across the unsteady table.

"Okay . . . ," I replied, my mind racing to terrifying thoughts that were just out of reach.

"We had been in contact with her due to some suspicions of Beck's involvement with Branson's death. . . ."

I leaned back. "Hold up, you're telling me that Beck is involved in all of this? You're crazy."

He gave a condescending smile, "We needed someone on the inside. And she had questions of her own," the man continued as he scooped up some residual chili with a spoon.

"But her mom and BIB are political allies," I said.

"Which is exactly why she was perfect. No one saw it coming," he explained. He paused for a beat and then said, "Until they did."

"Are you saying Ariel's death wasn't an accident?" I asked.

"I'm saying that Ariel was on the verge of confirming some very dangerous information about your boss. She said she was about to find something really big. And then she died."

"But she was with a drunk driver." I protested an increasingly viable reality.

"Well, we're not here to solve Ariel's murder . . . death," he corrected himself. "We're here because of Branson. Because I think Beck knew about Thativan—even encouraged it despite the risks. He was an investor in the company, after all, and all anyone could see at the start was money. But then people's brains started shutting down, and Beck had to get far, far away from it. And Ariel claimed she knew how."

"And then she died. What's stopping the same thing from happening to me? Why did you pick me?" I said, a slight tremor in my throat.

"Cameron, no offense, but you are a diversity pick for a summer internship. You're headed to junior college in a month and a half. Your dad is a landscaper, as long as he can keep that business together. And up until a month ago, so were you. No one is going to think you're capable of researching or even interested in a crime that happened six years ago. Interns are invisible. You're invisible. I bet there are people in the office who don't even know your name," he said.

"Okay, first of all, my dad's business is fine. He's fine." I weakly jumped to his defense. "And second, what's up with your knowing all of this stuff about my life? You basically know how much money the tooth fairy gave me for my second bicuspid, so why can't you figure out your little BIB theory on your own?"

"Cameron." he pushed aside his drink and leaned in across the table. "You have all access and no profile, which puts you in an even better position than Ariel to figure this out."

"So let me get this straight," I said. "You picked me because I seem like a nobody, because I'm the last person anyone would think could be smart enough to research an open case."

"Well, actually, Ariel picked you," he replied.

I looked at him, silent.

"She knew who you were before you showed up at the office. And she told me over lunch that you were smart. Smarter than anyone else realized, even though she'd only spent a few days with you," he said. "And that, if anything should happen to her, we would need someone on the inside to help. And she said that someone was you."

I was both stunned and oddly complimented. But I didn't want this. I didn't ask for this.

"I don't even know who you are," I said, my voice still tremulous. "Who do you work for, and why are you doing this? Who's this 'we' you keep referring to?"

"I work for the government," he said, leaning back and folding his arms. As if this answer were automatic, a reflex.

"What is that supposed to mean?" I asked. "So do I, kind of."

"In this town, when you hear people say *I work for the government* or *I work for the State Department*, that's when you stop asking questions," he explained. "Because there won't be any more answers. But I'll give you a hint. . . ." He opened his thick flannel shirt just wide enough to reveal what looked a lot like the FBI badges that agents flashed on TV.

Seeing the badge—the legitimacy—made me feel both more safe and more nervous.

"Look, Cameron," he said firmly. "Something tells me

whatever killed Branson killed Ariel. There is corruption there—mold, as I called it. And it will grow and grow, unless we shine a light on it. And you should care about that."

I wasn't sure that I did. I preferred the Katie Campbell fast-track-to-a-job-on-the-Hill version of this summer to being a mole for the freaking FBI.

"And if you need an extra reason to care," he said, accurately assessing that I did, "there's Central Valley State University."

"CVSU has nothing to do with this," I said. I felt an echo of my dad's disappointment for losing that landscaping contract.

"CVSU has a lot to do with your dad," he answered. "Lost that whole campus to some statewide operation. And he could have done it. He'd need to staff up a bit, but he could do it."

"Yes, he could," I said.

"And he will," he said. "If you help us indict BIB."

I felt a brief but massive wave of relief as I thought about my dad getting to work that campus. He'd be set for life. In a lower-middle-class kind of way. But then I wondered if it was all *legal*.

"Are you bribing me? That's a state-owned facility. You can't do that," I said.

"It's a reward. We use them all the time in my line of work," he explained. "And if you've learned something so far this summer, I hope it's that people win government contracts for all kinds of reasons."

"I need proof," I said. "That you have any ability to reverse the contract that's already in place."

"You'll get your proof." He rolled his eyes. "Now can we talk about what you're going to do?"

"Fine," I said. "But I'm not doing anything until I have some sort of assurance. . . ."

"You and your assurances, kid!" he interrupted, exasperated.

"Okay, what am I supposed to do?" I asked.

"Did she leave anything behind?" he responded.

"I don't know," I answered. "I sit at her old desk, and there's some personal stuff, a few files."

"Start there," he said.

"Did she tell you anything more?" I asked, incredulous. "You met with her all this time, and that's all you have for me? 'Start there'?!"

"She didn't want to tell me any more details. She said she was protecting someone. That it was best for only her to know," he replied. "And now, only you."

"I am freaking out right now, dude." I decided we were past any illusions of calm. I then thought that "dude" was probably not an appropriate way to refer to an FBI agent. "Um . . . agent?" I corrected myself.

"The name is Memo," he said.

"Okay," I replied. "Agent Memo. I just graduated high school and I wanted to come here to support a congressman, not to destroy him. I'm a kid from Lagrima." *He surely must have realized that, didn't he?* "I'm just an intern."

Memo pushed his plate aside and wiped his mouth with a napkin. "You're an intern who is going to make history," he said.

"I'll settle for an intern who saves his dad's business," I answered.

"That works too. Let me know what you find," he said. "And don't use that e-mail address anymore; it's not safe for more than a couple exchanges."

"How will I contact you?" I asked, suddenly feeling very vulnerable.

"Here," he said, pulling out a small black flip phone from his battle-scarred briefcase. "Secure line, but best to keep the texts to a minimum anyway."

"So you'll be contacting me from the year 2002?" I asked.

"Very clever," he said as he got up from the table and walked away. "Nice meeting you, Cameron. I think Ariel was right about you. And you're welcome for the half smoke."

As Memo walked out the door, I stayed seated at the table. And hoped Ariel was right about me.

14

I may have spent most of the weekend with Lena (an outdoor concert on the Mall, and an evening run around the monuments), which was a good thing because she was managing some Mexican-Caribbean relations event in Florida the following week.

"So I'll see you on the Fourth of July, right?" I asked her before we kissed good-bye at the end of our run.

"Well, actually." She hesitated. "I have another embassy thing. I don't think I'll be able to see you on the holiday."

"On the Fourth of July in the US Capitol?" I panicked at the prospect of an entire holiday weekend as referee for Zeph and Hillary's pointless spats. "What is it? Can't you get out of it, at least for the fireworks?"

"Look, I know it sucks, but I can't really do anything about it. My parents want me there, and I'm still living with them — remember? I'll see you again soon, okay? You'll be fine," she said, unusually obscure, while rubbing my arm up and down. I started to flinch away, frustrated by her vagueness. Mostly frustrated that I wouldn't see her for so long.

"I've never had a long-distance relationship with someone who lives in the same city as me," I said.

She answered with a kiss and another "soon" before jogging north across the Mall, back home.

As I walked back to my apartment, my thoughts shifted from disappointment about Lena to thoughts of what Ariel had left for me in the office before she died or maybe was murdered.

Late Sunday night, I talked with Berto and explained why we hadn't spoken in so long. "Dude, I had to look into that thing I told you about."

"Your little Watergate situation?" he asked, exasperated.

I looked around my room in the apartment as if someone was eavesdropping. I pulled down the shade of the window, which somehow made me feel better. Safer.

"Look, this probably sounds crazy, but we shouldn't talk about this on the phone," I whispered.

"Oh, so now you won't say anything about it to me, bro?" he asked.

"No," I said. The twisted carnage of that car and the shard of Ariel's yellow dress flashed through my mind. "I mean, I will talk about it eventually. If I can. But it's serious. It's complicated."

"If you can? Yeah, I guess you're right," Berto replied. "*You're* complicated now. Congratulations for sounding important. I'm just going to go back to bagging groceries."

"That's not what I mean," I protested.

"Look, dude, I gotta go," he said. And then, before hanging up: "Sunday-afternoon UNO game with the *primos*. You know how it is."

I did know. Because I was the reigning champ of Sunday-afternoon UNO before I left for DC. I enforced the compounding "Draw 2" card rule and always knew that Berto's cousin Julia hid one of her last two cards just to make you think she was almost done. And if it ever came down to just me and Berto's little five-year-old brother, Cesar, for a consolation round, I let him win.

Before I turned off the nightstand lamp to go to sleep, I reached for the small picture of my mom and slipped it into my wallet. I was going to need her with me for what lay ahead.

I woke up to a text my dad had sent that night, after I'd gone to bed: **CVSU is back in play. They said contract negotiations are stalled. We just might win the thing after all!**

I shivered as I realized that my lunchtime conversation with Memo two days prior had already taken effect across the country. This was a signal from Memo. This was his proof.

Wow! I responded. **That's great. When will you find out?**

They said they'll need until August, but I'll take it! Even the possibility has us real excited.

Until August. Just enough time for my internship—and Memo's investigation—to wrap up.

I bolted out the door, telling Zeph and Hillary that I needed to get to the office early in order to catch up on some research. But the real reason I rode the metro into work a little early was so I could have some time to search Ariel's remaining things in that desk before everyone came into the office. Now that Memo had confirmed the reality of my "reward," his questions seemed more real, more urgent. I imagined the clues Ariel might have left behind. Was there some code on the Post-it notes? A trashed gum wrapper with directions inside?

I found a stack of unclaimed mail at the base of the office's front door and picked it up as I tried to open the door. Nadia Zyne's heels clicked against the marble floor and she stood next to me. She did not offer any help with my balancing act, but she did offer a condescending "Looks like you've got a lot on your hands. Are you sure you can handle everything?" Cryptic and cold, she chuckled to herself, and I wondered if she knew of my recent interest in Wade Branson. Or maybe I was just paranoid.

She opened the door, vainly keeping it open for me for a half second with her index finger. When I heard her start a phone conversation with some reporter, I dumped the cluster of mail and went to my desk to open the drawer of Ariel's belongings.

The desk was empty.

I opened another drawer, just in case I had chosen the wrong one. This one was filled with my crap. I opened every drawer in the desk, hoping that I could find those Post-it notes, those movie ticket stubs, or even just that photo.

Nothing.

"Looking for something?" Nadia emerged from her office as Katie and some other staffers entered the front door.

"What?" I nervously replied, shutting all of the desk drawers I had opened.

"I had Jigar pack up all of Ariel's things Friday after you left," Nadia explained. "Nani wanted the last of Ariel's belongings, which I think is reasonable for a grieving mother. Or were you planning on hoarding the girl's stuff forever?"

"I wasn't hoarding it. I just didn't know what to do with it," I responded.

"Well, now you don't need to worry about it. Sorry for the inconvenience, but Ariel wasn't able to clear out her own desk, as you might have noticed."

A phone rang, someone turned on the other half of the lights, and the office slowly lumbered to life.

"That's not what I meant to say," I responded.

"Cam, I don't really ever know what you mean to say." She sighed. "Jigar!"

Just like that, Jigar carried an armful of files and Nadia's filled coffee cup and joined her in her office.

"The press secretary beating up on you again?" Katie asked quietly as she walked to her office.

Zeph dumped a weekend's worth of letters on the large table near the office supply closet, compounding the mini-mountain of magazines and packages I had retrieved from the front door.

I opened all of the desk drawers one last time, just in case there were any remnants of Ariel left in there.

None.

I went to the table and joined the mail brigade. As I tore open letter after letter and Zeph complained about Hillary for some reason, my disappointment turned to total relief. Now Memo couldn't expect anything of me. This thing was over, and it wasn't my choice. I couldn't help it if a mom wanted to see what her dead daughter kept in her desk.

Hillary very conspicuously made an inconspicuous entrance into the office, almost walking sideways with her back to Zeph and me.

"Did you shut off her TV show last night or something?" I asked Zeph.

"That girl is crazy," Zeph declared.

"You should have seen her back home," I mused.

Even though he was straight off a red-eye from the home district, BIB entered the office looking sharp and refreshed and bearing that invincible grin of his.

"Hi, everyone," he greeted us in a bold but earnest way, like an organizer at a volunteer event, humble and grateful that anyone showed up to help out. I tried to reconcile this magnanimous image with the murderous one Memo had suggested. As BIB walked through the office, I looked at him more closely than ever, as if my closer look could somehow expose a crime. So when he came over and asked if he could help open some mail with us, I was worried that if I looked him in the eye, he'd suspect that I suspected something.

"You kids aren't the only ones who know how to use a letter opener," he said as he tore into a few letters and assessed the messages therein. The most important man in the office spending some time with the plebeians—that had to say something about his character, didn't it? "I'm pretty sure this woman thinks I'm a senator, and this other guy managed to misspell 'liberal scum.'" He waved a couple letters in the air before carefully opening a handwritten note. "But this one, this is just a thank-you. No one's perfect around here, and I certainly don't expect the gratitude. But sometimes a thank-you is nice. . . ."

Nadia turned him away from the table of letters and said,

"We all thank you, BIB. You make it possible for us to do what we do every day."

She and Katie gathered around him and walked toward BIB's office. The three of them holed up in there to discuss the news and developments of the weekend.

Zeph and I made the rounds, delivering some letters and packages to other offices in the building. When we returned to BIB's office, Nadia almost tackled me with a "Where have you been, Cameron?"

"We were just delivering some correspondence . . . ," I responded.

"BIB asked for you," she said, as she guided me into BIB's office. "It's generally a good thing if you are here when he asks for you."

Questions stampeded across my brain in the few steps it took to get to his office. *Does he know about Memo? Can he tell I've been looking up Wade Branson?* I felt Nadia's guiding hand more strongly against my back as I filled with dread at the sudden, uncharacteristic summons.

"Please. Come in, Cameron." BIB waved me in with a quiet, welcoming gesture.

I was relieved to see that we were not alone. On BIB's couch, a couple held hands tightly, as if they were each other's handrail. The husband's weathered face and combination of shorts and white socks that reached well into his shins placed him in the forty-five- to sixty-year-old range. His wife's hair was a civil war between gray and brown strands.

"I want you to meet the Kluffs," BIB said. "They're from Lagrima, and I thought it would be nice for them to see a promising young man from their hometown."

"So nice to meet you." I reached for their hands, both of which were weak. Humble. "Did you come to DC to see the sights?"

The wife looked down and rubbed her mouth with her hand. The husband smiled a *we're getting through this* kind of smile—the expression I remember my dad giving people when they'd ask about my mom and I was still little.

"Cameron," said BIB. "Mr. and Mrs. Kluff's daughter died in Syria. Had some difficulty arranging for space in Arlington for her burial, so we stepped in . . ."

The wife lifted her head and smiled through glistening eyes. "Congressman Beck got our Linda the honor she deserved. Best representative our district's ever had. You learn all you can from him, okay?"

"I'm learning a lot about"—I coughed and corrected myself—"I mean *from* him. I'm really lucky to be here."

"Not many like him out here," said the husband. "Remembers his roots. Gets things done for the people back home."

"Just doing my job," said BIB, matter-of-factly, as Katie popped in the door.

"I'm afraid this is a bad time, but we've got a question for the congressman. Outside," she said, and then realized the somber scene. "You two can stay here with Cameron as long as you'd like."

BIB and the couple rose to their feet as the wife reached for BIB's hand. He gave her a hug, and she lost whatever composure remained. Tears of pain and appreciation wet his suit lapel. And I tried to reconcile this beloved congressman before me with Memo's serious allegations. In that moment, only the couple's gratitude for BIB's service felt real.

"Is it okay?" asked the man, pulling a camera out and looking at BIB for permission.

"Oh, of course it is!" said BIB. "Cameron, we already got some pictures together, but the Kluffs want some more photos in here. Can you be our office photographer after I run out?"

I obliged, reaching for the camera, as BIB said farewell and thanked me. "Our interns get to wear many hats during the summer!"

If he only knew.

BIB and Katie swiftly exited as I snapped away at the couple in front of BIB's desk.

"You don't think . . . ," said the husband as he sheepishly gestured toward BIB's chair.

"You want a picture in the chair?" I asked.

"Well, only if it's not going to get you in trouble," he responded.

I guided him behind BIB's massive desk to the chair, where he assumed a pose that was half state portrait, half cheesy tourist smile.

As I stepped back to take his picture, I saw a box that contained the photo of Ariel and her friend. And the stack of hair ties. And the Post-its. And files. It was a box of all of the items that had been removed from Ariel's drawer. Hiding behind BIB's desk.

Unwanted adrenaline stalked my veins as I realized I had one more chance to help out Memo. To help out Ariel.

The man cleared his throat. "Is everything okay?" he asked as I realized I had been studying the box and its contents for a few moments too long.

His words startled me. "Yes, of course." I grasped his early-generation digital camera and stood at a distance for a quick picture.

"Thank you for coming to visit," I said as I walked them to BIB's office door. "It was like having a little bit of home in here. Next time, bring some burgers from Vista Drive-In, okay?"

The couple both laughed on their way out and said something that I didn't listen to as I scanned the office and the visible hallway outside for any sign of BIB. He wasn't there. Just a cluster of staffers laughing at a YouTube video on Marcus's computer.

As if it were perfectly normal, I retreated back into BIB's office, left the door barely ajar, and went straight to the open box of Ariel's belongings. My brain was shaking, yet my hands were somehow steady. I figured I had a couple minutes to find whatever Ariel had left behind, before this box and any leads disappeared forever. I peeled off each Post-it note and figured that Ariel didn't mean anything special by reminding herself to feed her cat, make "10 copies of Ag Committee report," or the fateful "Capitol Sinny 9 p.m." I pulled out a cluster of hair ties and throttled through file folders that contained copies of very official-looking and innocuous congressional reports, travel schedules, and budgets. I flattened the few crinkled gum wrappers and found no hidden messages. Finally, I picked up that picture of Ariel and a girlfriend, their casual, beachside smiles almost taunting me. I shook the frame in my hand, as if Ariel's clue would somehow magically appear.

That's when I heard BIB's muffled but booming voice reenter the lobby of the office. The shaking from my brain shot right to my fingers, which suddenly trembled. As I held the framed photo in my left hand, I scanned the array of relics on the floor in front of me.

"*What were you so close to, Ariel?*" I whispered to myself as BIB's footsteps signaled he was walking toward his office.

As I simultaneously crafted an excuse for being in BIB's office alone, I stuffed everything back into the open box.

I did everything I could do, Memo. There was nothing in there.

Except, finally, there was.

As I placed the framed photo facedown, and I heard the creak of the opening door, I saw a tiny pink corner of a piece of paper peeking out from behind the matting of the frame. I grabbed that pink piece of paper, stood up, and dashed over to the couch where the Kluffs had sat—all in the time it took for BIB to fully open the door.

"They called and said they lost their umbrella!" I pre-emptively explained as I knelt down, looked under the couch, and secured the pink piece of paper in my shirt pocket. BIB couldn't even finish his sentence, "What are you doing in—"

"Do you think it's going to rain today? What nice people they were." I tried to deflect, to distract. "Thanks for bringing me in here to meet them."

"Well, you were an important burst of energy in here," he said. "Such a sad story, their daughter. . . ."

Out of the twitching corner of my eye, I saw that I had left the box of Ariel's stuff fully in view—not as I found it when it was obscured by BIB's desk. Amidst the OCD organization of the rest of his office, the misplaced box screamed, *I've been tampered with.*

Fortunately, Nadia did the screaming for me.

"Oh, this is good, this is good!" she shouted from the other room.

BIB turned his head just long enough for me to kick the box back into position as I exited his office.

"What's happening, Nadia?" asked BIB. I joined him and a group of other interested staffers around the door to Nadia's office.

"We're double digits ahead in the polls," she said. "You've got a nice little runway to November, Mr. Speaker."

"Well, don't get ahead of yourself," BIB cautioned humbly, though a glint of greed shot across his eyes. "What's the margin of error?" I was amazed to see how quickly he transitioned from congressman-in-mourning to campaign trail conversation.

"Oh, you don't even have to worry about that, BIB. Maybe Jigar's going to get an upgrade from that sad cubicle of his, come January!" Nadia squealed.

"You think?" Jigar pandered.

As the staffers congregated and dreamed of their larger offices and even larger career possibilities, I slipped out the pink piece of paper I had rescued from oblivion. I hoped it would be empty, a blank fleck of framing waste that got lodged behind that spellbinding photo. But somehow I knew that this was my next step. A clue.

I opened the folded paper and found a hastily scrawled

note in all caps. It looked as if Ariel had written it quickly, while no one was looking. Or before it was too late.

Four frantic letters: "FOR C." Plus a street address:

FRYE

1830 WALKER

VA BEACH

15

I found myself staring at the note on the metro ride home—and focusing on that offering or invitation or demand, "FOR C."

For me.

Ariel had thrown me a hot potato on her way out of this world, and it was starting to burn my hands and blister my train of thought. As we rocketed away from the Capitol South stop, I pointlessly looked around the subway car for another person to whom I could pass it on.

"Don't turn around," low-talked a voice from behind me. It was Memo. "Did you find anything?"

"Dude, you've got to stop sneaking up on me like that," I said in the direction of a random staffer who cautiously stepped away from me. "No, not you, I'm sorry," I apologized as she buried her face in her phone.

"An address," said Memo as he slipped the paper out of my hands. For a few stops, it seemed as if he studied Ariel's instructions, or compared it to other notes he had. By the time we hit the commuter crush of the Metro Center stop, I turned around to him.

"I'm going," I told him.

He urgently motioned for me to look away.

"Oh my gosh, do you really think the people around us are thinking we aren't talking to each other?" I said as I turned away. That staffer looked up from her phone and smiled at me.

"I think we should go together. Maybe just me," he said.

"Are you serious?" I answered. "Whoever 'Frye' is is not going to respond well to a creeper middle-aged man. An 'old friend of Ariel's,' however . . . They'll let me in the door."

"Okay, I may be on the other side of forty-five," he replied, shifting his weight slightly in protest, then leaning in to whisper, "but a creeper?"

I turned back to him, eyebrows raised. "My point exactly."

"How are you going to get there? What's your excuse at the office?" he asked, still standing behind me and speaking from a perpendicular angle.

We rounded the sharp corner of the McPherson Square stop and strained to stand straight as the train whipped left.

"First of all," I said, "I have an internship. And interns can have sick days. And I think I'm going to feel sick tomorrow."

I let out two small coughs. I could hear Memo stifling a laugh.

"And"—I leaned back closer to his ear as the train voice announced the stop at Farragut West—"I'm sure your employer can arrange for a car."

Memo got off the metro at Farragut West and told me he'd see me in the morning. I didn't bother to tell him my address because I was sure he already knew. I had gotten used to it—his knowledge of intimate details of my life. It didn't surprise me anymore.

What did surprise me was the janky Honda Civic parked in the red zone in front of my apartment the next morning.

"Idiot," said Hillary. "That guy's going to get a ticket."

"How do you know it's a guy?" teased Zeph. "You're sexist."

As we stepped down the stairs in front of the building, I looked across the street, where Memo made quick eye contact with me and did a casual *turn around* gesture with his right index finger. So by the time we were halfway across the street, a sudden and violent onset of food poisoning had rendered me debilitated for the day.

"Go ahead, you guys," I said, doing my best fake-diarrhea walk back toward the building. They wished me well, though Hillary looked mostly disgusted.

"You're going to miss the food-slash–tax policy panel tonight at AEI," she said. "Such a shame."

"Let us know if you need anything," added Zeph. "We'll get back home pretty late."

I waved good-bye from the steps and watched until they were out of sight. That's when Memo walked past the car and placed a set of keys on the roof without looking at me.

I wanted to go after him and ask if the beat-up car was a joke. Where was my government-issue convertible, or at least my sensible, new-model American car with a killer engine? I'd envisioned that's what the Bureau would have arranged. No dice.

However, it *was* surprisingly immaculate inside, given the bumps and scratches on the exterior. And it was my only way to get to Virginia Beach and back before Zeph and Hillary got home that night. I turned the ignition and was shocked by a too-loud adult contemporary station that Memo must have been listening to when he'd dropped off the car. Adele, wishing me a safe trip.

The city's driving ecosystem was not kind to me, but after a few angry honks and illegal turns, I was cruising south on the 95 freeway—the interstate spine that connected Maine to Miami. The four-hour journey was like driving through the pages of an eleventh-grade US history book. Civil War sites dotted the freeway, and I wondered what the warriors at Spotsylvania were thinking about the Waffle House and Starbucks that now christened the area. Lush, never-ending bunches of green leaves flanked the open road and defied the decades of smog that had battered them.

The Virginia Beach exit came faster than I expected and sooner than I wanted it to. It was just after noon. Multiple flags and mobbed fireworks stands and the subtle sting of salt in the air indicated that this was a party town getting ready for the imminent Fourth of July weekend. Every sign in sight seemed to point me toward "Beach," but I turned onto Walker Lane and meandered down the friendly looking, narrow street. I soon found myself in front of a butter-yellow clapboard house marked "1830."

As I walked to the door, I tried to think of it as one of the hundreds I'd visited during BIB's campaign back in Lagrima. Just another door. Except that this door led to the truth. This door led to the CVSU contract for my dad. *I've got this, Ariel,* I thought to myself. Whatever hermit conspiracy theorist or *Oh wait, Wade Branson didn't die—he's been living here all along!* or cryptic grandma lived behind this door—*I've got this.*

No such exotic character opened the door—rather, a thin man with short, graying hair, wearing a burgundy fleece jacket.

"Can I help you?" he asked.

"Hello, sir." I cleared my throat and went for it. "My name is Cameron Carter, and I worked with Ariel Lancaster. I . . . I think she wanted me to come here. Or she was going to come here herself. . . ."

The man covered his mouth with his hand as an equally thin and equally graying woman came to the door.

"What's this?" she grumbled.

"Honey," the man told him. "This is . . . was a friend of Ariel's."

"No, thank you!" said the woman, as she moved to close the door.

"Netsie, don't be rude," he intervened and held open the door. "Let's hear him out. What do you need, son?"

"That's the thing," I said. "I'm not sure. Ariel left your address behind. It was attached to . . ."

A startling and immediately recognizable framed photo interrupted my words. It was the photo of Ariel with her arm around a friend.

"It was attached to that same photo, but on Ariel's desk in the office."

The picture was surrounded by other Kodak moments of the various stages of a girl's life—water wings by a pool, posing as a *Nutcracker* mouse, summer camp, family vacations, volleyball team . . .

"Is that your daughter?" I asked. Then, urgently, hopefully: "Is she here?"

The pair studied me and then looked at each other with the silent flurry of communication that only a long-married couple can share with their eyes. The woman flapped her hands at the air and said to the man, "All yours."

"Come inside," said the man. "I'm Gerald Frye, and this . . ." She was already long gone, down the hallway of the modest house. ". . . *that* was my wife, Annette."

"Thank you," I said as I walked in the home.

"Daughter, yes," said Gerald. "*Was*, I guess is more like it. Caitlin died back in high school." He seemed to apologize for their quiet, clean house. "We've been empty nesters ever since."

I stood there, stunned, trying to piece together the scene: *Caitlin—the name she whispered at Capitol Sinny. Why did Ariel send me here? Who was this friend of hers?* The talkative Gerald was happy to help, as he motioned for me to sit on a buoyant, barely used couch.

"Yep," he explained. "Ariel and Caitlin were best friends. Met on the first day of kindergarten and never left each other's sides since. When Ariel's mom ran for office the first couple of times, Caitlin knocked on the most doors." He gestured to a series of photos that showed Ariel and Caitlin holding NANI LANCASTER FOR CONGRESS signs. "Never got to see her win, though."

"Can I ask what happened?" I said.

"Just saw Nani at Ariel's funeral a few weeks ago." He ignored my question. "I went up there and put my arm around her and told her our little angels are still cheering her on from heaven."

Gerald looked down to pick at a hangnail, and a pair of loudly ticking clocks spoke to each other as we sat in silence. I could hear his wife pacing in the nearby kitchen and the screams of children playing with a hose across the street. The house was perfectly, almost uncomfortably, pristine. And silent.

"Well, it looks like their cheering is helping," I said as Gerald dug away at his cuticle. "They say Nani could be the new face of the Democratic party."

Gerald raised his eyebrows and *hmph*ed to himself.

After another interminable few minutes of the clocks' tick-tocking, I offered an apologetic, "Look, I can leave. . . ."

Gerald fiercely ripped at his hangnail and sucked on the now-bleeding finger. "I think that photo was Caitlin's last good summer." He pointed to the campaign picture between sucks on his finger. "After that, she went dark. Not even really sad— just not really there. Ariel was the only one who she'd let in her room sometimes."

"Depression?" I asked.

"And it was Ariel who told her about Thativan," he continued. "Bless her heart, she just wanted her Caitlin back like we all did. So she did all this research. And she came in here"—he pointed to the entryway, as if Ariel's ghost were floating through the house—"and she told us about this new drug. Instant remedy, no more barfing, no fatigue, none of that brain crackling. FDA-approved and all. So we 'asked our doctor about Thativan'"—he imitated the pleasantly aggressive voices from TV pharmaceutical ads—"and put her on it."

His words were more a confession than a story. An admission of guilt.

"Didn't even ask her if she wanted to, we just put her on it," he said. "And then we had Christmas." He pointed to another photo of Ariel and Caitlin, proudly displaying an anemic snowman.

"Never snows here, but it did that year," he mused. "And then she was gone before New Year's. Those monsters killed our baby because they thought they were going to get rich. . . ."

Gerald's wife stormed down the hallway and suddenly appeared at the entry to the living room. She didn't acknowledge me and said, "Gerald, a moment, please."

I tried not to listen to their hushed voices in the other room but couldn't not. I could make out a few urgent phrases amidst the muffled words.

"We don't want any more of this," whispered Annette to Gerald. "Caitlin's gone, now Ariel, too—haven't you had enough?"

"You know there was always something questionable about . . ." I heard fragments of Gerald's whispers to his wife. ". . . that what Ariel told . . . find who's responsible . . ."

"It doesn't matter. . . . It's over. . . . You are so stubborn. . . ."

I could hear Gerald hug Annette before trudging back into the living room in his weathered slippers.

"Sorry about that." He smiled. "Where were we?"

"Look, I think I'm opening up some wounds here, and the last thing I want to do is hurt you," I said.

"No, no, don't worry. Any friend of Ariel's is a friend of ours."

"I know what it's like to lose someone you love," I said. "My mom died when I was little. And I know what the absence feels like. It feels like a ticking clock that won't shut up when you and the ones she left behind can't think of anything else to say."

I was telling the truth, but honestly, I was really just trying to find an angle. A connection. By using my mother's death. It felt a little cathartic and a lot manipulative. But I could tell that it had worked when I saw Gerald's left eye glisten. And heard Annette tiptoeing to the edge of the living room, just out of sight. Eavesdropping.

"Caitlin sounds like an amazing girl, and it's not your fault that she died," I went on. "And Ariel knew that too. And I don't know why, but I am pretty sure she wanted me to come here To see you. Maybe just to say good-bye on her behalf."

"Cameron." Gerald wiped his eye. "Ariel came down here for Easter with us. Just a few months ago. Said she was on to something about Caitlin. You see, after Caitlin died, Ariel felt responsible because she was the one who'd suggested that poison in the first place. We hugged and we cried and we looked at old cheerleading audition practice videos. . . ."

"Ariel was here?" I asked.

"She kind of became obsessed with the Thativan CEO's death—I never really understood why," he explained. "But now I know it was for Caitlin. It was always for Caitlin . . ." He trailed off and looked out the window at the playful antics of the neighborhood kids.

For Caitlin.

FOR C.

I wondered if that part of the note I found in her things was intended to address me, or simply a reminder of who she was doing it all for. The person she told Memo she was protecting. It was all for Caitlin.

"Will you be around for the Fourth of July?" He changed the subject. "They have this amazing fireworks show down by the water. Gets bigger every year."

"I have to get back to DC," I said.

"Well, we don't even compare to what they do up there."

I stood and thanked Gerald for his time.

"So soon?" he asked.

I heard Annette skitter away toward the kitchen, so I wouldn't see that she had been listening all along. Gerald had nothing to share but grief and memories, and it felt respectful to leave him there with them. If the only purpose of this visit that Ariel had envisioned was a farewell by proxy, I was happy to oblige. As I said good-bye to Gerald, I caught another look at that mesmerizing photo of Ariel and her best friend, Caitlin.

"Have a wonderful holiday," I said.

The door shut behind me, and I walked toward the car, which appeared to be baking in the hot, humid sun. Heat waves distorted the thick air surrounding the outline of the Honda Civic. I stepped into the driver's seat, and it felt like an inescapable oven blast.

As I started the car, I heard a knock from the passenger-side window. It was Annette Frye. I rolled down the window, and she started speaking before I could.

"Look . . ." Her stature was weak and her face apologetic as she searched for my first name.

"Cameron," I said.

"Cameron. I'm sorry you didn't exactly experience Southern hospitality in my home today. I hope you can understand, given the circumstances," she continued.

"Mrs. Frye, I'm so sorry for your loss. I think Ariel just wanted me to come and say good bye."

"I think I know why Ariel told you to come," she said as she put a manila envelope into my view. "We got this letter in the mail the day Ariel died. Never could get ahold of her to find out what it was or why she'd sent it. But now I think I know. I think she wanted us to give it to you."

Annette carefully placed the envelope on the passenger seat.

"I opened it up—just a list of names, I don't know." She

shrugged. "But maybe you'll be able to find something in there."

"Thank you, Mrs. Frye," I said as I pulled the stack of papers from the envelope. A simple handwritten list of names, just like she said. A quick scan revealed none of them to be remarkable or familiar.

"Anything for Ariel," she said and turned to walk back toward her house. She stopped and returned to the car as I rolled up the passenger window to keep out the oppressive heat. I rolled the window back down.

"Just wanted to say that I bet your momma is proud of you," she said and patted the passenger door with the lingering care of a mother whose mothering was cut short.

An unexpected lump in my throat prevented me from saying the thank-you I wanted to give her. By the time I gulped it down, Annette Frye had returned inside that happy-looking but sad butter-yellow house.

I figured I could spare a few minutes to go to the beach before I needed to hit the road and get back to the apartment unsuspected. I drove away from Walker Lane and followed the signs toward "Beach." Parades of families and friends crisscrossed the increasingly crowded roads. I parked and walked toward the sand, dodging generations of families for whom this place was clearly a summer tradition. Grandfathers gave shoulder rides to laughing little girls. A toddler dropped his ice cream cone on the ground and picked it back up, just before his doting mother could see the infraction. Two teenage girls walked hand in hand, laughing out loud and quieting each other when they realized I'd noticed them.

Ariel and Caitlin, I thought.

When I got to the beach, I rolled up my jeans and took off my shoes. The sand burned each footstep in the midafternoon heat. I pulled out my phone to call my dad, though I knew I couldn't mention where I was. And how it reminded me of our very rare but very fun day trips to Monterey when I was younger. And how I didn't miss home at all. It went to his voice mail. I hesitated before ending the call without leaving a message. Berto wasn't around either.

I searched around the idyllic summer scene in vain for a familiar face—but this was someone else's holiday, someone else's coast. As I walked through the shallow, lapping water, I considered tagging along with one of the large groups of friends and families that departed the beach. How long would it take them to notice that this stranger was crashing their pizza-party dinner, and then their games of charades, and then their late night donut run?

I was drawn to one such group that clustered at the water's edge a few yards away. As I got closer, it became clear that they were trying to help someone. Something. A group of parents and kids and friends and strangers stood helpless—about ten feet away from a baby whale that had washed upon the shore in the middle of an otherwise perfect beach day. One dad tried to shield his kids, but they just stood there—intrigued, horrified. Before I could fully register the swarm of flies that pecked away at its rubbery skin and the sour, wrong stench that emanated from that patch of sand, I looked away. Hundreds of other beachgoers laughed and chatted and continued with their days, either oblivious or indifferent to the nearby death scene. I watched as the group dispersed and listened as new gawkers came and went.

"Must have gotten lost."

"Should have left this area before it was too late."

"Whales don't belong around here in the summer."

At one point, it was just me and this dead whale, which rocked lifelessly in the occasional swell. The comments from passersby echoed in my head. And for a half second, I wondered if they applied to me as well. If this errant whale was an omen, a warning. *That's ridiculous*, I thought to myself. But half seconds of those thoughts multiplied and combined into two and four and ten seconds of those thoughts. I turned my back to the water and the whale and headed back to the car, hoping that those mutating musings would stay behind as well.

16

August 1, Seat 29J.

I lay on my back on the mattress in my room and stared up at a printout of my return ticket home. I envisioned that day—the In-N-Out Burger we'd grab on the way home from the airport, the welcome home party at Berto's house, the steamy hot asphalt smell of August in the Central Valley . . .

I had lasted a little over thirty days in DC—surely I could handle another month, right?

But I was now somehow walking the same path that led a girl to her untimely death. And an accomplice to an aggressive FBI agent, sniffing out a six-year-old suicide that didn't add up. And an instatherapist to grieving parents. And a boyfriend (I think?) to a girl who had better things to do on the Fourth of July than hang out with me.

And on top of everything, else, there was that dead whale on the beach. Just to make the situation a tad bit bleaker, in case it wasn't ominous enough, a dead *baby* whale.

So that return flight—that ejector seat out of this town— seemed tauntingly far away. In a weak moment, I thought about going home early. And maybe I was on hold with the airline for forty minutes, so I could find out how much it would cost to change my flight. But ultimately, I couldn't decide which was worse—the humiliation of telling everyone in Lagrima, *Yeah, I couldn't cut it out there!* or the astonishing airline change fee that probably would have required a few hundred mowed lawns.

It was Friday—a few days after my sick day/truth-seeking mission. A holiday, because the Fourth landed on Saturday. And I hadn't responded to Memo's eight increasingly intrusive and anxious text messages:

How was the beach?

Who is Frye?

???

Where is the car?

Okay, I'm outside your apartment, and I see the car. Where are the keys?

Hello?

Found the keys. On top of the back tire. Clever. Who is Frye?

I can see you have read all of these messages. Answer, please.

My lack of response wasn't because I didn't want to help him (well, maybe a little), but because I just wanted a normal summer internship. I found myself envying Zeph and Hillary's endless debates about trade sanctions and office gossip—while I daydreamed about Wade Branson and killer prescription drugs and what really happened to Ariel that night. I put the itinerary down and held up the list of names Ariel had sent to me, care of the Fryes. About forty names were written out on lined paper—randomly ordered Susans and Walters and Richards and Russells and Barbaras. The list meant everything and nothing, all at once.

I heard a dull *ding* come from the phone—announcing Memo's ninth text. This time, it was simply the URL for Central Valley State University—a not-so-subtle reminder of the carrot Memo dangled at the end of a very long and twisty stick in front of me. A carrot that wasn't even for me. But it was enough to break my texting silence.

You know your audience, I texted.

Who. Is. Frye.

I texted him all about the parents, the dead daughter/best friend, and the Thativan connection. And the list. "Too many names to text," I told him.

"Send pic," he replied.

Apparently, this dinosaur phone could send pictures. I

took a picture of the list and sent it back to Memo.

Two index finger taps at the door was the only warning Hillary gave me before barging in my room. I slammed the phone shut and threw it under the sheets of the bed. And looked very guilty as she stood above me.

"Caught you in a bad moment?" she asked, right eyebrow mischievously raised.

"No, no, just impressed by your respect for privacy. Are you sure you aren't interning for the NSA?" I asked.

She rolled her eyes: the expected response. "Are you coming tomorrow?"

"What?" I replied, doing my best to look fine and not at all preoccupied by what Memo would text next.

"The Fourth of July. Party at Marcus's . . . oh wait, you weren't there. He announced it in the office the day of your little diarrhea dance back into the apartment."

"Thanks for that, Hilly."

"You're lucky I told you about the party."

A *ding* from under the covers signaled Memo's reply. My hand instinctively reached for the phone, then stopped because of the audience in front of me.

"What is that?" she inquired.

"My phone," I said. "Any other questions?"

"Yes. If your phone just made a noise from your bed, then why is it sitting on the desk?"

We both looked over at my own, non-FBI phone—sitting quietly on the table. My reply was more forceful than the amateur liar shade of red flushing my cheeks: "Shut up. Get out of here, Snowden!"

I mostly ignored her taunting laughter as she walked away and I carefully opened the flip phone. Memo had replied.

Let the digging begin.

The next day, I waited for a different text. The one where Lena invited me to whatever embassy thing she was doing instead of hanging out with me on the Fourth. Or when she told me she was bailing on the embassy thing and said we should go back to the Washington Monument and watch the fireworks while we made a couple of our own in the observation deck. And when neither of those texts came, I settled for the Marcus party with Zeph and Hillary.

As we entered Marcus's glorified frat house residence, we heard a disturbing yelping noise from the backyard. "Is that a dying goat?" asked Hillary.

"No, it's Marcus," I replied.

The poor guy was wearing board shorts and a red, white, and blue Hawaiian shirt—and now the better part of a chicken marinade that had spilled all over him. As troubling billows of gray smoke emanated from the barbecue, he let out another pathetic scream that was halfway between a desperate call for help and a self-deprecating, mock *ahhhh!*—I took it for the former and walked over to help him out. Zeph and Hillary made a beeline for the well-stocked cooler and the group of BIB staffers who had gathered nearby.

"Have you ever barbecued before?" I asked him.

"Look, this is a DEFCON 3 chicken crisis, and we don't have time to make another run to the store," he pleaded. "This is not the time to talk about my outdoor culinary résumé—just do something!"

I winced as I opened the top of the barbecue and a mushroom cloud of disregarded cooking instructions formed a black haze over our heads. The other party guests marveled at the sight, though this was a basic Lagrima summer dinner situation for me. I quickly went to work, turning down the heat on the barbecue and starting to turn over the almost-burned meat. Disaster averted.

"Just like that?" asked Marcus, exasperated.

"Who's the intern now?" jeered Katie as she popped a potato chip in her mouth and passed by us. She was wearing blue-and-white-striped capri pants with a loose-fitting white blouse. She added, "So resourceful, Cameron."

"Who's the intern now?" parroted Marcus in a resentful, squished face, baby-voice kind of way. Followed by a sad whisper to me: "Do not leave me alone with this thing."

"Don't worry." I patted him on the back and tried to calm

him down, as Memo's text popped into my head: *Let the digging begin.* I looked at Marcus—knowledgeable, suddenly indebted to me, and just absentminded enough to tell me too much about people who may be connected to BIB.

"Nice place you've got here," I said as the early-afternoon sun sharpened its glare. Most of the other partiers walked inside for the air-conditioning while another group clustered under an umbrella on the deck, leaving Marcus and me as the lone keepers of the sizzling meat.

"Well, if you're going to live with nine other guys, a decaying Georgetown row house is where to do it." He shrugged, followed by a conspiratorial, "But if you see my landlord, it's only four of us who live here, okay?"

"There are ten guys living here?" I asked. The house was nice, but not big and certainly not ten-inhabitants big. I tried to find the right moment to hit him up for info.

"Not all of us are subsidized interns, okay?" he said. "DC is expensive. And besides, I'm lucky. I got the whole master bedroom walk-in closet to myself."

"You live in a closet," I stated.

"Yes," he said. "And this is how my parents can brag to their friends at home that their son is a big-deal Capitol Hill staffer."

"Big deal, indeed." I laughed as I turned the sizzling patties and juicy chicken on the grill. And then I went in for the kill.

"Oh, Marcus," I said casually, "you may be able to help me with this work thing. I was organizing some files, but I found this list, and I don't know where to put it. Has all these names—about forty or fifty people. . . ."

"Are you talking about the Fifty Hottest Staffers on Capitol Hill, because no, for the fifth time, I declined the offer to be featured." He chuckled to himself and gulped down sips from a triple-digit-ounce drink container.

"No, no, not that," I clarified. "I think they're friends of BIB or something. Susan McArthur, Walter Wendler . . ." I did my best to recall the names Ariel had written.

"Did someone say Fifty Hottest Staffers?" Hillary suddenly appeared, like an impish child who knows cookies have just been removed from the oven.

"No, Hillary, just grilling over here." I tried to swat her away, so I could have Marcus to myself.

"Because I heard that interns can be nominated." She wrapped her arm around Marcus. "But they have to be nominated by a full-time staff member. Marcus?" She fluttered her eyes at his sweaty face. "Deadline to nominate people is next week," she said sweetly.

"I think I recognize some White House staffers over there," I interrupted, and Hillary immediately darted her head toward the inside of the house. Anything related to 1600 Pennsylvania Avenue was the perfect distraction for her.

"One of your roommates works at the White House, right, Marcus?"

"Well, he's on the advance team, so he's never around, but he is here today." He pointed at a guy wearing a light blue polo shirt and jeans—and that was all Hillary needed to continue her social butterflying.

"Tootles, gentlemen," she said, followed by an all-business: "And remember to nominate me, Marcus. HillZone.com. There is this red button on the right side of the screen that says NOMINATE. So you click on that, just drag and drop a picture, and fill out the . . ."

As she prattled on, I peeked at the flip-phone screen and studied the image of Ariel's list of names.

"We got it, Hillary," I assured her and slipped the phone back in my pocket. She let out a gracious and totally sincere "Thank you" before prancing back into the house.

"Do you think these are ready?" asked Marcus.

"So, anyway, that list," I continued. "Do any of these names sound familiar? I could really use your help."

I listed off the other names I could remember, as Marcus prepared a plate for his finished product. He started to pull off the burger patties and chicken and delicately placed them on the platter.

"Ring a bell?" I asked, as Memo's persistent urging rang in my head.

Marcus was clearly more focused on showing off the spoils of his barbecuing.

"Lunchtime!" he announced, and suddenly a line of hungry partiers formed around the table where he placed his cookout masterpieces.

"Couldn't have done it without you," he commented as he put his arm around me. As if we had just built a barn together.

"Great burgers, Cam!" someone shouted, to Marcus's dismay.

He sighed. "Seriously?"

The moment had passed. Marcus's roommates gathered around him, the deck area swelled, and someone blasted Neil Diamond's "America."

"Today!" shouted everyone, as if on cue at the end of the song. Over and over, along with Mr. Diamond's earnest cheer, "Today!" Once the song finished, Marcus continued proudly shouting, "Today!" as the group looked at him with increasing alarm. He was *that* guy.

The day somehow got hotter as the shadows grew longer. And the group started talking about migrating to the Mall to watch fireworks.

"Lincoln Memorial steps are the best spot," someone announced.

"Only if you can get there in the morning," interjected another partier. "The steps fill up, and there's tons of security."

"I like this area near the Jefferson Monument," said Katie, smiling at me.

"No, no, no," added one of Marcus's roommates. "That's where all of the smoke goes. You can't see anything after a few minutes."

"We are going as close to the Washington Monument as we can get," declared Marcus with a newfound authority. "Optimal viewing, less security, a little more elbow room."

"That settles it," confirmed Katie.

These type A staffers took their fireworks viewing as seriously as health-care reform or negotiation over appropriations bills. What happened to a few Roman candles and ground bloom flowers on the sidewalk?

As the party closed down and the group headed for the door, I joined Zeph and Hillary on the long walk from Georgetown to the Mall. As we turned the first corner, Marcus pulled me aside.

"National Cancer Society, Americans for AIDS Relief, Diabetes Research Group," he listed.

"What?" I asked.

"Those names," he said. "You have at least three CEOs of health-care-related NGOs in there, probably more. I don't do health stuff, so I just recognize the well-known ones. . . ."

I closed my eyes for a long blink and continued walking with the crowd. A list of health-care NGO leaders?

"So, anyway, barbecue Jesus, hope that helps you out."

"With what?" I said, somewhat defensively.

"With the missing file?" he asked. "Remember?"

"Oh, yeah," I said. "Huge help. You really saved me on this one."

Marcus rejoined his pack of roommates. As I walked over to join Zeph and Hillary, I heard Katie's voice: "Overachiever."

"What?" I looked back and uttered an unconvincing, nervous laugh. She was a few steps behind me—a distance from which she definitely could have heard the conversation with Marcus. I tried to retrace my words, but she clearly wanted to talk.

"You're talking shop on a holiday, that's what I mean."

Though my conversation with Marcus was harmless on its face, no one else needed to know. The fewer people who knew about my extracurricular pursuits the better. Still: *What did she hear?*

I slowed my pace slightly to ensure maximum distance from Marcus. "Poor guy," I told Katie. "He's nervous about a report he's working on, just asking for help when something came to mind. I'm happy to help."

Katie's smile indicated she was 70 percent convinced of my story and 100 percent convinced of Marcus's ineptitude. "I don't believe that for a second."

Okay, 0 percent convinced of my story. Not good. I looked

away from her and widened my eyes, trying to think of a good reason to chat about a very specific set of BIB's friends with Marcus. . . .

She continued, "You're writing another report for him, aren't you?" she said. "You're running circles around that guy, even with a sick day."

"No, I'm not doing it for him," I said. "And what do you mean 'sick day'?"

And then I immediately realized she was referring to my faux intestinal challenges/trip to Virginia Beach earlier in the week.

"Tuesday?" she offered. "The day you didn't come into work?"

"Oh, yeah." I quickly recovered, or tried to. "I prefer to block that out."

"Oh, Cam, I can see you're flustered," she said. "You really don't need to be."

"I'm not," I answered.

"Well, you shouldn't be. BIB asked where you were on Tuesday."

"He did?" I asked, trying to wipe the guilt off my face. *Geez, one day out of the office and everyone notices.* It made me wonder what else people noticed.

"Cameron." She chuckled. "You're not in trouble. Don't worry. He wanted you to meet another group of constituents who were visiting. From Lagrima. He told me how impressed he is with you. Disappointed you're at the beginning of college and not the end, when he can hire you. Blah, blah, blah. This is good news. You should be very happy about hearing this."

She was trying to change the worried look on my face, I could tell. But not very successfully. Even though I knew Memo's questions and Ariel's trail led to something real—something bad for BIB—the man believed in me. He wanted to hire me. And I was searching for evidence that could bring him down.

"Really?" I asked. It was the best I could do in the midst of the conflicting loyalties in my head.

"The man knows how to spot talent," she said, and then added, laughing, "I should know. I'm evidence of that."

But does he know how to spot an inside man?

"Okay, something's up," she declared, no doubt in response to my lack of engagement. "Is Nadia bugging you again?"

"No, no, it's not," I protested. "She's not."

"Okay, well, I hope you can shake off whatever overachiever's curse you have going on in your head. Because you're doing just fine. You're family. And we're here for you whenever. *I'm* here for you whenever. Scary stuff happens in this town, and I want you to know you can always come to me with questions—even the crazy ones. *Especially* the crazy ones."

"Thanks, Katie. I will do my best to come up with some

crazy questions." Like, *what does BIB have to do with a defective depression drug?*

She patted me on the back and then our paths diverged slightly as she pecked away at her phone. The pat on the back—it felt ordinary, but really good. It felt good to be family. It felt easier to be the golden boy than the whistle-blower.

"Cameron! Buddy!" Zeph dragged Hillary toward me as we crossed the Rock Creek bridge on our way to the mall. "Tell me you know someone who's been injured by fireworks."

Hillary and Zeph yammered on about firework safety (because a lazy chat about reality TV never suffices with these people), and I occasionally added a detached "Yeah," "Wow," and "That's *crazy.*" In my mind, I tried to connect an increasingly beguiling set of dots. The partly cloudy sky burned a darkening and purplish orange as we crossed the Rock Creek bridge. And as we walked through GWU, hundreds of others joined us in an impromptu parade down Pennsylvania Avenue, toward the big show.

We arrived at the Mall just as the red blinking light atop the Washington Monument started to really contrast with the darkening sky—a teasing reminder of my private tour up there with Lena. Who was probably picking over shrimp at some country club buffet along the Potomac. Or whatever "embassy thing" meant. The Mall was packed. The normally expansive and clear area was covered with families and friends. It looked like a large quilt of picnic blankets with grass peeking through in between—not the normal, other way around. I texted her **Celebrating with the masses while you do an "embassy thing."**

"Elbow room?" complained Hillary to Marcus, as territorial revelers called us out whenever we set foot on even a corner of the land they had likely claimed hours earlier.

"Okay, so it's my fault the Fourth of July is so popular," replied Marcus.

We settled in a corner of grass, bound by a walkway. It seemed like the only remaining empty space on the Mall, likely because of the cakey mud that slathered anyone who dared to set foot in it.

"Okay, so now I know what pigs feel like when they see fireworks," continued Hillary. She trotted over to an unsuspecting family and sat on a corner of their blanket. "Hi, I'm Hillary," I heard her say to the confused but ultimately accommodating father, mother, and two kids. She rubbed her hands together in fake excitement to the children. "Fireworks!"

As we waited for the fireworks to start, I decided to check on the holiday on the other side of the country. I called my dad, but Rogelito picked up.

"*Que ondas, guerito?*" he asked. *What's up, little white boy?* I didn't love the nickname back home, but for some reason, I loved hearing it now.

"Hey, happy Fourth!" I said. "Is my dad there?"

"He's setting up some picnic tables for a dinner," Rogelito said to me as he simultaneously carried on a conversation with someone else in Spanish. "Big party! We miss you!"

I scanned the festive but overwhelming scene on the Mall. Latecomers started to join us in the patch of mud. There was literally nowhere else to stand. Hillary braided the hair of the little girl from the family whose party she crashed.

"Well, please ask my dad why he's never able to talk to me anymore," I half joked. Katie was standing nearby. She heard me and smiled.

Rogelito replied with a hearty laugh and a "No, no, put the hot dogs over *there!*" I could hear the splashes and squeals of a children's cannonball contest in the community pool. His voice grew clearer as I imagined him putting the phone back to his ear. "So, how is the big city out there? Are you putting all those politicians in their place?"

"Yeah, it's amazing," I responded as I played tug-of-war over my shoes with the muddy ground. "Huge fireworks show about to start. Way bigger than anything we have in Lagrima."

"Listen, that's great," said Rogelito, who sounded like he was much more interested in the hot dogs than what I had to say. I couldn't really blame him. "I'll tell your dad to give you a call. Have fun!"

The familiar sounds of a Lagrima Fourth abruptly stopped

when the call ended. In that moment, I wanted to jump through the phone and join them all back home.

Katie walked over to me. "So, what do you think?"

"It's incredible!" I mustered.

"And your family has forgotten about you?" she added.

"Yes, unfortunately," I said.

"Well, don't worry," she said. "I haven't. You have a bright future here, if you play your cards right."

If she only knew the proverbial cards I was drawing, then holding, clasping, creasing with my uncertain, clammy hands.

The first shot of light weaved its way through the sky and then exploded in a circular globe of sparks, followed by three more. The crowd cheered. The show had begun.

"No better place to watch fireworks in the whole world," she commented as we looked up to the progressively illuminated night sky.

"Yeah." I nodded hesitantly—thinking that the ground blooms and sparklers back home weren't all that bad.

Sparkly white lights hovered in the air and strobed through the sky. And every minute or so, a massive globe of fire rattled the sky and lit up the crowd in reddish hues. Looking at the dots of fire shot toward the masses made it feel like the ground was actually lifting us toward the sky.

I closed my eyes, and I envisioned my mom.

For some reason, a slide show of all of the photos of her in

DC went through my head. That picture of her and my dad in front of the National Air and Space Museum. Her model-like gaze into the Tidal Basin. A playful salute at a dot in the sky, which my dad later told me was President Clinton's helicopter. A shot of her back and her hair in the breeze near the Washington Monument—just a few hundred feet away from where I stood. I could feel her there with me. And then I could feel okay with not being at the Lagrima party. I was with her.

"Open your eyes!" nudged Katie.

"Sorry," I instinctively said.

The blasts increased in frequency and intensity, eliciting *oohs* and screams from the crowd. I looked around and saw everyone's smiling, jaw-dropped faces turned heavenward.

Except for one.

From just across the cement walkway, I saw Lena. Looking at me.

When we briefly made eye contact, she looked away and up. I smiled and started to walk across the path and talk with her when I noticed that she was with a guy who placed his arm around her shoulder. His arm, which was adorned with a very expensive-looking watch.

Embassy thing.

She quickly glanced back at me as I rejoined the BIB crew in the muddy knoll. She turned her head toward the douchebag who embraced her and shot him a quick, guilty smile. I instantly hated him. And his Rolex, which gleamed even in the dark.

The show climaxed in a horrendously beautiful and chaotic blur of light, followed by silence and nothing but a blanket of smoke in the air. The crowd applauded and some people started to stand up. I turned back to look at Lena, but exiting crowds already clogged the walkway and obscured the view.

I tried to decide the appropriate mix of *What the hell?* and *Did you have a nice date with The Watch?* for my text to her.

17

Ultimately, I decided to send no text at all.

Let her text me.

Let her think that I didn't care. That she and that guy and his fancy timepiece weren't bouncing around my mind and my holiday hangover.

But the only texts that came the next day were pictures of my dad and friends at the community pool back home. And, of course, from Memo.

What's the connection? rang a text from the flip phone.

My homework was due. And though Memo's persistence was annoying, it was a convenient distraction from Lena's radio silence.

Nonprofits, I typed back. **I think mostly health-care sector.**

Tell me something I don't know, son, he snapped.

I hesitated, then wrote, **That's as far as I got in the last 22 hours, including a holiday. Sorry if that's too slow for you. Maybe you should find another intern.**

There was a pause. I filled the silence with **In fact, yes, please find another intern. I'm going to enjoy the Fourth of July weekend.**

He responded immediately, **What's more patriotic than investigating the possible malfeasance of a congressman?**

This time I paused.

Memo continued, **A congressman who made five-figure donations to everyone on Ariel's list in the years before his tenure on the Hill?**

I paused again. It was just the nonanswer Memo needed to know that he had my attention.

I'm going to keep texting here, so I hope there's someone on the other end to read . . . , he wrote.

Fine, yes, whatever, go on, I blurted back.

So, what's the connection? he asked.

What do you mean? BIB gave them money. That's it, I responded.

BIB gave them money, Memo answered. **What did they give BIB?**

A tax write-off? These are charities, not donors, I figured.

These are people BIB gave money to. And this was the final step Ariel took toward finding out what happened to Wade

Branson. Before, she, you know. Was stopped. So, we need to find out if anyone on this list had a particular . . . The texting stopped momentarily. Then another message: **. . . utility for BIB.**

Okay, I carefully typed.

Another pause.

This is the part where you thank me for doing your work for you and tell me that it's your turn to contribute something, he responded.

You seem to have forgotten my day trip to Virginia Beach.

That's over now, he snapped back. **Ariel Lancaster died because of one of those forty names. You tell me which one. Ready, set, expose.**

I glanced at my other phone to see no word from Lena. The growing daylight weaved through the building next door and into my bedroom window, promising a beautiful Sunday. But there was something about Memo's text that motivated me to stay inside.

We were close.

I broke out a clean spreadsheet on my laptop and put on my headphones. It was a Barry Manilow kind of morning.

I moved my head back and forth to the beat of "Copacabana" and then stopped to confirm the door was locked and neither Zeph nor Hillary would stumble upon my investigation into BIB's bad behavior. Then I resumed the head grooving and dove into Ariel's list. Barry's eternal question in the song took on new meaning: *"But just who shot who?"*

I typed out the names from the list and looked up their corresponding organizations and, where possible, photos . . .

Susan Stein, chief development officer of the National Cancer Society, looked like a kind grandma who eats half of the cookies before she gives them to her grandkids. Not exactly useful to BIB.

And then Lena emerged from her cave of shame, tiptoeing onto my computer screen with a simple **Hola** on MessageNow.

I stared at the word and wished she had written more, even as I closed the message window and kept researching. She was going to have to come up with more than *Hola* to get a response from me.

Richard Rudd from the Diabetes Research Group was pictured on the organization's impressive website, surrounded by what looked like several kids and even more grandkids. His background as "Pennsylvania's pediatrician" did not fit the ominous profile Memo was hunting down.

I can explain popped up on my screen. A full sentence this time.

Still not enough.

Betty Ann Barrington founded Americans for AIDS Relief and was a vocal supporter of related causes, after losing her young son to the illness in the mid-'80s. So far, it looked like BIB had selected a lot of legitimate recipients.

Well, maybe I can't, she added, increasingly dividing my attention from the research. **But I'm sorry.**

I researched a few more completely innocuous-looking suspects before answering Lena: **He does have a much nicer watch than I do.**

She replied quickly: **I knew you were going to say that. It is obnoxious.**

Apparently just obnoxious enough to make you want to spend the holiday with it. I mean, with him, I replied.

I continued to plug away at the Barry Manilow catalog and check out lots of smiling bureaucrats with sterling public records.

He's my ex, she wrote.

Didn't look like it last night, I answered.

He was in town for the holiday weekend. On a plane back to London now.

Fancy, I wrote.

This will be easier to talk about in person. Can I see you? she asked.

I wanted to type *YES NOW PLEASE WHERE?* but that would probably sound more pathetic than the four words looked in my mind. So I continued researching the list. It felt selfish and bad and right to make Lena wait. And squirm. A little.

I searched for a Russell Meteer and found that he started

National Oncology Warriors. "NOW," neat acronym. Except Betty Friedan got to it first.

I skipped "Can't Smile Without You," because even though it's one of Barry's most beloved hits, it's also a horrendous song. A rare miss, Mr. Manilow.

And then I noticed that National Oncology Warriors didn't have a website like the others.

I ignored another message from Lena: **???**

Russell Meteer did not have a Wikipedia page of his own, like the others on the list. The "image" search results turned up thirty different faces for the name. No sound bites in news articles, no list of awards. I scanned through more search results for any clues on this guy. One Russell Meteer was a junior high school pole-vaulting champ last year. Another owned an art gallery in Sedona.

As I clicked through page after page of not-helpful search results, I noticed that Lena had signed off MessageNow. I couldn't decide if I'd won or lost the standoff.

And then, based on a site tucked away on page nine of the search results, I instantly knew who Ariel's Russell Meteer was. Who *our* Russell Meteer was. The identity clicked in my mind, and the likely backstory crawled through my mind like angry, mutant ivy.

I picked up the flip phone and texted Memo.

7-11 near GWU. Now.

I didn't care how secure Memo's phone was. Meteer's identity felt too dangerous to be in my head—let alone typed out and sent into the air.

As I approached the local 7-Eleven where we agreed to meet, I saw Memo sitting on a bench outside—a Slurpee in each of his hands. Knee tapping aggressively up and down. When I sat down next to him, he wordlessly handed me the thick cup, which perspired in the hot evening air.

Then, as if he were talking to the passing cars, "What do you have for me?"

"Russell Meteer," I said, staring ahead in return. "Founder of National Oncology Warriors. Except there is no website, and he's not well-known like the other people on the list."

"Just because he's a nobody doesn't make him somebody to BIB," Memo said dispassionately.

"He's an ex–Navy SEAL, Memo," I offered. "Listed in some Navy SEAL reunion booklet buried online."

Memo cleared his throat and apologized. "Sorry. Slurpee headache . . ." He smacked his palm against his forehead and harshly squinted his eyes. Then it passed. "Okay, continue."

"Honorably discharged over a decade ago. Founded his cancer nonprofit four years later," I continued. "The same year—"

"Branson died," Memo finished my sentence.

We sat in silence, though I could almost hear Memo racing through the possibilities.

"Anyone else?" he finally asked.

"Only if you're looking for pudgy grandmas, famous family men, or saintly AIDS moms," I replied and took a confident slurp of the already watery slush.

"Okay." His tone was the vocal equivalent of a lion squaring its sights on its prey. "So now we—"

"Try to find Meteer," I cut him off. "I know."

"'We' isn't just you and me anymore, Cam," he said. "'We' is my employer. When Ariel tried to find Meteer, she was . . . ended. You've been walking in her footsteps, and this is where her footsteps stopped stepping."

"Are you asking me to bow out? Even though Ariel sent me to Virginia Beach—not you? Even though I got the list, and I identified Meteer?" I protested anxiously. And then, the root of my frustration: "And is CVSU off the table now too?"

"Calm down," he said. "I'm just saying to tread lightly. And about CVSU—that's only happening if we get our guy."

"BIB," I clarified.

"Yes, BIB," he answered, just before abruptly standing up. "But first things first. Meteer. And as for you—go be a normal intern for a while. Let me look into this guy."

He mechanically looked at both sides of approaching traffic, and then darted across the street.

"You left your Slurpee!" I shouted.

But he didn't turn around.

"You're acting very perky for the Monday after a holiday weekend," slurred Marcus as he looked up at me from his desk. In addition to a wrinkled, too-small plaid shirt, he was wearing the entire weekend on his face.

The slightly retracted corners of his mouth made him look ridiculous. And vulnerable. Practically begging for me to pump him for all kinds of sensitive info.

Even though Memo had instructed me to be a "normal intern," those regular intern tasks and research were far less exciting than they used to be. There was something much more interesting about tracking down Meteer and solving Ariel's "end" and Branson's "suicide." And I could still follow Memo's warning to tread lightly, to some extent. Normal interns searched for contact information, right?

So I asked Marcus for a list of BIB's contacts so that I could "verify constituent and donor addresses in advance of the final election fund-raising push."

"Hey, Zeph and Hillary," announced Marcus in a louder voice. "This is what it means to be a true intern! Cam over here's verifying all of the—"

"Shut up, dude," I whispered. "I don't like to brag."

Idiot almost blew my story.

"And he's humble, too!" Marcus shouted.

Zeph and Hillary had been desensitized into not paying any attention to Marcus, and fortunately, this morning was no exception.

"Here." Marcus guided me to the computer of a staffer who had called in sick that morning. "Full contact list is only on a few computers, but I know the password."

His facility with the various computer menus belied his completely unkempt appearance that morning. After a few efficient clicks, the entire database of BIB's contacts appeared before my eyes. "Have at it," he said.

I immediately scrolled to the *M*s, then to the *ME*s. There was a "Metchick," and there was a "Meyer." No "Meteer."

As if he'd heard my thoughts, Marcus leaned back toward me and said, "And if you can't find someone on the digital database, just check out BIB's Rolodex. That's where all of the old friends are."

You're making this too easy, Marcus.

"Where is that?" I asked, as I envisioned Memo's shock at how easily I would produce Meteer's home address.

"Nadia keeps it in her office."

Okay, you're not *making it too easy*, I corrected myself. I glanced in Nadia's office to see her filing her nails while barking away at someone on the gilded phone headset she was wearing. The apparatus looked like one of those microphones boy band members wear onstage. And it was gold. Then I saw the smudged plastic dome of the Rolodex, planted in the center of her desk. I saw that Jigar hadn't come into the office yet.

"Hillary." I sauntered over to her cramped desk while devising a plan. "What if I told you I would forgive you for all of the times you sprayed me with that hose while I mowed your parents' lawn? Help you shed the last vestiges of Hilly . . ."

Zeph looked over suspiciously. Hillary stood up and led me to the office supply room. "What are you talking about, Carter?" she asked gravely.

"I need you to distract Nadia . . . to talk with Nadia for one minute," I said. "Out of her office."

"Why?" she asked.

"You see, that's where the whole 'forgiving' thing comes into play. I can't tell you," I said.

"This sounds shady." She rubbed her index finger over her chin.

"It's not," I assured her. "You just have to believe me. As a fellow Lagriman."

"Like that means anything?" she responded.

"It means everything," I said.

"Okay, whatever. I'm bored, so I guess I'll do it." She dismissed me, and we both returned to our desks.

Flashing red text indicated that Lena had written me on MessageNow: **It's really unattractive for a guy to sulk.**

I wasn't sulking. I responded, annoyed, quickly: **It's really unattractive for a girl to CHEAT WITH AN EX.**

Her rapid-fire answer: **It's really unattractive to have conversations like this. But I guess it means we both care . . . ?**

I looked away from the screen to check in on Hillary's progress. I gave her an urgent look, and she slowly lifted both hands in a strange Zen pose that seemed to say, *Brilliance can't be rushed.*

A few more minutes passed as I realized that I was now on Hillary time. The blinking MessageNow cursor seemed to poke me in the chest with each blink. It was my move.

I guess it does, I replied.

Then can I see you? she asked.

Messaging with Lena while trying to steal Meteer's address made me feel like a radio going back and forth between a familiar love song and one of those investigative reports on NPR. I couldn't pay full attention to both—too much static in between. But there was something about Lena—something about the song—that made me feel calm. Confident. Like I wanted to turn the dial completely to just the song, just her. I tried to break the tension with my response: **Promise not to bring the ex along with you?**

As I clicked send, Hillary's performance began.

"Oh! Mr. Speaker!" Her voice was raised and somewhat tremulous. "I'm so sorry for thinking you were that creepy guy from the hamster shop! One moment, please."

She gracefully pranced over to Nadia's office and said that the Speaker of the House was calling for BIB, "but I can't transfer the call to anyone for some reason." Hillary literally pulled her hair out from the sides of her head in feigned frustration.

As Nadia emitted a guttural sigh and walked toward the malfunctioning phone, Hillary conspicuously winked at me. When Nadia picked up the phone, I casually slipped into her office.

"I was told it was the Speaker," I heard Nadia say.

I flipped open the Rolodex to the Ms and then to the MEs. Again, no "Meteer" among the tattered and faded cards.

"Why is he calling the receptionist? You know he has my direct line!" Nadia pouted from across the office.

I carefully peeled each M card back in hopes that "Meteer" would materialize.

"Where's Patrick?" Nadia asked, increasingly frustrated. "If I can't talk with the Speaker, get me Patrick!"

I found it at the front of the Ms. One of the cleaner cards in the stack, "Russell M." My hand was shaking, but I held it firm as I took a picture of the card and then quietly shut the Rolodex.

I slipped back out of Nadia's office and sat at my desk— watching to confirm that no one had seen me. Gulping down the illicit excitement of my discovery and suppressing the very deep breaths my lungs were fighting for. I noticed that Zeph was gone.

I also noticed that Lena had left four messages before sign-
ing off MessageNow:

**I'll be at Georgetown Waterfront Park on Friday night.
Sunset. Gives you a few days to calm down. Come if you want.
I hope you will. PS: The ex will only come for a few minutes.
He wants to meet you.**

Then: **Just kidding, the ex isn't coming. That was a joke.
Do you remember what those are?**

Then: **Okay, I'm sorry, that was mean. Okay, I'm out. See
you on Friday, I hope. Are you there anymore?**

Then: **I'm a dork. I should stop typing. You're really not
there, I guess. Ugh. Embarrassing. Bye.**

By the time I'd finished reading the messages, a grudging
smile had crept onto my face. And—weak moment with an ex
or not—I really liked Lena again. I don't think I ever didn't.

As I looked up from the screen, my smile retreated and I
saw Hillary's profuse apology to Nadia: "I'm so sorry, it must
have been a mistake."

"Excuse me?" asked Nadia.

"Maybe the lines crossed, I don't know?" Hillary shrugged.
"Maybe it wasn't even the Speaker? But I swear I heard
'Speaker'! 'It's the Speaker calling for Nadia Zyne.'"

Nadia suddenly looked at Hillary as if she were speaking a foreign language. She brushed the front of her olive-
green satin pantsuit in a symbolic gesture of wiping away the

moment. She returned to her office, where I had stood twenty seconds earlier, closed the door, and likely called "Patrick" to get to the bottom of the mystery.

Zeph returned to the office, and Hillary proudly gestured as if to say, *It was* him *on the phone with Nadia!* Followed by a self-congratulating silent laugh.

I could barely look away from that picture of "Russell M.'s" number on my phone, though. Ten digits that led to the truth, or at least the next step. Ten digits that Memo was looking for, that I already had. Ten digits that seemed to say *Call me.* Like any other call I made on behalf of the congressman. Mundane and quick and easy. I would verify that the number was functioning, that's all. "Hi" and "Bye." Memo would be grateful, maybe even impressed. Definitely impressed.

It was one of those adrenaline-soaked ideas that got better and more appealing—more right—the more you thought about it. The kind of idea that snowballs into bold action, usually around two a.m. Except it was two p.m. And the snowball was already barreling down the hill, picking up speed. Picking up size.

I grabbed my phone and walked down the hallway, down the stairs, and outside into the inner courtyard of the Rayburn House Office Building. I dialed the number.

After seven rings, I almost hung up. And then a tired voice answered.

"Hello?"

I did my best eager intern cold call, like Hillary had taught me hundreds of times: "Hi, I'm Cameron, and I'm calling from Congressman Beck's office. We're just confirming everyone's addresses for the upcoming election, and we wanted to make sure you get the latest and greatest info about Congressman Beck!"

A clumsy skittering noise came through the phone, like a cat was playing with the handset on the other end.

The man's voice was suddenly much more upbeat, saying, "Oh, you're calling for Russell?"

"Yes," I stated. "Russell Meteer. Is this the right phone number for Russell Meteer?"

"Well, Rusty's not exactly available at the moment, but can I let him know you called? What's your name? Where are you again?"

"I . . . I'm calling for Congressman Beck. Just to confirm your address. . . ." I hesitated.

"What's your name, boy?" The voice was unsettlingly firm.

"Ray . . . Burns," I said, picking apart the building's namesake as printed on a nearby sign. *That was convincing, right?* I told myself.

"But don't worry about having him call back," I backtracked. "I can just call again."

"Oh, are you certain?" the man asked.

"Yeah, yeah, no problem," I said, now restless to end the call. "Have a nice day!"

I ended the call and stepped toward a bench in the courtyard that was barely shaded in the midday sun. Closing my eyes, I retraced the conversation from the start. Memo would need to hear everything. Memo would be proud.

And then I realized that "Ray Burns" had introduced himself as "Cameron" at the beginning of the call.

18

Tell me you're joking.

After the call, I texted Memo a vague **Have Meteer update**, nothing more. Apparently frustrated by my failure to provide more detail, Memo had intercepted me at the exit of the Foggy Bottom metro station that muggy evening. As Zeph, Hillary, and I surfaced, I saw him leaning against a light gray concrete ledge. A slight twitch of his head demanded that I come over to talk.

"Go ahead to the apartment," I had told an oblivious Zeph and Hillary. "I need to make a quick run to the store." And by that, I meant, *I need to go talk to my other boss for the other life I'm living this summer.*

"Tell me you did not call Russell Meteer," Memo insisted.

"I found a phone number for him, Memo. I'm officially

past where Ariel got—and I'm still alive!" Halfway through the word "alive," I dramatically decreased my volume—partly to avoid attention, mostly not to jinx things.

"It's one thing to do a little extra research, to come up with an interesting theory," said Memo. "But when we find a guy whom we think may have been involved in the death of Wade Branson, you do not call him up for a little chat."

"I said I was calling him to confirm his address for an upcoming election mailer—just like any other call I do at the office," I claimed.

"Cam, this wasn't just any other call. This guy isn't just another constituent. When this guy gets a call from BIB's office, a big bright red flag gets hoisted up the flagpole," Memo said as he pantomimed raising a flag. "Thank God you didn't tell him your name."

I slowly nodded.

"Wait," added Memo. "You didn't tell him your name, did you?"

"Of course not!" I barked back. *What kind of idiot would do something like that?* The lie was a heavy boulder that quickly sank and settled into my stomach.

"Good. Because all this guy needs is a name," warned Memo.

"To do what?" I too eagerly asked.

"To find someone, to be *very persuasive* with someone,"

Memo said, with a particularly sinister emphasis on "persuasive."

Sweat gurgled up through the pores of my palms as I envisioned Russell Meteer tracking down this loser intern "Cameron" from BIB's office. I innocently slipped my hands into my pockets and shrugged my shoulders. "So what's next?"

"Well, for now, good work." Memo patted me on the back. "Not with the phone call, but everything else. We might have our guy. So now I get to work and you just let me know if anything weird happens."

"What do you mean, 'weird'?" I exclaimed.

"You'll know it if you see it." Memo nodded confidently as he jumped on the downward escalator back into the metro.

Comforting.

Though "weird" had kind of become my new normal that summer, the closest I got to especially "weird" in the following days was Zeph and Hillary's newfound mutual hostility toward each other. They pulled me into stupid fights about some senator's position on campaign finance reform, whether Uber was more expensive in DC than San Francisco, and Zeph's tendency to dodge questions about himself.

"It's because one day you're going to be governor and you're preemptively clearing out all of the skeletons from your closet so the reporters have nothing to find, right?" prodded Hillary.

Zeph smiled a *there she goes again* smile.

"Cameron, meet your first of many baby politicians," she said, hands grandly presenting Zeph. "The guy who feels like every day he's writing his biography. Whose carefully edited Facebook photos look like you're walking through his presidential library gallery. Who is already carrying around a mini copy of the US Constitution in his shirt pocket. Show it," commanded Hillary with an accusing, pointed index finger.

Zeph sheepishly pulled out a folded-up US Constitution—as was the tradition of most elected officials. "It's a really amazing document," he defended.

"Anyway, these baby politicians are impressive at first, but mainly just impossible to know and in the end kind of boring."

And so on.

For a few days, I looked over my shoulder to see if I was being followed by a stranger. But there was no stalker, no gun-wielding intruder hiding in my closet, no "weird." Just another week of work, free food at receptions, my first constituent tour of the Capitol (much less titillating and more factual than Hillary's version), and checking Smithsonian museums off my list. Refreshingly, Memo left me alone.

And when sunset rolled around on Friday night, I made my way to the Georgetown Waterfront Park to meet up with Lena. Of course I did. She was beautiful and she felt guilty and she was sorry—which somehow made her seem more beautiful.

As I scanned the park benches, I saw her see me and then pretend not to see me. She was in a long sundress (I wondered if she had any outfits other than these long, flowy, beautiful dress thingies) with light brown sandals.

"Hey," I said to Lena.

"Hey," she said back. "Ex couldn't make it. Last-minute change of plans."

"He's busy trying to get more followers on Instagram with pictures of his watch," I said.

"Okay, are you for real right now? You are obsessed with his watch. He doesn't even care about it."

"I don't really want to talk about him," I said.

"Okay, well, I do. For a second. I think it will help you understand. Our dads were college roommates at Princeton. His dad owns a bank back in Mexico, and our parents decided we were going to make grandchildren for them before I was in junior high."

"Wow," I said. About the Princeton dad, the owning of banks, *and* the preteen arranged marriage.

We started walking along the path. The day was waning, and the leafy riverside promenade swelled with tourists, families, and people getting off work. Kids frolicked in the fountain structure, which was a series of spouts shooting out from the sidewalk and forming a low tunnel of water.

"And—he's nice. Just finished his freshman year, so he

has a lot of good college advice. But he's more of the same. He's oblivious. Doesn't even know how much that watch costs, because his dad gave it to him. And his finance internship in London this summer—he doesn't realize that the only reason he got it is because his dad did some deal with the company."

"Must be rough," I observed.

"Anyway, we dated," continued Lena, telling the story like I was her therapist. Purging her privilege. "If you can call it that: long distance, high school. Me here, him in DC. And he was in town over the holiday weekend and wanted to see me. And my mom and dad wanted me to see him."

"You mean they didn't want you to hang out with the commoner from California?" I asked.

"Cam, that's not fair," she said. "And besides, you are anything but a commoner. You're different. I like you. Did you hear that? *I like you.*"

She kicked off her sandals, lifted up her long dress, and walked through the splattering row of water. She rejoined me, her wet footprints evaporating from the path she left behind her. She was playful, carefree, sexy. And she'd said she liked me. Twice.

"Well, you're in luck, because I kind of like you," I said cheekily. "I mean—if you're around. It's convenience, more than anything. You fill my downtime."

"Shut up!" She slapped my arm with greater force than

one would expect from a joking hit. She was strong. When I didn't say anything, she quickly followed up, with the kind of neediness that is irresistible, not scary: "It's more than convenience, right? You were joking?"

I answered: "I was joking if you are ready to move on from high school boyfriends."

We walked away from the crowds and closer to the water, toward some large steps that led to the lapping waters of the Potomac River below. The sky looked like a finger painting of baby blues, lavenders, and faint reds—plus some wispy clouds in between. The hulking white mass of the Kennedy Center glowed orange in the far distance. We both sat down on one of the steps.

And even though a few minutes had passed, her "I'm ready" came eventually and decisively.

"I'm glad," I said.

"Besides," she added. "It's a lot more attractive when a guy gets a big internship on his own instead of because of Daddy."

I laughed as she silently leaned forward with her elbows on her knees. But she wasn't joking. She rested her chin on her hands and looked out at the water. As nice as the night was, it was more beautiful to look at her taking it all in. The darkening river began to reflect the lights of the shore, which started to dance off her delicate profile.

"The real world, you know?" She stretched out her arms

in the thick evening air and leaned back toward me as she uttered this non sequitur. I listened happily, just glad to be there. "You read about it, you hear about it from older friends, you watch movies—but you don't really know what it's like. And soon we'll be there. You already are, basically."

"Princeton is the real world?" I asked, dubious.

"Anywhere away from my parents is the real world. Where I decide who I hang out with on a holiday is the real world. Like what you're doing, Cam—out on your own, across the country. You must be loving it," she suggested.

My eye followed the bank of the river on my left. To the site of Ariel's car accident, just beyond the Watergate complex. The red lights of cars whipped by, oblivious to the events that transpired there at the beginning of the summer.

"You are loving it, right?" Lena asked. "No more of that— what was it—pushing over poor cows in fields?"

"Yes, it's great being here," I told her as I envisioned how Russell Meteer could have made a murder look like a drunk-driving accident. He did good work. "It's great. Mostly."

We sat together in the warm night as the crowds in the surrounding park thinned out. And I felt the weight of my charade, especially with her. Even more unexpected, I felt a wave of homesickness and nostalgia.

"Mostly?" she asked. "Cam, is everything okay?"

"I guess the things you resent the most turn into the things you miss the most," I said. "The curfews, the boring familiarity, the empty dirt fields, the sameness of every night."

"Is this the same Cameron I met at the beginning of the summer?" she asked. "Now you're missing that sad little town of yours?"

"It's not sad," I replied. "It's small and it's in the middle of nowhere and I can reasonably predict the careers of most of my graduating high school class—if you can even call them careers. And I know that sounds cheesy, but I feel like I forgot to bring something from home when I came here. Like shoes or a suit or my photo ID—something important, something missing. But I'm making do without it—like I don't need it anymore. And I'm beginning to realize that what I left behind was my home. And it feels wrong to be okay without it. Does any of that make sense?"

"Kind of," she said. "Theoretically—for me."

"I guess leaving home is a bigger deal than I realized when I did it. And you can't really go back to how things were. So enjoy your parents, enjoy the obnoxious friends, enjoy now. Before you change. Before the real world changes you." I wondered if there were Caitlin Fryes and Russell Meteers and Memos in Lena's future. I hoped there weren't.

"You're a funny one, Cameron Carter," Lena said as she quickly and suddenly kissed me on the left cheek. My eyes grew big and I hoped that the darkness of the sky hid my reddening face. We sat in silence for a few minutes. And I felt like I could tell her more. Memo, Virginia Beach, Wade Branson, my call to Russell Meteer. I wanted to tell her everything. But we were one hour into rebooting our relationship—our summer thing, whatever you want to call it. We were cheek kissing, easing back into things, and I didn't want a crazy rant to derail anything. My mind was racing for something to say. Lena was calmly playing with her hair.

Even so, I was seconds from talking about the man in the fishing vest who cornered me during a Capitol tour when she said: "Well, you can thank the ex for one thing." She broke the silence and pulled out a photo ID from her purse. A fake one. "He says this is more important than your school ID in college. I don't know . . ."

I looked at the very pretty picture of Lena on the card. And the name—"Marisol Castro, from Indiana. Just turned twenty-two."

"Well nice to meet you, Marisol," I said and pulled out my own contraband. "I'm Chester Arlington Vanhille III."

"From Alabama!" she shouted.

"I think we should put yours to the test tonight," I said.

"You mean they really work?" she asked.

"Of course," I said. "I've been 'Chester' all summer— never get any questions."

We both stood up from the steps and she let out a giddy laugh.

"Okay," she said as we walked up toward the string of bars on M Street.

We strolled along a narrow but deep canal that ran parallel to the Potomac River. Our hands brushed each other and then linked together. Like magnets—flailing, then locked tight.

"This is the C and O Canal," she explained to me. "It's superlong and used to be for shipping things up and down the East Coast. Now it's just for little tourist boats. And romantic evening walks. It's swelling this year because of all the rain."

It looked charming but somehow stark in the orange industrial lights. One other person walked in the opposite direction—otherwise, the whole stretch of the canal was deserted. We crossed a small walking bridge and went up to the livelier M Street, where Lena stepped up to the first bar she saw. She proudly displayed her fake ID to a burly man standing by the door, like a child showing off an "all-As" grade report to her parents. The bouncer just waved her in. From inside the bar, she looked back at me and waved with a guilty grin. I flashed my card and proceeded to enter the bar, as I had multiple times before that summer. The firm, fat arm of the man came down and stopped me. He nodded at another man with a shaved head, who came over and put his arm around me.

"You think we serve alcohol to minors here, son?" the shaved-head man said to me.

"I showed my ID," I claimed, my voice quavering slightly.

"Don't lie to me, kid," he said as he guided me to a stoop under the entrance of the bar. I looked up and saw Lena peering down at me from a window. She looked confused and awkwardly alone. Then I noticed that the first man I'd talked to was no longer standing by the bar door; he wasn't anywhere in sight.

The man with the shaved head got on his phone and informed someone on the other end that "we have an underage drinker here."

"Please don't call the police," I pleaded and wondered why Chester had failed me after a successful summer of fooling all of the other bars. Why when I was with Lena? Why that night?

The man didn't respond and just stood there. Over me. I wondered who was giving him orders. My face flushed with embarrassment and, for the first time, fear.

"I need to talk to my girlfriend." I raised my voice at the man.

He put his index finger over his lips and stepped away for another phone conversation, all the while staring at me. It all seemed a bit wrong.

Weird, as Memo had warned.

Suddenly, an aggressive Latino man in a suit approached the man with the shaved head. At first, they looked like they were calmly conspiring together, but things escalated as they began to shout at each other. The Latino man flashed a badge that seemed to scare the man with the shaved head, who then became deferential and even courteous.

"Sorry for the misunderstanding," he said as he turned me over to the custody of the man in the suit. I didn't know whether this was a good thing, or if everything was about to get worse. When I saw Lena waiting for me in front of a black SUV, I figured she had played a role in my rescue. She ran to me and gave me a hug. "Meet Oscar," she said. "Head of security at the embassy."

The man's stern expression threatened to give way to a slight grin as we shook hands.

"I guess you were right about enjoying those things that I currently resent," she said as she patted Oscar on the back. "Diplomatic security detail has its privileges, especially when your friend gets busted for a fake ID."

I simultaneously wondered why she didn't say "boyfriend" and if the fake ID was really the reason I was detained.

"Listen," she said. "Oscar's already doing me a big favor by coming here, and"—she elevated her voice—"he's not going to tell my parents about this."

Oscar flashed a disappointed but supportive look at her.

"So he's going to drive me back home. Are you okay getting back to your place?" she asked.

"I'll be fine," I said, still shaken from the encounter with the bouncer, or whoever that guy was.

With that, Lena entered the car, and Oscar slammed the door. He hopped in the driver's seat and whisked her back to the embassy.

The pulsing music of the bar became more muffled as I quickly walked out of eyeshot and into an empty street block. Closed clothing shops and restaurants were faintly lit from the streetlights as I realized it was almost midnight. I headed west on M Street, and saw a man across the street who walked at about the same pace. For three full blocks.

I turned right, heading down a sloping, narrow road that intersected M Street. I looked back to see that the man had crossed M Street as well. He followed me down the road, toward the canal. I began to hear the scratching of his footsteps against the loose pavement. He was getting closer.

I made an abrupt left and hoped to find someone — anyone — else walking along the canal. But the only things that greeted me were the hollowed-out tourist canoes that gently banged against one another in the standing water. Within seconds, the man made the same left turn and now followed me from less than a block behind. The various industrial lamps and spotlights of the canal cast disorienting, long shadows that at once made him seem far away and disturbingly, increasingly close.

When I started to jog, he did too.

I approached a footbridge and tried to cross the canal, but it was blocked by a firmly closed gate. Trying to open the gate only made me lose my lead. The man was now close enough for me to see that he was over six feet tall and wearing a black hoodie. I stepped back to the pathway and started to run in and out of the pools of light created by the streetlamps above.

Three blocks ahead, I noticed two people walking together, just out of earshot. When he got close enough for me to hear his labored breathing, I leaped to my right—into the serene stream of water.

I hit the shallow floor of the canal, and a punishing shock jolted from the heels of my feet to the top of my spine. For a moment, I was sure both legs were broken, but I treaded water toward the couple that approached me, which signaled they were okay. I could hear the hurried and worried footsteps of the couple increase in speed. Without looking back at the pursuer, I started to shout at the people above, "Help! I can't swim!"

The couple must have quickly concluded that I was just another drunk GWU student when they saw that I was clearly standing in about three feet of water. They guided me toward a ladder. My legs quivered as I lifted my sopping wet self up each rung. When I reached the top of the ladder, I panted, "And there's this guy following me!" I pointed to the other side of the canal, to find the full stretch of pathway completely empty.

"Yeah, sure there is." The man and woman laughed to each other and continued their midnight stroll. "Make sure to have a swimming buddy next time," the man mocked.

I studied each empty block of the other side of the canal. The man was gone. I wrung out the thick, mossy water from my shirt and pants and bolted west along the canal. I could barely manage more than a frantic limp as thick needles of pain shot up my concussed legs.

I reached the main bridge and crossed it back up to M Street, realizing I was leaving a trail of sloppy wet footprints behind me. I saw a taxi emptying out some late-night arrivals into a hotel and jumped into the back seat. I urgently commanded the driver to get out of the area—now. When he asked me for an address, I told him the closest thing to a safe house that I could think of.

19

I did not breathe for the three blocks it took the speeding taxi to jet across the Georgetown Bridge. As we careened down Pennsylvania Avenue, the growing distance from that hopeless canal alleyway was directly proportional to the growing depth of my breathing. We crossed the street that led to my apartment, where I knew I couldn't lead the stalker in case he was still somehow following me. I grabbed the flip phone and started texting Memo.

Got busted for fake ID for the first time ever. Man chased me in Georgetown. Out of control. What is going on?

We blew past the Mexican embassy, where I envisioned Lena dumping me for good if she knew the additional drama of the night. Besides, she had grown up with a security detail and wouldn't exactly know what to do with a stalker other than retreat behind the embassy walls. Better for her to think I was just an unlucky underage bar patron than the mark of a hitman. The taxi shot down to the Mall, which was empty and vast in the warm summer night. Memo did not respond. I had to push my head against the window to see the top of the Washington Monument as we drove by. Memo still wasn't responding.

I DID NOT SIGN UP FOR THIS, I texted Memo again.

We passed the bone-like columns of the National Archives Building, and then the glowing white Capitol building came into view. I turned to look out the back window, just in case that man was somehow running after the taxi at fifty-seven miles per hour. He wasn't, but I wouldn't have been surprised if he were.

No response from Memo. Very convenient for him that he could always find me, but the one time I needed him, he was radio silent. . . .

The taxi screeched to a halt on a dark block behind the Capitol. I threw too much money at the driver and didn't wait for the change. I winced at the unplanned splurge and ran into the lobby of a four-story building that looked like it was shedding layers of stucco on the outside. A gaping yellow water stain adorned the wall of the elevator that took me to the third floor. As I knocked on the door of apartment 310, I realized that it was past midnight.

"Who is it?" her voice promptly inquired from inside as I looked down both sides of the dim hallway for signs of anyone else.

"It's me, it's Cameron. Please let me in now," I low-talked into the crack of the door.

Katie opened the door. Her initial surprised smile was replaced with total confusion as she asked, "Why are you soaking wet?"

"It was the canal . . . ," I uttered.

"And what are you doing here at twelve thirty a.m.?" she demanded. "Get inside!"

She ushered me into the apartment and triple-locked the door behind me.

"One second," she said as she disappeared down a narrow hallway. The small living room belonged in a much nicer building than the dumpy-looking one outside the front door. A marshmallowy gray couch dominated the room, along with a lamp that looked like a praying mantis, modern-looking tables and chairs, and a tragically too-small TV. She may have fancy taste in furniture, but Katie clearly didn't appreciate the value of a big old TV.

"Here." She handed me a light purple bathrobe, which matched her own.

"Purple," I said.

"Listen, you look like a sea creature, and you're not sitting on my couch in those hideous wet clothes," she responded.

"And yes, these are his-and-hers robes, but it was two for one at this store, and I figured maybe one day there would be a 'his' in here. And now there is, but not exactly how I had envisioned it. . . ."

"Should I change in your bedroom?" I asked.

"No, no, no, no." Katie laughed. "It's a mess. I'll go in there while you change in here. Just shout when you're done."

I peeled off the sticky layers of canal-watered clothes from my body and threw them in a pile on Katie's kitchen floor. The blasting air-conditioning rocked my body with a deep, long chill. I put on the "his" robe, which had the softness of a sweatshirt that's never been washed before.

"All clear," I shouted.

Katie bolted down the hallway. With her hair up in a messy bun and feet wrapped in oversize slippers, she was a much more relaxed version of herself away from the office. She eyed the mountain of knitting supplies on her coffee table and quickly gathered them into a basket.

"No comments about the knitting on a Friday night, please," she said, without looking at me.

We both plopped into the fatty folds of the gray couch. It was the kind of couch that embraced you so generously that it required dedicated core exertion to get out.

"Okay, what are you even doing here? And how did you get my address?"

"You gave me your contact info. That night at the George Mason Memorial—remember?"

"Okay, well, I was expecting the occasional text, not a midnight swamp thing knock at the door. What's going on?"

"I just needed a place to go," I said, still feeling the adrenaline from the chase coat my veins. "Really, no big deal. I fell into the canal in Georgetown, and I needed a place to go, that's all."

"You fell into the C and O Canal?" she shouted. "What's wrong with you?"

"It was the only way I could get away. . . ." I stopped short of saying more of the evening's events. Talking about that chase was the first pulled yarn that would undo the ugly sweater Memo had crafted for me.

"Someone was after you?" she asked gravely.

"I don't know," I said. "Can we talk about something else?"

Katie took a deep breath. She looked at my hair and instinctively pushed it to the side of my forehead before rapidly rewinding and pulling back her hand.

"Purple is not your color," she apologetically assessed.

"Thanks," I replied.

"So." She stood up and headed for the kitchen. "I'm actually glad you're here. Because otherwise I would still be having a counseling session on the phone with my college roommate about how she can keep her marriage together despite the ravaging effects of a home remodel."

I leaned back into the gray cloud couch and looked to her for permission to put my feet up on the coffee table.

She hesitated for a moment before saying, "Of course! So, yeah, she married this tech king, moved to a gigantic home in Palo Alto, and now her full-time job is choosing tonally complementary wainscoting."

"What?" I asked.

"It's not even worth explaining," Katie dismissed. She leaned forward to straighten a stack of magazines that lay on the table and then sat back and said, "Okay. So that was me lightening the mood. Now it's your turn to talk."

Memo, Ariel, Wade Branson, the man by the canal—it all seemed to churn throughout my stomach. Like I had swallowed a mouthful of finely chopped glass, which slowly sliced through my intestines. Needing to be expelled. Exorcised. A voice inside told me to "just explain a little" of what was going on. A little won't hurt. It would feel so good. Just how that first sip of beer won't do any harm at the first ninth-grade party where alcohol showed up. Try some. . . .

"What's going on, Cameron?" she implored, now quite serious, even insistent.

I thought about how she said I was "family." How she *gets* things—the city, the office politics, the starting-from-nothing thing. She understood things—certainly more than my dad or Berto. She understood me—or at least the me I was trying to become. And she *had* told me to come to her with any concerns. . . .

"Well, you know how you told me I could always check in with you—even about the crazy questions?"

She nodded warmly.

An unstoppable chunky tidal wave of verbal gastric acid shot up my throat as I blurted out, "I think Ariel's death maybe wasn't an accident. . . ."

"What? Why would you think that?" interrupted Katie, her voice and posture now more befitting a chief of staff.

I looked straight ahead and let out a deep breath. "This guy cornered me during a Capitol tour. He said he talked with Ariel before she died, that Ariel was looking for someone and had probably left a clue for me. . . ."

"A clue? Cameron, do you realize how crazy this sounds? There are so many paranoid weirdos all over this town, and if you engage, they'll follow you around like lonely stray dogs." She closed her eyes and took a deep breath—her reaction a little more aggressive and dramatic than I had expected. Then she leaned forward so she could look me in the eye. "Have you told anyone else about this?"

"No, and I know I'm supposed to tell Nadia about anyone who approaches us, but something tells me she would not be happy about what I found," I replied.

"No," she said. "Don't tell Nadia anything. And what do you mean, 'What you found'?"

"In the things she left behind in her desk. There was this note that said 'For C,' with an address. In Virginia Beach."

"You're kidding me, Cameron. . . ."

"Look, I do know how stupid this probably sounds: I went to that address. I didn't even know if I would knock on the door, but I did, and it was the parents of Ariel's best friend, who died when they were teenagers. Died of this drug overdose because a CEO put the drug on the market before it was ready. Wade Branson . . ."

"Branson," she said in unison. "You asked me about him in a text that one night."

"So you know who he is?" I asked.

"Of course I do. But I already told you: We don't talk about Wade Branson in the office. Anyway, that was like eight years ago. What does he have to do with anything?"

"*Six* years ago," I corrected her. "And I think there's a connection between Wade's suicide and Ariel's accident. Like, what if it wasn't a suicide?"

"Cameron, you sound like a conspiracy theory Reddit thread right now. You realize this, don't you?"

"Yes, I know," I said. But it felt like kicking off uncomfortable new shoes as I told her. Memo and his secrets and—let's call it what it was—his bribery felt constricting. Talking to Katie felt like discovering an escape hatch—a back door out of the house Memo had lured me into. And even if I would never bail on Memo, it felt good to know I could. I continued, my breaths deeper and my face less strained with every word: "Ariel left this list of names, and I called one of them—used to be a Navy SEAL—and tonight I basically got arrested for a fake ID, which never happens, and next thing I knew, I was getting chased down a Georgetown alley-way, and the only thing I could do to escape was jump in the water to get these random people's attention."

Katie slowly dragged both hands down the front of her face and sighed.

"Now I think this guy might be after me," I said. "And that is why I'm knocking on your door at twelve thirty a.m."

"Cameron, you need to stop." She put her hand on my knee. "You need to stop, and hope that this guy will stop too."

"But what if there really is a connection? What if Wade Branson was killed? What if Ariel was killed? And I'm next?"

"Ariel Lancaster died in a drunk-driving accident," Katie clarified.

"I know, but she died right after she wrote that list. She died when she knew things. And now I know more than she knew when she died."

"Do you know Rose Mary Woods? Oliver North? Mary Jo Kopechne?" she asked.

"What are you talking about?"

"Exactly," she said. "Collateral damage left behind by the political machines that you *do* remember—Nixon, Reagan, and Ted Kennedy."

"Whoa." I cut her off. "Who's the conspiracy theorist now?"

"Look, all I'm saying is that people who poke into things don't always fare well in this city. They turn into accomplices, fall guys. They die. And once you touch this stuff, the bad stuff, you can't ever really wash it off. Better to stay away."

"You speak from experience?" I asked.

"I've seen a lot," she replied. "Enough to know that you don't want to keep peeking inside Pandora's box for an answer to a question that isn't even a question. You should be taking selfies with the ruby slippers at the Smithsonian and going to Screen on the Green this summer, Cameron. Not being taken advantage of by some mysterious guy who corners you and puts questions into your head. Who was that guy, anyway? And who did you call who is suddenly following you? How does all of this connect to Wade Branson?"

Three questions too many. Even though Katie only wanted to help, I seized up as I thought of Memo and the secrecy he had always insisted upon. The secrecy I could no longer bear. And even though it felt good to talk with Katie, I knew I had to answer to Memo.

And that I had to backtrack. A little. Somehow.

"I'm sorry, Katie," I said. "Thanks for looking out for me."

She looked like she was still waiting for me to answer her questions.

"I think I just need to get home. Put a good night's sleep between me and what happened tonight. Leave the conspiracies behind."

My newfound resolve, however feigned, successfully convinced her that I wasn't going to answer her questions. That would only impede my penitent progress, I hoped she thought. It seemed to work.

"I'm driving you home," she said. "You look ridiculous, and part of me would find a little bit of pleasure in your taking the metro in a purple robe—but I will spare you that indignity."

Not to mention, spare me from the madman trying to track me down.

I followed Katie to her car, wearing only the purple robe and sludgy shoes, with a heavy garbage bag of wet clothes in my hand. As I stepped into her aging Toyota Camry, Katie was already starting the ignition. Which triggered Cher blasting out of the speakers: "Do you believe in life after love?" Katie snapped the radio off and made a fierce hand gesture that preempted my inclination to critique her music selection.

I entered my address into her GPS, and she started cruising across the deserted streets.

"A lot of people say DC was built on a swamp," she commented. "And, look, you know from the Capitol tour that there are lots of made-up stories about this city. But even if it wasn't built on a swamp, it can feel like one. Deep, thick mud. Bugs that suck on you, and you can't see them until it's too late. Alligators perfectly content to watch you fumble around the distractions until they decide they've waited long enough." She accelerated through a yellow light near the Lincoln Memorial and banked northward toward GWU.

"Anyway, I don't even know what I'm saying. It's two a.m., and you kind of blindsided me tonight, Cam."

"Can we not talk about it again?" I asked her. More of a demand than a request.

"Gladly," she answered. "How 'bout you start by not giving us anything more to talk about on that subject?"

A kind robot GPS voice in the car announced that we had arrived at the destination.

I opened the passenger door and turned toward her.

"I'm serious," she urged. "I don't want to lose two staffers this summer."

"Thanks for the ride," I responded. "And the chat. You're right. I'm done asking other people's questions." *What she wants to hear*, I thought. *Whatever makes her think I'm not going to poke around anymore. . . .*

She kept the car in park until the front door of my apartment building clicked behind me. As I walked toward the door of our unit, I pulled out both of my phones. There was a text message from Berto on my phone and another from Memo on the flip phone. I checked Memo's first.

You told him your name, didn't you?

Followed by, **You've stepped in the mud with your socks on. Can't get dry now. . . .**

As I clicked the key in the lock of the door and started to open it, I heard a rumble on the other side, followed by the crash of a lamp and a light bulb. Then total silence. With the door completely ajar and darkness beyond it, I froze. The hallway light framed me from behind, and my soft shadow fell on the ground in front of me. Whoever had knocked over the lamp was watching me from the deep black inside. Our standoff lasted for about four deep breaths before I flipped on the living room light, like the click of a revolver in Russian roulette.

I heard the scream before I saw who it came from.

It was Hillary. Sitting on top of Zeph. In what appeared to be the middle of a very romantic moment. Screaming at me.

"Close the door!" shouted Hillary as Zeph leaped from the couch. Caught. "Can't you knock?"

"I live here," I said, my eyes still taking in the bewildering scene.

"Well, hardly anymore," Hillary snapped. "And what's with that granny housedress nightmare situation?"

I froze and wondered how much of my night was given away by my alarming appearance. "Long story, involving an aggressive sprinkler system and a very solicitous night clerk in the CVS clothing section." I shrugged it off and deflected back to them. "You guys . . . So this explains all of the fighting."

"Um, yes," admitted Zeph, before breaking into a deep belly laugh.

"Well, what do you expect us to do?" asked Hillary. "Now that you've abandoned us and never tell us where you go anymore!"

Zeph laughed harder.

"Don't laugh, Zephy," demanded Hillary. "Seriously, it's not funny," she said as she picked up the pieces of the broken light bulb and let out a snort.

"Zephy?" I asked.

They both exploded into laughter. She playfully hit Zeph. He kissed her back.

"You've outed us, Cam," he said. "And in a very Hitchcockian fashion. That was quite the dramatic entrance. A robe and a heavy bag of . . . something . . ."

"My clothes," I explained.

"Ugh, weirdo," moaned Hillary as she dragged Zeph into her room.

"Good night!" chirped Zeph as Hillary slammed her bedroom door.

I locked the front door and cleaned up the rest of the shattered light bulb.

Then checked to make sure the door was locked.

Then checked four more times, before closing my own bedroom door. My heart thumped in response to every creak of the wall, window crack, and chortle of the air-conditioning. All night long.

20

Washington, DC, did heat with great pride and creativity. Every summer day, the city found new combinations of temperature, humidity, and furnace-like breezes to make people question whether they would actually die before walking another street block. They were not the dry, hot pool days of Lagrima; these felt like Mother Nature burping out a thick blast of hot breath on the mere mortals below.

A little over a week had passed—a thankfully uneventful stretch of days where for moments at a time, I actually felt like a normal intern. And never more "normal" than when I was parked on the Mall—the southwest corner of Constitution Avenue and Fifteenth Street to be exact. I was fulfilling the distinguished intern task of reserving a softball field for our office's weekly face-off against some Texas rep's team that afternoon. Having used up the junior staff, Hillary, and Zeph already, Jigar informed me that it was my turn to race to the base of the Washington Monument and squat on the field for two and a half hours—just as the sun hovered directly overhead. I barely made it. By the time I was sitting in the office's ancient folding beach chair, I saw other lucky interns racing to the empty fields. Like a desperate land rush, to which all of our professional futures were somehow linked. The first intern who arrived to find that all of the seven fields had been taken shouted multiple expletives and stormed back to Capitol Hill, where ridicule and ostracizing no doubt awaited in the office.

"You can't just leave a pylon or a pile of stuff in the middle of the field and walk away, because someone *will* take it from you," Jigar had instructed. "You must sit in the middle of the field, the entire time. No pee breaks, no movement at all."

"And don't talk to strangers." Nadia laughed, with a knowing gaze that made me give her a double take and myself second thoughts about going out there for so long, alone. I would be a sitting duck, and it wasn't strangers I was worried about. It was someone about whom I knew too much.

Though I cursed Jigar's name, I obeyed and watched a slow drip of sweat from my forehead splat down on the increasingly wet dirt. The accumulation of sweat formed a tiny mud puddle, which a parade of ants efficiently bypassed as they went about their day. I envisioned the long, sizzling days in

Lagrima, when I drove from lawn to interminable lawn. I could even hear my lawn mower, chugging away at the tufts of grass. Getting the job done. One hour closer to dinner at Berto's house. . . .

I looked up to see that I was actually hearing a real lawn mower trekking across the Mall. The man rode in a shaded John Deere ZTrak Zero, and I was instantly jealous. Those things cost a fortune. My dad laughed at me when I suggested that we buy one. I tracked the beautiful lawn mower as it neatly combed the broad swath of grass. Left and right, and left again. And though I'm usually quick to critique others' lawn mowing, this guy was good. An artist. Never crossed the same patch twice, nice racetrack finish, continuous flow. I told myself that the next time he drove near my field, I would get up and talk with him. I didn't care if we lost the field; I had to talk to someone normal for a few minutes. Maybe he'd let me do a test drive.

And then I heard a low, calm voice from behind. "You will not get up. You will not turn around."

My shoulders swiveled slightly before I could process the words and froze in place.

"You will listen carefully to every word I say right now."

His voice was quiet but commanding—and urgent—like an angry but restrained surgeon methodically issuing instructions in an operating room.

My body temperature instantly shot up. My subtly shaking head felt like it was in a vise, ready to pop open.

"Who are you?" I asked, clearing my throat halfway through the question.

"You should know. You called me," he replied with a chuckle. "I'm Ray Burns."

Though he didn't have the unsettlingly upbeat tone from my hasty phone call, I could tell this was the man I called. It was Russell Meteer. It felt like the bottom of my stomach opened up and all of my insides crushed the parade of ants below. I futilely scanned the Mall for Memo. And as the lawn mower man drew near, I wanted to shout to him.

"You will not draw attention to us." As if he knew my thoughts.

I looked down at his shallow midday shadow on the ground and saw that he was gently swaying back and forth.

"What can I do for you, Mr. Meteer?" I asked.

He let out a short gasp when I mentioned his name. Or was it a cough? Followed by, "The last time someone called that phone number, it was a nice little girl by the name of Ariel Lancaster. You know her, I presume?"

"Yes, I know her." I sat captive and felt the dark, sorrowful weight of his presence behind me. "*Knew* her."

I watched as the lawn mower crossed a dirt pathway and drove closer to the Capitol. Away from me. Away from us.

"Such a shame what happened," he said. "The roads aren't safe. . . ."

I imagined that he was holding a tiny needle that would inject some poison into my body that would make it look like I'd died of heat stroke. Surely people like him had access to things like that. Or a simple snap of my neck and he's on with his day. A man who was really good at killing people in broad daylight stood inches from my back, the heat from his body radiating along my shoulders.

"I was supposed to meet Ariel the day after her body smashed into a dashboard of the car that uprooted that tree along the Potomac. Did you know the tree's still there, all tilted? Halfway out of the ground. Visited it this morning . . ."

"What do you want?" I asked. Even though I was sitting down, I knew my heart was beating faster than that of a panting, athletic woman who jogged by. She obliviously glanced at me and smiled.

"You can help me," he stated.

"I'm not going to hurt anyone for you," I said. "I won't do that."

"You're not going to hurt anyone who didn't have it coming anyway," he clarified.

The lawn mower was now a tiny green-and-yellow speck, chugging along two football fields away on the Mall. I wanted to follow it—I wanted to go home. I cursed every step that had gotten me to this impossible place—my stupid phone call, Memo, coming to DC, getting the offer from that lady in the district office. I wanted to undo all of it. Nothing was worth this.

"We need to talk, somewhere more secure," he said. "When your teammates aren't minutes away."

"Interns aren't even allowed to play. . . ." I brooded.

"We need to talk," he repeated.

"I'm not coming alone," I told him.

"You want to bring Memo?" he asked. Of course he knew who Memo was. "Sure, bring him. He can help too. Wasn't much help to Ariel, though . . ."

"Did you do something to her?" I asked.

"The Awakening. Thursday at sunrise."

"What did you do to her?" I repeated, just a little more boldly.

He ignored me. "And no crying to that pathetic chief of staff of BIB's. I can see how much you look up to her. . . ."

"She's not pathetic," I said, as I realized my hiding place at Katie's was not as secure as I had thought. Nothing was as secure as I had thought. When you don't know who's watching you, you don't know what's being watched.

A strong breeze drew a patch of dirt high into the air, where it dissolved. My eardrums were thumping with every beat of my heart.

"What is The Awakening?" I asked. But there was no response and no shadow at the base of my chair. I took ten deep breaths before slowly turning around to see that there was no one standing there.

Russell Meteer had disappeared.

"Nice work, Cam!" shouted Marcus from two fields away. "You picked the best softball field!"

Zeph and Hillary were close behind, pinkie fingers discreetly linked.

I ripped the flip phone out of my pocket and texted Memo:

He found me. He wants to talk with us. Thursday, sunrise.

Marcus balanced the bases with a bag of bats and balls as he speed-walked toward me, already sweating profusely. "Thanks," he said, before walking around the field to put each base in its place.

"Sure." I flashed him a quick smile, an annoyed smile. And stared at the screen of the phone, where Memo's reply appeared.

Are you okay? Where does he want to meet?

I typed back quickly, **Yes, fine. He wants help. Said something about The Awakening.**

I'll pick you up Thursday at 5:30-ish. Be ready, Memo answered.

"Did you bring the orange slices?" asked Marcus, already out of breath.

"Jigar didn't say anything about . . ." I trailed off.

"Just joshin' ya." Marcus laughed before exploding into a violent coughing fit.

The rest of our office team showed up, along with the Texans. I continued to sit in the middle of the field, staring at the dirt.

I saw Katie's feet on the ground in front of me before she asked a loaded "Everything okay?"

"Yeah, yeah," I replied and looked up at her. A lump grew and settled into the bottom of my throat. And she heard it.

"What's happening, Cameron? You look pretty shaken up," she assessed. "You're not . . . ," she said as she made particularly concerned eye contact with me.

I couldn't talk to her. Meteer said so, and he was probably watching from nearby. I couldn't talk to anyone. I had to get away. I stood up and acted out what I guessed he would want to see.

"Well, I've been sitting in ninety-five-degree weather with ninety-five percent humidity for three hours so all of you can play softball. So excuse me if I'm a little out of it."

"Cameron . . ." Her voice was as worried as it was disciplinary.

"I don't have to stay for the game, do I?"

"No, but we could use some help in the cheering department," she responded. "The Texans are intense."

"Good luck," I said as I folded up the chair and walked away from Katie, to home base. I dropped the chair near Marcus's stash and walked toward Constitution Avenue.

"You're not staying for the game?" whined Jigar. I didn't respond. Didn't even look at him.

The one time I looked back at the field, I could see Katie, still staring back at me with her head slightly cocked to one side.

21

When one is planning to meet a likely hired killer at a mysterious location at sunrise, it seems sensible to give a heads-up to someone close to you. In case of disappearance, dismemberment, or, you know, unintentional "suicide." Or a conveniently fatal drunk-driving accident. At least someone would know where I was going and what was going down. So the truth wouldn't die with me. So this viral infection of knowledge could be passed on to someone else.

At that point, Berto would not have understood. And if he sensed any real fear (which he would definitely sense), he would go running to my dad. And Dad probably would have called the Lagrima Police Department, which would have been the opposite of helpful. Katie was out, because she thought I wasn't "asking crazy questions" anymore.

Zeph and Hillary were nowhere to be found. Probably making out in some abandoned corner of a Smithsonian museum. Love in the "Textiles from the 1700s" room. And the only thing Hillary loved more than hearing secrets was telling secrets—like a quartet of viper grannies at the nursing home bridge table.

This left Lena.

And explains why I found myself back in Kramerbooks on the eve of my little chat with Russell Meteer.

As I walked in the door, the scene was remarkably similar to that first date with her. Loner bibliophiles wandered the aisles, new sets of girls' nights out complained about their boyfriends or lack thereof, and a guy and a girl onstage (he with a ukulele, her with a Casio keyboard) proudly announced themselves in unison as I walked past: "We are Crack Is Whack."

Lena was sitting at the same table as before and had taken the liberty of ordering for me.

"Apple crumble pie, which has raisins you will pick out like a surgeon. And extra vanilla ice cream so you don't run out this time. Did I get that right?" she asked.

"Impressive memory," I said as I sat down and saw that there was just one plate on the table. "No vegan pecan pie for you this time?"

"Not bad recall yourself," she commented. "How cute! We both remember each other's orders from our first date."

The band earnestly jumped into a song about children and the future and inner beauty.

"What's their deal?" I asked Lena.

"It's just DC's best Whitney Houston cover band, that's all," she described. "Maybe the only Whitney Houston cover band. Name of the band is a little crass, but at least they're honoring her memory. It's a shame, you missed 'Exhale (Shoop Shoop).'"

"I am finding it hard to follow anything you just said," I admitted, as I looked down at my vibrating phone, which announced "Humbertonius" was calling. I declined the call.

"The parents are major Whitney fans. She's kind of the soundtrack to my childhood. Or, at least, childhood road trips. And every Saturday morning. And junior prom, when my dad hijacked the DJ and dedicated 'All the Man I Need' to me and said the song was about how I felt about him."

"Obscure family culture, I get it," I said. I did. "Do you know Barry Manilow?"

"Didn't he run for president in the 1960s?" she asked.

"No, but we're even in the weird-family-music-obsession department," I responded. "And it's 'Goldwater,' by the way."

"Oh, right! That poor little girl holding the daisy, no idea that Barry Goldwater was about to obliterate her with an atom bomb . . ."

"The birth of the modern negative attack ad . . . ," I mused.

"LBJ was a bastard," she added.

"LBJ was a pragmatist," I countered.

"Okay, we're being way too 'DC' right now," she declared. "This is the conversation I'm supposed to be eavesdropping on and making fun of—not having myself."

Our forks intertwined on the plate as we simultaneously reached for a bite of gooey, crumbly pie. I pulled my fork away and motioned, *Ladies first*. I thought about telling her the truth about my summer right then, but these last few moments of her ignorance were sweet and comfortable. So I batted down those thoughts in my head—like trying to plunge a basketball to the bottom of a pool. Only a short matter of time before it bursts out . . .

As Lena gulped down her small bite of pie, she commented, "I hope you're grateful for your freedom, by the way. I used up pretty much every ounce of goodwill I have with Oscar to bail you out. And then to get him not to tell my parents that I'm dating an underage drinker who can't even get a functioning fake ID . . ."

"I swear it has worked every other time!" I protested.

"Oh, I'm sure." She nodded condescendingly. "But let's avoid the alcohol-serving establishments in the near future, okay?"

"Fine with me," I said.

"Anyway, I hope you aren't too shaken up from your brush

with the law," she said to me as my eyes followed a tall man who briefly made eye contact with me and then disappeared into the cooking aisle. Meteer? I had suddenly found myself wary of anyone taller than six feet. I leaned forward to see the man disappear down the aisle.

"Are you interested in gourmet food now?" asked Lena, seeing my abrupt fascination with what was going on in that part of the bookstore.

"No." I looked back at her and let out a nervous laugh.

I thought about a version of this night where I didn't mention anything about the Other Summer I was having, which Lena didn't know about. A conversation where I didn't tell her what could be my last words. A version of the night where we just sat and listened to some hipster covers of light '80s R & B and got a second helping of pie and went on a long stroll home instead of taking the metro.

But it couldn't be that version of the night.

"Lena." I looked her in the eye as she looked back at me with a faux-serious glare. "Something else happened after you left the bar that night."

She shot me a confused smile.

"Someone chased me," I said.

"Are you kidding me? What are you talking about?" she said, loud enough for Crack Is Whack to shoot her a disciplinary glare.

"Shhhh," I replied. "I just need you to listen right now and not draw attention to us."

"You're scaring me," she said.

"Can you just promise me that you'll listen and keep this to yourself and not do anything based on what I tell you?"

"Sure, sure, whatever," she responded and pulled her hands back into a crossed-arms formation. "What is going on?"

I told her everything. The interrupted Capitol tour, researching Wade Branson, the briefing at Ben's Chili Bowl . . .

"This has all been going on since we met?" she asked, incredulous.

I continued with the trip to Virginia Beach, the Ariel Lancaster connection, and then my not-so-smooth call to Russell Metecr. Everything I had told Katie over a week ago. Except talking with Katie felt like fessing up to an authority figure—comforting but anxious, fumbling for the right words. Talking with Lena felt like writing in a diary easy, calming, in a shorthand we both somehow understood.

"Wait, so Ariel died because she was investigating some evil, suicidal CEO? But it was an accident. . . ."

"I don't know, Lena," I said. "And I don't think it was suicide, and I don't think Ariel's death was an accident. Because the next thing that happened is I got busted by a bouncer for the first time this summer and then got chased through half of Georgetown."

"Well, you *did* give this hitman your name . . . ," she explained. "What are you going to expect?"

"Okay, I get it. I shouldn't have given him my name," I exclaimed.

And then I described the meet-up on the softball field. And my appointment at The Awakening, which was less than twelve hours away.

"I'm going with you," she said. I had expected a more cautious response, along the lines of Katie's or that of a normal person. She added, "This is amazing." I was both impressed and concerned at her willingness to help. Impressed that she'd want to join my investigation. Concerned that she'd actually do it, regardless of my caution.

"No, you are not," I insisted, even though it would have been nice—even fun—to have her there. "Remember the part where you couldn't act on anything I say here, just listen?"

"Cam, do you realize what you're looking into?" she marveled. "A congressman who is about to be the next Speaker of the House, who had a donor killed in a cover-up six years ago, and then did away with a staffer whose proactive work ethic proved a little inconvenient. This is huge."

"Yes, I am aware," I said, lowering my voice in an attempt to get her to do the same. "I'm just wondering if I'll be the third person BIB makes disappear."

"But you're not going alone, you'll be there with the FBI guy, right?" she clarified.

"Yes, he's coming with me. But I'm just saying that if you don't hear from me by tomorrow night, here's the phone number for my dad and my best friend back home." I passed Lena a piece of paper with the contact information. She nodded and slipped it into her purse. "And keep the embassy doors locked at night. And maybe have Oscar do a little digging."

Lena's eyes darted around in a combination of intrigue and worry. And disappointment. That she couldn't do more.

Or maybe Oscar could do a little digging now.

I remembered Lena's guard friend from the Washington Monument. And the guys from the embassy, who monitored all of the security cameras. Lena knew people. Who knew other people. She could help. She wanted to help. I realized I had been stupid not to ask for it sooner.

"Unless," I continued, "you're interested in doing a little research yourself?"

"Yes!" she exclaimed. "Yes"—quieter this time—"I want to help."

"Research," I stated. "Nothing more. I don't want to pull you into this. But you do seem to have a disproportionate number of friends who are also security guards and have access to street camera footage. Or know people who would."

"Okay, so I guess it's an unusual group of friends for a

teenage girl," she admitted. "But they are bored, so we had that in common. Until I met you. Anyway—they're bored. They get paid to be bored. So I'm pretty sure they would be very excited about any kind of . . . investigation. . . ."

"But you can't tell them that part," I said, starting to worry about keeping things confidential.

"What can I tell them, then? Where do we start?"

"Ariel Lancaster. Her last days—who she met with, where she went. Everything leading up to that night at Capitol Sinny," I said. "Look, this could be a bad idea. I don't even know if you're going to find anything. . . ."

"If there is something to find, my guys and I will find it," she assured me.

"Thank you," I told her. "And if I don't see you again, please tell your parents I really wasn't that bad of a guy."

"Are you already speaking of yourself in the past tense?" she asked. And then laughed to herself. "And I thought my life was interesting with dorm room accessory shopping. I'm going to miss you when I go to school, Cam."

"Humbertonius" called me again. I declined the call again. Like an athlete wanting to avoid distractions the night before an event, I told myself I'd call him soon. After the main event.

She added, "That is, assuming you'll still be alive after your romantic sunrise meeting."

"Well, you could always transfer to Lagrima Junior College," I offered. "They have some phenomenal vocational programs. I see construction management in your future. . . ."

"All of the gossip blogs in DF would eat that up." She contemplated. "Ambassador's daughter ditches Princeton to head to some hillbilly junior college in . . ."

She stopped, because I think she realized that she was calling my future educational institution a "hillbilly junior college."

"Cam, I didn't mean that," she apologized. "I'm sorry. That is gross. I'm a terrible person."

Crack Is Whack boldly started their encore: a strangely samba-infused "I Will Always Love You." What appeared to be their only fan loudly cheered them on from a few tables away.

"Saved by a song." I smiled to Lena.

We silently took in the full song in both horror and wonder. I sported a very thoughtful look, which made Lena cover her mouth to block her laughter. When the duo finished the song and bowed multiple times through their heavy breathing, Lena and I gave them a standing ovation.

I paid the bill, and we walked toward the front door. I saw the tall man purchasing a stack of books at the counter. Once I heard him gushing to the clerk about how "okra is the new kale," I confirmed that he was definitely not my hitman stalker.

"I'm dating the modern-day Woodward and Bernstein," teased Lena.

"Can I at least be Bernstein?" I requested. "He always looked cooler, with the long hair and everything."

I opened the door as we both felt a blast of warm night air and saw the cars whooshing around Dupont Circle.

"You're Cameron Carter," she said, as she put my hand in hers. "And that's cool enough for me."

"So," I responded, "you're not worried? Because I thought you weren't going to let me go through with this. Maybe that's what I secretly wanted you to say. . . ."

"I'm not worried at all, Cam," she said. "You've got it— you're so close. And you have to go through with this."

Her confidence in me felt more empowering, more real than any flattery Katie had imparted from BIB. As I started to walk toward the metro station, Lena pointed at the black SUV that was waiting for her around the corner. A security guard waved at us from the driver's seat, with an unnerving smile that told me not to try anything with Lena. Not there, not now.

"That's my ride." Her smile was apologetic as we both realized that the night would be ending with an audience and a chaste hug.

At least it was a long one. I reached forward and held her closely, each second of the hug somehow building my courage for the next morning.

"Thank you," I whispered into her ear.

She rubbed my back with her hands and responded with

a hushed "Thank you." They were the first words she had spoken that evening that sounded worried. She climbed up, popped into the back seat of the gargantuan SUV, and closed the fortress wall of the car door.

As the car took off, I walked extra slowly toward the metro station. As if I was somehow slowing down the seconds that remained between me and Memo and Meteer and whatever he was going to say or do to us when the sun came up again.

22

Memo was surprisingly calm as he drove south on the 295 free-
way—shooting out of DC along the Potomac River. A steady
rain began to fall. I thought about the Honda he had lent me—
where it was and if it was really an undercover FBI car (if so,
well done, FBI; you had me fooled). But aside from a "You
will let me take the lead" when I got in his car, we didn't say a
word to each other. The questions and scenarios in our minds
were too loud to say or hear anything else. Like whether Meteer
wanted to talk to us or silence us. And how Memo could handle
a former black-ops guy, if it came to that (one glance at Memo's
office belly, and my money was on Meteer. . . .). It was just
before six a.m., and the opposite direction of the road barrier
was already clogged with type A commuters getting their days
started. Far fewer people were headed in our direction.

Even fewer were at the National Harbor, a touristy shopping center situated on the Maryland shores of the Potomac River. Dim lights, closed storefronts, and empty restaurant patios lined the walkways—like the mall was some sort of sea anemone that had closed up and didn't want to be disturbed.

"We're here," said Memo as he parked in a loading zone across from a glowing row of CLOSED signs.

"We're meeting BIB's hitman at a Rosa Mexicano franchise?" I asked.

"Down there." He pointed to a small strip of sand by the docks. Emerging from the beach was a huge, cast-iron sculpture of a man, mostly buried by the sand and straining to get up. Only a hand, an arm, a foot, a raised knee, and his head remained visible. In the gray-blue light of the early morning, I could almost see the poor giant moving—making progress with his escape from the sand that covered him.

"The Awakening," Memo added.

We flopped open a couple of pocket umbrellas from the back seat of Memo's car and jogged across the deserted street. After stepping down a few broad steps, we walked toward the center of the sculpture, muddy sand caking our shoes. It was just us and the 85 percent buried giant—no Russell in sight. I walked over to the massive, sand-coated head of the statue—his mouth frozen in an angry shout, and his eyes locked in a desperate glare. Tiny drops of water flicked at his face, and as

I leaned in just inches from the gaping mouth, I could have sworn I heard his labored, defeated exhale.

"He's not here," called Memo from twenty feet away. "Guy got cold feet, dammit."

I turned to look at Memo, whose back was to the giant's foot and upraised leg. As I trudged over to him, I could see that Russell Meteer had not been scared away after all. I walked past Memo and heard the crunching of his shoes in the sand behind me.

The man was standing under the makeshift triangular shelter provided by the giant's bended knee—similarly frozen and somehow bursting with rage like the giant was. We approached him slowly, both probably thinking the same thing: that this man could suddenly burst to life, like one of those seemingly sedentary scarecrows in a haunted house. The closer we got, his extraordinary height became more apparent. Well north of six feet. His silhouette against the gray sculpture was identical to the one that chased me along the C and O Canal. I felt a flicker of relief that I had survived that encounter, followed by a pang of panic about the current rendezvous. He wore only gray sweatpants and a thin white T-shirt, which grew increasingly transparent with the falling rain. A complicated geometrical tattoo snaked its way up his entire right arm. I looked more closely to see odd, squeezed, drooping distortions in the design—indicating that this guy had gotten inked

at the bulging height of a since-atrophied physical condition.

I moved forward to cover him with my umbrella.

"Don't," barked a protective Memo.

I stopped short and put the umbrella back over my head.

The first and only things that moved were his lips: "I don't want it anyway." The intensity of his eyes belied his immobile stature. Only his eyes looked alive. The more I looked at him, I felt less physical danger. And the more I could tell he had dangerous things to say.

"Are we alone?" asked Memo.

Russell started to talk but got caught up in a coughing fit—a bout of superficial, unsatisfying hacks that went on for half a minute. "Don't worry, this isn't an ambush," he finally said after clearing his throat.

Memo's eyes darted around the empty, hazy predawn pathways and buildings.

We were completely alone.

I looked at Memo with uncertain eyebrows; he was staring straight into Meteer's eyes. Meteer wouldn't look directly back at either of us, his eyes fixated on the small waves in the river. "Some people say this thing is a symbol of hope—this giant emerging from a sandy grave."

We stood in silence as Meteer fought off a twitch of emotion in his cheek.

"But now I know better. He's not emerging from anything.

He is sinking. He's going, going . . . almost gone," he added, his voice as fragile as damp tissue paper.

All we could hear was the incessant dings and thwacks and bips of the raindrops against the cast-iron kneecap. Meteer's shirt was now completely drenched and revealed his surprisingly skinny body. The air was getting slightly brighter as the sun was rising, somewhere. Memo shifted his weight back and forth on his feet. Nervous. Impatient. Hungry.

"What are you going to tell us?" he asked. "Why are you stalking my friend and why are we here?"

His questions seemed assault-like, given Meteer's weak state.

Meteer obliged the interrogation. "Nothing like a fresh Navy SEAL retiree to get the donations flowing," he said, focused and disconnected all at once. "There I am onstage, lung cancer—the nonsmoker kind—just my luck. All these folks eating their stuffed chicken. Standing next to the smiling congressional candidate Billy Beck."

"What are you talking about?" I slowly asked.

Memo raised his hand to silence me.

"You see, Billy—I still call him Billy. Always will. Billy was a philanthropist before he got elected. Raised money for all sorts of causes—and he needed a mascot for this cancer fundraiser event he did with his pharma friends. Enter the strapping, tragically afflicted serviceman. Got everyone all excited. Raised a few hundred thousand in just that night."

Meteer's voice grew stronger as he went on.

"But I never saw any of it. Coverage ran out, insurance vipers wouldn't listen to me, got thrown out of the VA when I had a little disagreement with my idiot doctor. Didn't have enough money for this experimental treatment. Still looked and felt pretty fine, but the system just turned the other way."

Memo held his umbrella between his chin and his shoulder as he brought out a pad of paper that he wrote on.

"And that's when Billy calls me again. I thought he wanted me to raise more money for him. But this time, he wants to give me money. For my treatments. I just needed to do one thing."

"Wade Branson . . . ," uttered Memo.

"'Take care of him,'" blurted out Meteer. "That's what he said to me. Take care of this guy I didn't even know. With my 'unique set of skills.' I guess he was in a bad place, about to rat out Billy and a bunch of other people who knew about a drug that was rushed to market. Made people's brains mush . . ."

"You're telling me Congressman Beck paid you to kill Wade Branson?" asked Memo.

"Paid my foundation." Meteer cleared his throat. "He told me to set it up. National Oncology Warriors, I called it. That way, he could give me annual donations—he could give a bunch of foundations money—and it just looked like he was a generous guy. Got me out of the woods, that money. Clean bill of health."

Memo's jaw was increasingly lax. "This is insane."

"So I went to Boston. Fresh Pond . . ." He stopped, replaying a scene in his mind that he would not verbalize for us. "Exercised the skills my government taught me. And then disappeared. That's what we are trained to do, after all. Mission complete."

"Why are you telling this to us?" I asked.

Meteer's taut cheeks blew up with indecision. He let out a slow exhale and proceeded. "Because Billy went all Washington on us. Forgot about causes. Focused on getting votes. Getting money. Because I called and called, and he never returned. I showed up at his office one day, and he looked right through me. With a smile on his face. Because the cancer came back. First day of spring, this year. Don't get me wrong, I can still get around. I can still run on a good day—junior here knows that pretty well, don't you?"

He managed a partial smile as I recalled that nighttime chase with dread. "But the good days are fewer and fewer now. And I don't want another man's death to be the thing keeping me alive."

The rain retreated upward, and the first sly wave of morning heat slathered itself over us. Memo and I closed our umbrellas.

"And then there were the calls from that girl . . . ," he continued.

"And you . . ." I searched for the words. "'Took care of her,' too?"

"Hell no," Meteer quickly rebuffed. "Branson was my last assignment. I didn't touch that girl. Didn't even see her in person. Didn't want to, at first. But she kept calling me. And then I got my diagnosis, and I was like, 'Screw it, I'll talk.' So we spoke on the phone. Was supposed to meet up with her in person—the day after someone else took care of her."

"Someone killed Ariel?" I asked, my heart leaping at our proximity to answers, real answers. "All reports said it was a car accident. . . . It looked like a car accident. . . ."

Meteer emitted a light chuckle that gave way to a punishing burst of uncontrollable coughs. "Very . . ." He paused. "Convenient," he eventually said, carefully filling out all three syllables of the word.

A distant, cold slap of metal signaled the early arrival of a nearby shopkeeper who raised the retractable grate covering a store. Meteer's head snapped in the direction of the noise, and his subsequently tightened body indicated displeasure with the company—however far away.

"So you're dying, and you want to bring BIB down," stated Memo. Even though we were talking about a murder for hire, his conclusion sounded particularly insensitive.

Meteer did not respond. He didn't have to.

"You know what this means? Press, trial, sentencing,

prison, and then capital punishment . . . ," listed Memo.

"Doctor gave me two months two weeks ago. So I think I've got my own death penalty on its way," said Meteer.

"Can I get a recorded statement?" asked Memo, incredulous.

"Put me on the freakin' YouTube, I don't care. I'm done. And it's time Billy is too," said Meteer, his soft voice disguising a sour kind of revenge.

The giggles of a pair of jogging girls indicated more signs of life in the area. I saw an anxiousness fill both Meteer and Memo, and I knew our time was short.

"How can I reach you again?" asked Memo.

"You don't get to ask that question, mister," scolded Meteer. "I'm dying, but I'm not stupid." He cocked his head toward me with a fleeting flash of sarcastic emotion.

"I'll find *you*," he reminded us.

He leaned forward from the iron triangle of the giant's bent leg, the surface now shining in the morning light.

"Thank you," I said, reaching out my hand to his.

Meteer brushed past me without saying a word. He was not proud, but he was visibly relieved. We watched him take a few steps and then stop. He turned around and looked at me. In the eyes, for the first time in the whole conversation.

"And don't you talk about this with anyone in that office." He ominously held up his left hand, index finger outstretched.

"Because Billy owns everyone there, to some degree or another. Everyone there owes him. And he makes them pay, sooner or later."

A heavy tremor of guilt reverberated through the sentence. He shuffled through the drying sand and stepped onto the dock, which led to a dozen resting boats. Memo and I turned toward the steps and walked to the car.

I looked back and squinted as a ray of sun ricocheted off the giant's upraised arm and into my face, obscuring my view of the ghostlike Meteer, who appeared to be walking to the end of the dock.

We got into Memo's car, and I looked back at the patch of sand, the giant, and the dock.

Meteer was gone.

Only the giant remained. Sinking into oblivion.

23

Dear Mr. and Mrs. _____,
On November fourth, the ballot boxes will open in
Lagrima County, and I am asking for your support.
We have come far together. With your vote[s], we
can continue this journey.

A news anchor–worthy head shot of BIB filled the upper-left corner of the page. "A Generation of Service" was written in a slick font next to it. Red, white, and blue (obviously). Katie said the election letters were going out in a week. She needed someone to proofread the document, and I offered to help.

This November, you can send a message to
Washington: that you have been supporting a

murderer. That I paid a dying former Navy SEAL to kill Wade Branson and make it look like a suicide. And then, when my hot staffer started to figure it out, I somehow made her die too. This time, I made it look like a drunk-driving accident. And then my crazy press secretary planted some story that I was screwing the girl, so the press would ask different questions. I didn't care that the girl's mom is a close political ally.

"Try to have a normal few days. Don't talk about this to anyone in the office," Memo had me told before dropping me off three blocks away from the Rayburn building, the morning we'd talked with BIB's penitent hitman. "I need time to formalize Meteer's statement, and I need you to act like you're continuing to have an amazing summer interning for your congressman. Replace copy machine toner. Give tours. Write form letters. We'll keep an eye on you. You'll be safe."

"A normal few days," he'd said so effortlessly. Normal, even though the man whose name was on the plaque outside the office hired at least one contract killer in his life. Normal, even though I'd spilled a particularly volatile pile of beans to this same man's number two. Normal, even though I was keeping secrets that had gotten others killed.

So I kept my head down, all the while bracing for impact.

And I'd had taken the liberty of tweaking Katie's election form letter. It felt good to get the truth on paper, even if it would only be heard by "Mr. and Mrs. _____."

> A vote for me is a vote for our children, for health care, for our senior citizens, for covering up a six-year-old murder and an eight-week-old fatal car accident. And most important, for my perfect hair and that smile.
>
> So thank you. Thank you for being complicit in a crime that is the foundation of my political career. Thank you for knocking door to door and getting the word out. Thank you for never asking questions. Because if you do, maybe you'll be found with a gunshot to the head under a bridge. Or wrapped around a tree on the side of the road.
>
> Try me.
>
> Sincerely,
>
> William "Billy" Irman Beck
>
> Member of Congress

"Cameron," Marcus called gingerly as he sauntered over to my desk, third afternoon coffee in hand. "So I could use some help with that literacy report, if you have a second?"

Just before he reached my side of the desk, I quit out of

the election letter and clicked "Don't Save" any of the edits I made. "Mr. and Mrs. _____" would have to find out the truth about BIB some other way. And, by the way, was it really taking Marcus an entire summer to assemble some report about literacy? Was *he* literate?

"Is this the same report you were working on in June?" I asked.

"Yes," he murmured, lowering his voice and making sure no one else in the office was hearing. "Look, it's a really complicated report. And I've had all these other things going on. . . ."

"Like a Fourth of July barbecue," I teased.

"Yes," he replied. "No! What? Why do the interns always end up mocking me? It's supposed to be the other way around. Please can you just get these statistics? You're only here another week!"

My internal countdown had been inactive for a while, as it hit me: it was my last week in the office. Maybe it was Lena and our mutual denial that summer was ending, and with it, our unlikely time together. Maybe I was actually enjoying the hunt with Memo. Equal measures of relief and knotty anxiety competed in my stomach. Soon I'd be out of this mess. An intriguing mess, but a mess all the same. Just a few more quiet days and my plane ticket would make the decision for me.

But deep down, I knew my remaining time wouldn't and couldn't be quiet. I felt the momentum of Memo and my efforts—an undertow that was drawing us closer to the end of something. Or someone.

Marcus shoved a bulleted list of questions on my desk, the slap of the paper jolting me back to the task at hand.

"Yeah, sure . . . ," I said to him, trailing off a bit as I noticed a text pop up on my phone.

It was Lena. Confirming that my final days in DC would be anything but quiet.

"Of course . . . ," I said, my eyes now firmly fixed on the message from her.

We need to talk. I found something, and you need to get out of that office, she had typed.

Ha-ha, I wrote back. So clever of her to play along with my little spy hobby. **If you want to go out tonight, you really don't need to make things up.**

Her reply came back strong and furious. **This is real ASAP immediate 911 not a joke.**

I read the sentence over and over, before she added another one for me to read. She hadn't acted this way before. I moved my phone low, beneath the desk, as if that would keep her news—and me—more secure.

Cameron, you're not safe. Not if what you told me is true.

Where? Mexican embassy? I texted back promptly.

Not safe? Simultaneous thoughts darted down moldy rabbit holes of possibility in my mind. Was Meteer's confession a front, a favor for BIB, a trap? Had Nadia reached a critical mass of my incriminating actions through her network of PR spies? Panicking on the inside, I casually looked around the office for who else or what else could explain Lena's grave warning.

Can't meet there, she indicated and then paused. **Where you had your first edamame . . . experience.**

Nice of you to bring that up, I replied.

And then, before I could write *The National Press Club?* in response, she wrote more.

Don't write the name of the place in this text. We both know where. And we don't know who else is reading.

When? I asked.

Now, she shot back.

"A few personal errands" sounded plausible enough at four p.m. on a weekday, so that was my excuse for leaving. Katie said she needed me back by five thirty p.m. for the traditional summer interns' photo with BIB. I ran down the Capitol South metro station escalators and barely got through the train doors before the mostly empty late-afternoon train whisked me to Metro Center. I shared the subway car with a couple families of tourists and a lone, jacked-up guy in workout clothes who looked at me enough times to make me think either he was going to hurt me, or I was officially paranoid. It turned out to be the latter, as he slipped out the doors one stop before me. I got to the National Press Club in twenty-three minutes, door to door. Lena was waiting outside, wearing a yellow tank top and jeans and an alarming look of concern.

"What took you so long?" she asked.

"Your driver was unavailable," I said, exasperated as sweat dampened the roots of my hair. "Can you just tell me what is going on? I'm really not supposed to be raising any questions in the office right now. . . ."

She scanned the area and didn't appear to hear a single word that I said. She grabbed my hand and led us both into a plus-size middle-aged women's casual wear store.

"Are you kidding me?" I asked. "Are we going to try on caftans and scarves together or something?"

She tore through the store, arbitrarily picking up four different items off the racks before leading me straight to a dressing room. An upbeat Gwen Stefani jam filtered through the speakers from the ceiling. A store employee who was wearing a flowy, flowery blouse sang along and bounced to the beat before noticing that we were in there with her. She initially smiled and then, sizing up Lena's sticklike figure, shot us a look of confusion and then disgust.

"You have to come in here with me!" cried Lena, for the employee to hear. "I'll miss you too much if we aren't togeth-errrrrr!"

Lena pushed me into the cramped space and quietly closed the door.

"You are a crazy person," I told Lena.

She threw the armful of clothing on the floor and then lifted a small electronic tablet from her deep purse.

"What is this?" I asked.

"You asked me to see if I could find anything on Ariel in the days leading up to Capitol Sinny."

"What was she doing? What did you find?"

"Nothing," she answered. "Nothing before the party at Capitol Sinny. But I found what happened after."

She dropped the tablet on my lap.

"Press play," she said, crossing her arms.

"Fine!" I responded and touched the triangle-shaped play icon on the screen. Grainy black-and-white security footage suddenly filled the small screen. "Why did you take me into retail hell to show me a security video?"

"Scroll forward to eleven forty-nine p.m.," she instructed.

And then I noticed the date on the screen: June 4. And the location: Eighteenth Street NW. As I slid the time stamp over to 11:49 p.m., a familiar girl came into view.

"This is . . . ," I uttered, frozen in anticipation.

"The security footage near Capitol Sinny on the night of Ariel's death," she answered. "I mean murder. You're welcome."

Murder.

Ariel's flowing yellow dress practically glowed white in the security camera footage. She and her male companion for the night meandered down the sidewalk and then stopped to kiss. The kissing went on until 11:52 p.m., at which point they appeared to be saying good night.

"Guy had game," observed Lena.

When the clasp of their outreached hands broke apart, the guy got into his car and turned on the lights. Ariel dropped out of view, away from the camera. He started to drive away, alone.

A loud knock at the dressing room door jolted both of us upright and startled. We looked at each other in trapped terror for a few seconds before a husky voice inquired from the other side.

"Are you going to need those in any other sizes?" It was the store employee.

"Umm . . . ," stalled Lena. "Yes. Smaller!"

I looked back down at the screen and saw another person run at the retreating vehicle to stop the guy. The person had their back to the camera and gestured for someone else to come closer to the car. Then a reluctant Ariel ambled back into view. They stood outside the car for a minute before the person basically pushed Ariel into the passenger seat and slammed the door. The car tore off in a zigzag pattern, away from Adams Morgan.

And into a tree, three miles away.

A rip of vibration tore through my pocket, and I pulled out my phone to see that Berto was calling. I declined the call and swore to myself I would call him later. *Always at the worst time.*

The person who pushed Ariel into the car stood in the vacated parking spot and did not move.

Berto called again, and I declined again. For a flicker of a thought, I wondered if something was urgent or wrong at home. But nothing felt more urgent than the video in front of me.

"You can fast-forward this part," indicated Lena, hinting that the best/worst was yet to come.

As I quickly scrolled through three minutes of footage, the person's body gently swayed back and forth. Groups of other weeknight revelers shot in and out of the screen. Cars zoomed by.

Berto called for a third time. I almost picked up the phone, but then the person turned, their face illuminated by the head-lights of an oncoming car. Her face.

Lena reached down and pressed pause as Katie Campbell's face came into crystal clear view on the screen. And even though it was recorded from a security camera probably attached to a lamppost several feet in the air, her face read excitement and relief and guilt and exhaustion, all at once.

"Katie Campbell killed Ariel," I said in a low voice.

"After Ariel said good-bye to that *borracho* — after," empha-sized Lena, "Katie dragged her back to the car. Insisted that Ariel drive with him."

In that moment, I heard in my mind Russell warning me against telling anyone in the office. *Everyone there owes him. And he makes them pay.*

And I also heard Katie's dismissal of my offer to walk her to the metro station that night after we walked around the monu-ments together. "There are cameras all over this city."

And worst of all, I recalled my stupid, pathetic, and — did I say stupid? — confessional at Katie's apartment. Which she'd no doubt been dissecting since.

Lena picked up the tablet from my weakened grasp and put it back in her bag.

"How did you get this?" I asked.

"A girl can do a lot with security guards for best friends and some free time." She shrugged.

I wondered how much more Lena and her security guard besties could have helped had I told her what was going on ear-lier that summer. Her street smarts surprised me. She was good.

The employee started knocking nonstop at the dressing room door. "Okay, lovebirds," she said. "Out of there."

Lena sheepishly opened the door and shot the clerk an apologetic smile. I played along and followed Lena out of the store, shoulders slumped in feigned shame.

The sidewalk was swelling with foot traffic from the early-evening commute. Lena's demanding eyes seemed to ask, *What now?*

"Lena . . . ," I reluctantly admitted, "I told Katie things. I told her—"

"You what?" she snapped. "Do you realize—"

"I know, I know." I cut her off and finished the sentence in my head. Whatever I told Katie will be used against me. Katie belongs to BIB. She knew all along. Katie is a killer. Then I saw that it was just after five p.m., the photo shoot with BIB less than a half hour away. "I need to get back to the office," I said to myself.

"You can't go back there," Lena warned.

"Memo said I have to continue as if everything's normal," I told her. "And besides, if I suddenly disappear, they'll think something's up. And believe me, they'll find me."

"Look, I know I said you should look into this, dig deeper, whatever." She placed both hands on my shoulders. "But I think it's time to leave this alone. You confided in the devil."

Twin chills shot from my upper back and through the sides of my head, then ricocheted throughout my brain. Katie Campbell. Mentor. Murderer. Very poorly chosen confidante.

"Thanks," I said, easing away from her. "Keep that video; don't show anyone. I need to tell Memo. I need to get back to the office before . . ."

My footsteps and thoughts were frantic. I bumped into some lady in a pantsuit, who sighed loudly in response. I kept walking and pulled out my phone to text Memo the latest. There were seventeen missed calls from Berto.

I dismissed the calls and started texting Memo. **Katie Campbell killed Ariel. Have video.** Followed by, **Do u have statement from Meteer yet?**

The phone screen filled with Berto's name. This time I picked up.

"Berto. What the hell?" I said, almost jogging to the entrance of Metro Center. "What's going on?"

"That's my question. I've been calling you for days. You don't answer my calls anymore? What's going on?" he shouted.

I answered: "Look, I can't really talk right now. I'm—"

"That's all you ever say to me these days," he interrupted. "I'm sick of it."

"There's no way you would understand," I explained.

"Oh, nice. So you go to Washington, DC, and now you are all grown-up, and the stupid friend you left behind in Lagrima wouldn't understand. And I have to call you three thousand times to get you to tell me that."

"Look, this is insane political stuff. You work in a grocery store—," I said and then immediately regretted as I stepped down into the Metro station.

"*Used* to work at a grocery store," he cut me off.

I stopped just short of losing cell signal in the cavernous station below.

"What?" I asked.

"They're shutting down the store," he explained. "I lost the job. My mom doesn't know how we're going to pay the rent. But I'll stop there. You wouldn't understand. . . ."

I heard the whir of the advancing train. My last chance to get back to the office for the immortalized close-up with BIB. And if I wasn't there, they would start asking questions. BIB, Katie, whoever else . . .

"Berto . . . ," I said. "I'm sorry, and I suck, but I have to go."

"You did it," he said, somewhat defeated.

"What do you mean?" I asked.

"You became a douchebag," he responded.

"That isn't fair, Berto," I retorted, as the braking train announced its arrival at the station. "Berto?"

There was no response. He said what he needed to say. He had ended the call and maybe our friendship.

I ran down the escalator and was the last person to get on the train headed back toward Capitol South. And even though I looked around the train for signs of any threat, all I could see was Katie's frozen, illuminated, criminal, black-and-white face.

24

I made it to the southeastern corner of the Capitol exactly one minute before Katie led a parade of BIB, Zeph, Hillary, and a geared-out photographer to the site of the traditional summer photo. Even though I had run from the Capitol South stop and my light blue shirt blotted perspiration from my stomach, I tried to appear calm and cool. And blissfully unaware of Lena's discovery.

"Sweaty much?" taunted Hillary, who had gone full-on skintern for the occasion. She looked as if she had prepared to walk the red carpet at the Teen Choice Awards show—some ponytail Mohawk thing going on in her hair, fresh coat of severe makeup, and an all-black outfit that was Congress on top and club below. She self-consciously pulled down her skirt, while pushing away a dutiful Zeph, who was attempting to fan her with a manila folder.

"Nice" was all I could muster to communicate my diminished tolerance of Hillary and amazement at Zeph's advanced stage of emasculation.

"Hi, Cameron," said a cheery Katie, who held BIB's briefcase and a clipboard of files while the photographer readied the congressman for his close-up.

She knew I knew about Branson. But she did not know that I had just seen her in the dooming, final moments of Ariel's life. It took all of the manufactured warmth I could muster to respond, "Hey, what's up?" I didn't look her in the eye.

Act normal. Memo's admonition rang in my head.

"Well, are we going to do this or what?" said BIB, with the golly-gee enthusiasm of a grandpa about to take pictures with unruly grandkids. He looked sharp and shiny. Too electable to be trusted. "We've sure loved having you with us this summer."

The photographer positioned Hillary and BIB in the center, with Zeph and me on either side. The massive Capitol building behind us was the rich butter yellow of late-afternoon sun. Hillary let out a giggle that seemed to indicate her glee at this seminal moment in her life. Then a louder, naughtier squeal confirmed that her excitement was more connected to Zeph's likely grabbing of her butt.

Without warning, the photographer began clicking away. As the brief session proceeded, BIB slowly moved his left arm around my back, his hand covering my shoulder. His hand felt uncomfortably heavy, as he let out the kind of fake laughter that people do when they're trying to have a natural smile in a photo. The only thing that stopped me from lurching away was the permanency of the record that was being taken. I smiled back.

"Looking good!" approved Katie from behind the photographer. "Okay, we're done."

Hillary leaped over to the photographer so she could see the digital results.

"Zeph, you look so handsome," she said, now publicly embracing their once-hidden relationship.

BIB shook his left hand as if he was flicking something off of it.

"Boy, you really are sweating," he said to me. I looked down at my two-toned light blue and dark, sweaty blue shirt.

"See, Congressman Beck, I said that too!" commented Hillary. "Are you mowing lawns in your free time, Cam? You're so good at that. . . ."

Before I could reply to the insult part, BIB added, "You know what Truman said . . ."

Katie chimed in, "If you can't stand the heat . . ."

"Get out of the kitchen," followed BIB, his eyes seething. The pithy political quote sounded more like a warning. A mandate to get the hell out of his business.

"We've got to prep for your committee meeting in the

morning, BIB," said Katie before placing her hand on the lower part of his immaculately suited back and guiding him toward the Rayburn building.

As Zeph, Hillary, and I walked back to the office, I glanced at the phone Memo gave me and saw a missed call from him. Now disputing the chemical content of elementary school cafeteria hot dogs, Hillary and Zeph didn't seem to notice that I stayed outside as they walked in the door. Memo picked up after a single ring.

"What is this video?" was his greeting.

"Katie," I told him. "She killed Ariel. I have it on tape."

"What exactly do you have on tape?"

"A security camera—it shows Katie pushing Ariel into the car of this drunk guy. Just before she died."

"That's a friend opening a car door for another friend," he said. "Hardly homicide. And how'd you get access to security camera footage, anyway?"

"You have to see it, Memo. Katie knew that Ariel would die, or get hurt. Isn't that what BIB wanted? To get Ariel out of the picture? And this makes it look like he didn't do anything at all."

"Which is exactly the problem. Good luck connecting those dots for a grand jury."

Katie's intention and guilt—so clear to me in Lena's video—were fading under the microscope of legal scrutiny.

"You haven't answered my question, by the way. The tape?"

"It's my friend Lena, the Mexican Ambassador's daughter. She has all these security guard friends and—"

"Excuse me?" interrupted Memo. "Now you have an assistant in all of this?"

"I thought she could help. And you're not exactly the most pleasant person to work with, if no one's told you before. . . ."

"Okay, I've gotten the unpleasant thing before. Whatever. And this tape might be helpful supporting evidence, assuming your *amiga* did her homework and obtained it legally. But you need words—a confession—to seal the deal. And you need to not tell your little girlfriend about our . . . project. Look, kid . . ."

I shrugged off the word "kid" as I heard it through the phone. *I'm your partner in this, dude.*

"One murder at a time, okay? I told you to lie low. Our goal here is the Branson thing. Once we take care of that, the circumstances of Ariel's death will fall into much better focus."

"But we can't let them get away with this, Memo! A girl died because it was convenient for BIB. And Katie made it happen."

"Do I need to be concerned about you?" Memo asked. "Look, I really appreciate your help this summer, but now you need to just be an intern and let me do my job."

"You're able to do your job because I'm more than just an intern," I reminded him.

"Fine, yes, you're right," he admitted. "But so am I. Please. Eye on the prize. And the prize is Branson. Gotta go."

He hung up, and I put the phone in my pocket. As I walked the wide marble halls back to the office, I glanced around to make sure no one was there and then kicked the wall as hard as I could. The cold white surface, of course, bore no bruise as a result. And I realized that, as much as I wanted to expose the Branson scandal, it was Ariel's death I really wanted to avenge. She had taken me under her wing, after all—if only for a week. She was trying to help Memo, just like me. She was just a few years older than me. And Memo dismissed my efforts with a first-things-first philosophy that sounded more bureaucratic than brave. And I know it's selfish, but I thought about the CVSU contract, and how the Branson thing could get caught up in court for years. Ariel's death was more recent, and news of BIB's role in the accident would sink him in the court of public opinion, which is what really matters anyway. And sinking BIB meant my dad got the contract. Memo had promised.

I took a deep breath before walking back into the office, where twenty minutes stood between me and the end of the day. I sat at my desk. Ariel's desk. My left shoulder throbbed from BIB's aggressive grip and my jaw clenched from the letdown of Memo's response.

As much as I wanted to deny, it had been a summer of uneasy smiles. Of triple meanings and double lives—myself included. It was a foggy maze—you couldn't see the next level of bad until it was six inches away from your face. And it looked right back at you.

While I studied satellite Google images of Lagrima, my desk phone rang. It was the first time anyone called me the whole summer.

"It's for you, Carter," Hillary said from the reception desk. "Some weirdo insisted that I transfer the call directly to you. And you're lucky, because I almost didn't answer. It's closing time."

She joined the prompt end-of-day exodus from the office as I picked up the line.

"Cameron Carter?" a young, nasally voice inquired.

"Yes," I replied. "Who is this?"

"This is Congresswoman Nani Lancaster's office," he said. "She'd like to see you now. Longworth building."

"What is this about?" I asked.

"I'm sorry, but Congresswoman Lancaster said it's urgent and that you shouldn't mention it to anyone over there. Okay?" He abruptly hung up the phone.

The last time I had seen or heard of Nani Lancaster was her mournful but resolute interview in the aftermath of Ariel's death. Had she discovered that there was more to her daugh-

ter's accident than a plastered law student? Could she help?
I thought of my own mother, and the excruciating lack of
answers that surround any fatal car accident. What if they had
been driving three seconds later? What if the car battery had
been dead? What if the chief of staff hadn't pushed her daughter into the passenger seat of a drunk driver?

I started texting Memo about the invitation, to let him
know. To ask his permission. But he had communicated his
priority: Branson. And this was a meeting with Ariel's mom—
perfectly timed and irresistibly ambiguous. I deleted my text to
Memo. He would have said no, and I wasn't willing to accept
that.

Ariel wouldn't, and neither would I.

I left the office, joining the wave of workers that exited
the Rayburn building and then weaving my way against the
departing throngs, into the Longworth building. It was the
runt of the congressional office buildings, dwarfed by the
Rayburn on one side and the Cannon on the other. Even still,
the marble interiors and row of representative state flags down
the hallway were bright and majestic. I followed the directory
until I reached Lancaster's state flag—the royal-blue banner of
Virginia. I looked more closely at the text on the flag, which
read SIC SEMPER TYRANNIS. I tried to recall the meaning of this
phrase and why it sounded so familiar when a slender, balding
staffer emerged from the office.

"You're here," he said. "Right this way."

The foyer of Lancaster's office was bathed in a cheap, fluo-rescent hue that belied the stately hallway steps away. A coffee table was covered with year-old *People* magazines whose brittle cover wraps clung to the other pages like a sheet of dead skin you suddenly notice on the arch of your foot. The yellowing walls and mismatched couch and chairs confirmed that junior representatives get the last pick of offices and furniture. The staffer led me into Nani Lancaster's cozy office, which glowed dark amber in the twilight hour. A malfunctioning light panel flickered spastically above.

"Representative Lancaster, I can't tell you how glad I am to see you," I said as I walked closer to her desk.

"Virgil!" she shouted. "This light. Please, someone fix this light. Strobing away. Someone's going to have a stroke. It turns this place into Studio 54 after dark."

Or a haunted house.

"Sit down," she instructed coldly.

The office door clicked shut behind me. I eased my way into a flaky old leather chair, which crunched as I sat down.

She was a pale imitation of the strong and confident woman who had spoken to me and the families of America on TV earlier that summer. Far from the attractive and trust-worthy-looking leader in her congressional photo, she sported bags under her eyes and silvery roots that revealed her rich brown hair was an expensive disguise. It was like when a person posts an old photo for an online dating site, only to reveal a much more haggard and hazardous reality in person. My first instinct was sympathy—to provide consolation for this poor woman who probably just wanted justice for her daughter. Justice and answers.

"I am so sorry about your daughter," I said. "You know, she was my first friend in the office. Only one who really went out of her way and made me feel at home the first week I was there."

She looked down and took a long, slurpy sip from her mug. Then she looked up at me while licking her teeth behind her closed lips.

"Cleo Beauregard," she enunciated, fighting back a hint of slurred speech. She placed her mug on the desk and then leaned her head on a tall leather chair, the back of which towered at least two feet above her.

"Pardon?" I asked.

"Old coot." She laughed oddly to herself. "Record thirty-two terms in Congress. Can you believe that?"

She had issued an urgent invitation to talk about the most tenured congressman in history?

"Up and resigns from Congress one day. And guess who they ask to take his spot?"

"Your special election?" I answered.

"B-I-N-G-O," she sang-spelled and chuckled to herself. I began to suspect the contents of her mug. "School board president, beautiful daughter, malleable husband with a respectable but not too demanding career. A few lost elections under my belt, but I wasn't taking things too seriously then. I was clean, ready."

"The perfect candidate," I observed.

"The perfect candidate," she concurred. "And then you know what they tell me about Beauregard? Senile as a swan the last ten years he was in office."

I questioned whether swans could suffer from dementia as Lancaster droned on.

"'But no one can know,'" she air-quoted. "'Need to uphold his reputation. Need to keep the party happy,' they told me. We all tell the stories we want to believe. The stories we need others to believe."

She slurped from her mug again and reflected on her own words.

"So I make it to DC, big fanfare and all. And I meet BIB. And he takes me under his wing, shows me the ropes, as they say. Invited me into conversations where a junior rep—let alone a female junior rep—just didn't belong. He made me."

"That's what he does," I observed. "He makes people."

Even though the room was overpoweringly air-conditioned, I felt my palms start to sweat. Lancaster took off her sweater to reveal a sinewy, bare set of arms and a billowing, sleeveless purple blouse. She rolled her head around her neck, simultaneously enjoying and suffering through each *crack* and *pop* that ensued. And then she looked at me with the suddenly fierce clarity of a symphony director.

"Do not make my daughter die all over again."

"That's why I thought you brought me here," I replied, relieved. "Representative Lancaster, I know how your daughter died. It was an accident, but that's not all. . . ."

"Don't." She held up her right hand, which trembled slightly at the urging of whatever was coursing through her veins—caffeine, alcohol, vengeance, rage, guilt? "I told Ari the same thing. It's okay to leave some questions alone. It's okay to believe other peoples' stories."

My body tightened. "Are you saying that Ariel came to you before she died? She asked for your help?"

Lancaster bitterly swallowed her own saliva. "If you ask those questions, you're going to find answers you don't like. You're going to find answers that *I* don't like," she said. "That's what I told her."

"But you're still BIB's right hand, so it's okay? Is that how it is?" I took her on.

"I got the cutest phone call from one of my constituents a couple weeks ago." She coldly changed the subject. "Netsie Frye. You've met, I understand. Nice little afternoon chat . . ."

"Caitlin's mom . . . ," I muttered, as I realized my visit to the Fryes was not as off-the-record as I'd thought. "Why did she call you?

"Because my supporters are loyal and they call me when strangers start snooping around the past." Her words were damning. Angry. And then light as sweet tea: "'Nicest boy came by the other day, asking about Caitlin and Ariel,' Netsie told me. I almost didn't take her call. She still thinks we're in the PTA together and can gossip every day about the neighborhood. I feel sorry for her."

"I feel sorry for *you*," I blurted out.

"Cameron." She laughed through her nose to herself. "Do I need to remind you that you are a charity case this summer? That BIB saved you from two months of who knows what in that dust-bowl district of his?"

"You don't know what you're talking about," I said, even though she had a disturbing grasp of my background.

"Oh, I think you know I do," she barked back smugly. "You're not the only one who gets to do background checks. One thing Virgil is any good at . . . ," she mused as she glared at the still-flickering light. Then she fixed her eyes directly at me: "Anyway. Follow my example, and show your congressman some gratitude."

"The people in my hometown—that dust bowl you're referring to—are real people. And it's them I owe my gratitude to, for showing me how messed up you are by comparison. You watched your daughter die because it meant you'd be politically protected. . . ."

I stood up and turned toward the door. Though it was less than fifteen feet away, the exit out of her office seemed to grow more distant with each step I took. By the time I grasped the doorknob, I realized that the door was locked. I turned back to see her smug grin again.

"That Virgil is helpless," she mused. "Leaving me with this crazy light, locking my guests inside my office. So inconsiderate . . ."

"Open this door," I told her.

"Oh!" She smiled in phony surprise at my boldness. "Charming."

She pressed a button on her desk that caused the door to buzz. I nearly fell outside the office as the thick, tall wood surrendered to the weight of my body.

"You may leave now," she calmly declared.

"Who else knows?" I turned to ask. Her face appeared to pulsate with intensity in the flickering light of the malfunctioning bulbs above.

"About you?" she clarified.

"No. Ariel," I corrected. "Your daughter."

"Wrong question, young man," she said and then pondered to herself, "Who else knows about *you* . . ."

I looked outside the office windows to see that night had fallen. And recalled that my bag and wide-open laptop remained at the office, ready for anyone to poke through. I had to get back.

"Enough," she said. "Enough people know about you."

I darted out of her office, briefly glancing at Virgil who shot me a menacing, knowing smile. I remembered the meaning of the Virginia state motto, emblazoned on the flag by the front door.

Sic semper tyrannis.

Thus always to tyrants.

The words John Wilkes Booth shouted before he shot Abraham Lincoln.

25

I was about to knock on the locked front door to BIB's office,
when a janitor wearing a blue vest opened the door to exit. She
was the only other person I saw on the deserted second floor of
the Rayburn building.

"I'm an intern in this office," I explained to her. "Just need
to pick up my things."

I volunteered my badge as proof, and she waved me in. As
I walked over to my desk, she rolled a clunky chest of cleaning
supplies outside and closed the door with a loud *bang* that
echoed throughout the empty office. I picked up my phone to
text Lena. A message from Memo was waiting. Finally.

**Meteer on record. Stay away from BIB and Katie now.
Stay away from the office. Lie low.**

Not helpful, I thought to myself as I looked around the

vacant expanse that now seemed to be closing in on me. Everything looked different in the dark. With the exception of a few desk lamps, the lights were off, shadows at anarchic play. The suffocated moonlight barely sneaked in to feebly showcase the stately tall ceilings above.

Is the Mexican embassy offering good rates on asylum these days? I texted Lena.

Then I alerted Memo: **Leaving office now. Nani Lancaster called me to meet with her. She knows BIB responsible for daughter's death.**

It was when Lena replied with **Weeknight special just for you** that I realized I was not alone.

"I told you. He knows."

It was Katie. And even though that's the first thing I heard, I knew who "he" was, and I knew what "he" knew. "He" was me.

"He knows, William. Enough time has passed since I told you. What do we do now?"

No one called him "William." But it was late and it was dark and they thought it was just them in the office, so maybe the rules were different.

Katie called him William.

There are places where you don't expect to see people this late—places and times where people don't belong. The abandoned chairs, the sleeping phone switchboard, the snoring water cooler—everything said, *This is not a place for people.*

Not right now. Offices are meant to be empty at night. Offices and graveyards. But in this office—this graveyard—there was a thin line of light that painted the dark wood floor. A glowing band of illuminated ground emerging from a small crack in his office door—leading to, pointing at me.

Get out now, glowed a message from Memo.

"Wade, Thativan, the girl—he's probably even meeting with Russ . . . ," Katie explained.

But I couldn't leave. Not now. As Memo's message faded away on my phone, I crouched low to the ground and listened to every unbelievable, damning word.

Words that established guilt. Words that connected the dots, as Memo said.

"Stop."

And she did stop. Because when he wanted something—someone—stopped, it stopped. Sentences, budgets, resolutions, bipartisan cooperation, heartbeats.

"Russell," he said calmly. "That name. He doesn't exist."

I slowly reached for my phone and activated the video function, my shaking left finger struggling to tap the correct icon on the screen. This would be evidence that Memo couldn't deny. If I could just get the right angle.

"William, look, I'm on your side, and this kid is"—she hesitated—"a kid, but what he knows . . . what he knows could end you and . . ."

Her words were instinctively silenced by the ricochet of distant clicking heels against the invincible marble corridors outside. I didn't know whether to be relieved that someone might be coming to defuse the scene, or angry that this person was going to foil my one chance to get BIB and Katie on tape. The happy, tinny footsteps gave way to guttural, droning echoes.

For a moment, there were no more incriminating words to eavesdrop. The only thing that broke the silence was the frantic blood pulsing throughout my body and nudging my eardrums outward each time my heart sputtered away. Were they listening? Could they hear the beating in my ears, this nonsound that filled the darkened corner I eased out of?

I winced in anticipation of a creak in the floorboards with each step closer to the crack in the door—the angle for my perfect shot. BIB's face seemed to look directly at me, though it was Katie's unflinching profile he was talking to. I lifted the phone, hit record, and watched the conversation continue through the screen.

Katie resumed: "What he knows could end you, and if something is to be done, it needs to be done now."

That nothing little word "something" had never sounded so evil.

"'It needs to be done,'" he said. "You and your passive voice. Like you never have a responsibility. Your convenient grammatical trick to make yourself think your hands never touched any of this."

"If something is to be done," she stood corrected, "*we* need to do it now."

"Then do it," he said. "Like you did to the girl."

His loafers shuffled across the rug in his office, followed by a sad, long crunch as he settled into his leather couch. Katie's facial expression signaled that BIB's statement was incomplete.

"Fine. Like *we* did to the girl," he revised. "You and I. And the plastered law student you handpicked for Ariel."

"You know, she didn't want to get in the car at first," she said.

"And you made sure she got in there," he added. "I know, I know, like you already said. Are you gloating over her death now, Katie? Have I made you that jaded?"

My hands shook with both triumph and terror as I tried to steady them. I couldn't have Memo rejecting this video because it was out of focus or something.

"'He's so cute,' I said to her. 'He only had a couple drinks,'" she explained. "It felt a little cleaner than calling up your sad friend from black ops. You know, you can't be so heavy-handed anymore, Mr. Speaker. I was just trying to protect you from your own impulsiveness, and there was this perfect opportunity right in front of me. In front of us."

"It's turned out better than we could have planned," he

assured her. "Job well done. But now we have the boy. Like that little turd that sticks around in the toilet bowl after you flush it. You think he'll go away, but he's still there. It's always the young ones who think they can just blow a whistle and make everything right. Do we call Randy?"

"You're thinking about bringing the chief of police into this?" she questioned.

"The man owes me a favor. Or we could call that friend of Russell's. . . ."

The phone nearly slipped out of my hands as I started to hear them plot my own demise. I stopped the recording. Now I just needed to get out.

And then I knocked over the garbage can.

My retreating footsteps had collided with a heaping trash can that the janitor had left. As it tipped over, I reached to halt the impending crash, but the can seemed to be in fast-forward. This container filled with garbage and things no one wanted anyone else to see anymore was tipping over. About to release its rancid contents. I think there was a metaphor in there somehow, but before I could connect those dots, a distinct "CRONK!" filled the office and blared through the sliver of air between his office doors.

Urgent and annoyed, BIB ordered Katie to "go see what's out there."

By the time Katie emerged from BIB's private doors, I was

standing at the other side of the office, out of hearing distance. Putting my stuff into my bag. Trying not to let her see my quaking frame.

From behind my desk, I watched her scan the relatively dark office, her view becoming clearer with each second that her eyes adjusted. Like a nocturnal predator.

"Oh, Katie!" I feigned surprise as she flipped the main office lights on. "Didn't think you'd be here so late. Janitor let me in because I forgot some stuff."

My thumping heart seemed to scream to my frozen muscles *get out get out get out get out*.

"Well, I guess I shouldn't be surprised you're here late," she uttered as she crossed her arms. "You've always been such an . . . overachiever."

A gregarious *glug-glug-glug* of the water cooler broke the heavy silence. Our faces remained locked on each other, tenuous smiles on each. I couldn't read her—did she know that I had heard every word of her conversation with BIB? Or did she believe the hack improvisation that I was just picking some things up?

I didn't want to wait to find out. "Well, I won't keep you any longer. I think I have everything." Now both of us were speaking with loaded language.

"Okay, then." She watched as I moved toward the front door.

I exited, just as I saw her lean down to the toppled trash can—whose proximity to BIB's office revealed that I had in fact been in earshot of every incriminating word.

"Cameron?" I heard her call nonchalantly as the door clicked shut. It was a sinister-sounding enticement to stay a little longer. *Let's talk through some things.* . . .

My footsteps down the hallway were soft and small at first, but then fast and frantic as I got farther away. Building security—and apparently the whole police department—would do whatever BIB instructed, and I knew Katie and BIB were furiously debating their plan to legitimately contain me. As I turned the corner toward the stairs, I nearly slammed into a Capitol Hill policeman who walked the floor.

"Whoa, there. Everything okay?" The guard reacted and then studied my badge. "You know, interns are not supposed to stick around after hours."

"I'm sorry, sir," I said, trying to make my voice sound calm. "Just finishing up a big project before the summer's over!"

"Do I need to walk you to the exit?" he said.

"Oh, no. I'll leave right now," I replied.

I heard a muffled message on his walkie-talkie as I headed for the stairs. Was he being alerted to look for an intern? Five ten, medium build. Maximum risk.

I bolted down the stairs and casually waved at another security guard, who stood watch at the front entrance of the building.

I was almost out the front door of the Rayburn when the guard called me back to his station.

"We need to look through bags when people of your level leave this late," he said as I handed over my bag.

With excruciating care, he unzipped the bag and dug through my stuff. He seemed to handle my phone with extra interest before grabbing for the phone Memo gave me.

"Two phones!" he said to himself.

"Yeah" was all I could muster.

Get out get out get out get out.

"This is one of them old ones!" He held up the phone from Memo. "Only folks I see carrying these around anymore are government types, FBI . . ."

I let out a nervous laugh and an even more nervous, toothy smile at the sound of those three letters.

The guard shrugged and continued to rifle through my things at a punishing, languid pace. I watched his desk phone, waiting for a call from Congressman Beck's office to appear.

"Okay, all clear," said the guard. Followed by, "You interns are gonna be wrapping up soon!"

I nodded and pushed the front door open. Somehow the late July night air felt hotter than the daytime.

I heard the security desk phone ring just before the door closed.

I was a good forty yards from the building entrance and

hidden in the shadows beneath a tree, when I watched the security guard burst through the front doors. Looking for the kid who was at his desk seconds before. The kid whom BIB probably had claimed was a danger, a hazard, and must be found. The kid who must be contained.

He scanned the exterior of the building, at one point staring right at me. But he didn't see me, and he walked back inside.

It was less than three miles to the Mexican embassy. The metro was out, because it didn't run as often at night, and the stations were completely covered in security cameras. Taxis left this part of town alone on weeknights. My only remaining option was the most conspicuous one.

I ran.

26

I wasn't even a hundred yards away from the Capitol when I felt the first tingling of a blister. Then four more. Surprise: My dress shoes were not cut out for three-mile dashes. It had been a while since the track-and-field season, and my cramping shins let me know it. I tore across the Mall anyway, toward the White House, which was now about halfway between me and the thick, protective concrete walls of the Mexican embassy.

I weaved in and around clusters of tourists admiring the bright white monuments and the smoky gray sky that reflected their glow. As I looked over at a much-better-equipped runner, who sported bright orange shoes and a tight black outfit, I stepped into a patch of mud. The slick surface propelled me forward and I nearly slammed into the murky slush before leaning out toward the neatly trimmed grass next to it. The mud didn't bring me down, but it had left its mark—big fat splatters of Jackson Pollock–like blobs all over my pants and shirt, sneaking up to my neck. As a group of shocked women watched and tittered to themselves, I wiped myself off and ran even faster.

I saw the first policeman near the back of the American History museum. He looked bored, which is not how you want your policemen when you want to go unnoticed. I wondered if BIB had alerted his friends at the police station yet, and if the APB about an eighteen-year-old intern-slash-spy-slash-terrorist-slash-whatever worked to get their attention had reached this cop. In an effort to minimize any suspicion, I slowed to a brisk but noncriminal walk. I realized that the mud splatters and my blister-induced limp didn't exactly lower my profile. The cop looked me up and down, furrowed his brow, and was about to speak to me when I talked first.

"Rough day," I said, shaking my head with a beleaguered smile.

The policeman took a breath. His expression grew sympathetic. "You and me both, kid." He smiled back. He would not be smiling in a few minutes when he got the message and realized that he let one of DC's most wanted just stroll on by.

As I got farther away from him, I picked up my pace until I was at a full sprint again. I crossed the gigantic, oval-shaped grass field in front of the White House, without even thinking about the significance of the structure. Architecture starstruck no more. As I neared the street lights of Seventeenth Street, more people began to stare. I couldn't blame them when I saw my messy reflection in a glassy office window. I looked like a confused private who'd worn Costco business casual instead of his fatigues into the heart of battle. Or a particularly creative haunted-house employee, fully embracing Zombie Intern. People laughed and/or shielded their children as I ran by them. Then they went on with their evenings.

But there was one who didn't look away.

I saw him first as I banked left onto Pennsylvania Avenue, just two and a half breathless blocks away from the embassy. He stood on the other side of the street — abnormally tall, hulking, and lean. Like a former Navy SEAL. Like "that friend of Russell's" BIB had just mentioned to Katie. Ready to pounce.

Waves of traffic streamed between us, a wide, protective moat of speeding and honking cars. I bolted up the street. Every breath was a blowtorch blast down my arid throat. He reached the next block well before I did, as if he moved in fast-forward. Finally, the embassy came into view.

As did a police car, lurking toward me from a side street. The two patrolmen looked straight at me. Their faces changed to animated, angry *stop right there*, as I realized my description had likely hit the wire.

Two long blocks from the embassy, I did an about-face

and ran to the building, as I saw the tall man calmly jogging through and navigating a buzzing Pennsylvania Avenue. That's when the flashing lights of the police car bathed the northern side of the street in electric blue. The speaker from the car shouted something.

I looked back at the street to see the tall man two lanes from the sidewalk, eyes locked on me with a dispassionate, robot-like gaze.

He was reaching inside his jacket when the car hit him. It was a tiny car—a smart car or an especially mini Cooper. Looked smaller than him, even. But the car won. A slow crunch of bones softly echoed against the buildings on the street as the man flipped high up into the air and then slammed down on his side. For a few seconds, the pursuing policemen turned toward the accident as traffic slowed down and bystanders tiptoed into the street. A middle-aged woman stepped out of the car and held both hands to her head. The horrific scene proved a sufficient diversion for me to run the remaining block and a half to the embassy door, where I was initially greeted by a confused and defensive guard.

I banged on the bulletproof glass as Lena appeared on the other side and convinced the security guard to let my sorry-looking self inside. I didn't look back to see if the police had seen me enter the embassy doors.

She gave me a hug. It was tentative at first, due to the mud caked all over me. Then it turned into a full-on embrace. I felt my body collapse a little in her arms as the fatigue and the shock of the last three miles caught up with me. I peeled myself off her to see that the mud had transferred to her bare legs, shorts, and oversize button-up shirt. We grabbed each other's hands and headed into an elevator.

"You're lucky my parents are gone tonight. Otherwise, I wouldn't be able to harbor a fugitive as easily." She pushed the third-floor button, but a familiar face reached through the doors just before they closed. "Or this very assertive FBI agent who I convinced the security guards to let in here earlier. I guess you're friends?"

"Such a shame that drivers don't see pedestrians anymore. Didn't even hit the brakes, did she?" It was Memo, snarky as ever. Grateful that a couple of kids were apparently doing all his work. "Glad you decided to wear some clothes with that mud, by the way."

"What are you doing here? You're supposed to leave her out of this," I told him.

"We were both supposed to leave her out of it, if I recall correctly," he replied. "Nice choice of asylum, though."

His contagious laugh infected Lena, as they both chuckled. I laughed too, more relieved and in shock than amused.

"What is it about you and elevators?" I asked him.

"Convenience, mostly." He shrugged. "Anyway, you

piqued my interest in this little lady's security footage. So I decided to drop by."

We reached the third floor and Lena guided us to a conference room. Lena and I eased into the oversize chairs that surrounded the table. Memo remained standing.

"Compelling stuff," he said as he held the same tablet Lena had used to show me the footage. "And it's now in FBI custody. I know I must have sounded ungrateful earlier, but this will definitely help us when we move on to the Ariel case. So thank you, Cameron. And Lena."

I reached for my phone—for the footage of BIB and Katie that I had just taken.

"Let me know if you come across something a little more . . . hard-hitting," he said to Lena. "Surprise me."

"Actually . . . ," I interrupted, and they both looked at me. But then I put my phone back in my bag. If I told Memo about the video, he'd confiscate it as well. And "FBI custody" sounded so boring. I changed gears. "I think we've had enough surprises for a summer."

"Meteer showed up at the bureau after we spoke today, by the way," he said. "Deposition in progress. As is his new identity and booking at an alternative treatment facility in the quaint coastal village of . . . well, I suppose that's privileged information, now, isn't it?"

"That's very decent of you, Memo," I said. "Are you going

to arrange for a new identity for me as well? Or just the CVSU contract for my dad?"

"BIB confesses, and your dad gets the contract. That's the deal."

"You're right. First things first," I dutifully parroted Memo's philosophy. "Well, I hope a confession surfaces soon," I said both wistfully and knowingly. I felt for my phone under the surface of my bag, just to make sure I still had it. I felt the contours of this little stick of dynamite that I had in my possession. *Yep, still there.*

"Now, if you'll excuse me, I need to go hammer out the details of an arrest warrant. That's my favorite part—the look on these devils' faces when they're suddenly surrounded by eight feebs. The surprise. We're competitive about this stuff at the bureau. Maybe someday you'll get to issue one of your own. . . ."

"Someday. . . ." I smiled back.

"Okay, that's a little sadistic," Lena intervened and stood up to show Memo the way out.

"Wait a second," I said. "How am I supposed to get out of here with DCPD chasing my head shot all over town?"

"When the police find out about BIB, you won't have to worry about them anymore," explained Memo. "I'm sure Ms. Cruz can find you some comfortable accommodations for the evening. . . ."

Lena rolled her eyes and walked him down the hallway.

Memo popped back into the room for a word of farewell. "It's been nice working with you, kid. Your mom would be proud."

By the time she had finally said good-bye to the chatty, upbeat Memo and returned to the conference room, I had connected my phone to a bank of audiovisual machines. The TV screen in the room had come to life, revealing a wallpaper image of a wicker basket filled with kittens and balls of yarn.

"Seriously?" I teased.

Lena initially tried to change the image, but then sat back in pride. "My parents never let me have a cat, so I made this the default background image on all of the screens in the building."

"Brilliant," I commended her. "Oh, and by the way, there's one more thing." I pointed to a video file that appeared in the corner of the screen. "Press play."

She clicked play, and the conversation between BIB and Katie began.

Katie's voice was more tremulous than I remembered: *"William, look, I'm on your side, and this kid is . . . a kid, but what he knows . . . what he knows could end you."*

Lena leaned in, eyes widening with every sentence.

Katie went on, *"If something is to be done, we need to do it now."*

BIB joined the conversation: *"Then do it. Like you did to the girl. . . . Fine. Like we did to the girl. You and I. And the plastered law student you handpicked for Ariel. . . . It's turned out better than we could have planned."*

"This is unbelievable," she commented. "Wait, this is BIB's confession. And Katie, too! Why didn't you give it to Memo?"

"Memo's focused on Branson right now," I said. "He actually told me to hold off on the Ariel thing, if you can believe it."

"I think the FBI can handle these things on their own."

"Clearly, they needed a little help this summer," I said, gesturing at her and me. "You know how he said maybe someday I'd be able to deliver my own surprise to one of the bastards in this town?"

"You're making me nervous, Cameron," she said.

"Let's make someday come sooner."

27

It was ultimately Lena who clicked send. Well, mostly her.

We had watched the video a few more times together—each time more amazed at how commonplace the conversation seemed. BIB and Katie were so calm, so matter-of-fact.

"Do it . . . Like you did to the girl. . . . Fine. Like we did to the girl."

"Are you gloating over her death now, Katie? Have I made you that jaded?"

"It felt a little cleaner than calling up your sad friend from black ops. You know, you can't be so heavy-handed anymore, Mr. Speaker."

It was well past midnight as the video sat there on the screen—fifty-eight seconds that were about to ignite the world. And a very bad man's very good reputation. Never ceasing to surprise, Lena displayed a disturbing facility for wiping video files of identifying metadata and setting up fake e-mail accounts; this one was named "lasirenita." *The little mermaid* in Spanish. Our subtle way of letting Ariel break the news, if only by way of a corporation's cartoon.

La sirenita's note was about to show up in the "anonymous tip" inboxes of four DC bloggers.

Hovering over the send button with the cursor felt like massaging a bomb detonation trigger—irreversible power and destruction, one tap away. Lena and I talked about holding on to the video, giving the video to Memo after all, selling the video instead of giving it away—and I was halfway through describing what I'd do with the money (new house for my dad, a couple of ATVs for Berto and me, *no, just kidding, Lena, I mean weekend trips to Princeton*) when Lena pushed my hand down and the upload bar started to fill. Pixel by poisonous pixel, displacing white for black, until it was done.

Not for long.

We both held our breath as lasirenita's "sent" box changed from zero to one. We looked at each other with a mix of nausea and *WHATTTT?*

Lena broke the silence: "So how does it feel, intern? You

made a difference after all this summer. Or rather, you're about to."

Her fingers had remained on mine after making The Click, and we were now holding hands.

I answered, "You know when you let out a fart, but it's totally quiet, and there's like ten seconds before anyone else smells it?"

"Gross," she squealed. "Are you giving me a warning or something?"

"And you know it's really bad, and people are going to react. Audibly."

"Classy," she noted.

We visited all four blogs, just in case there was an eager insomniac editor. Each site moaned the dirge of a slow news day (a trumped-up gerrymandering "exposé," "Top Congressional Recess Vacation Spots," and HillZone's reminder about the upcoming Fifty Hottest Staffers list). The headlines were about to get much more interesting.

"Anyway, that's how I feel right now. There's this fart cloud about to cover the city, the country, and maybe the world. And no one knows it's coming," I explained.

"A fart of truth and justice," she added.

"Yes, exactly. See, you get it," I said. "This analogy has been brought to you in part by three a.m."

"Very nice," she said. "I wonder what else three a.m. is sponsoring tonight?"

I wheeled my rolling conference chair closer and answered her question, leaning forward to kiss her and closing my eyes. I didn't feel anything in response.

Keeping my eyes closed, I said, "This offer expires any second now."

"Just messing with you," she said before meeting her lips with mine.

Waves of chills flowed from my head to my fingertips and back up to my head as we kissed. Not a tentative *Is she liking it?* kiss. Not someone else's aggressive movie kiss. It was a simple, comfortable Cameron-and-Lena kiss. Kisses, to be precise. Six of them. And they were perfect. We both opened our eyes to see each other's smiles.

"You've certainly learned a lot this summer," she remarked.

"Well, I had to learn pretty quickly, because we are going to be in opposite corners of the country soon," I said.

"Right now, it's just us and here and now," she replied.

"And a very romantic conference room," I added.

She moved from her chair and sat with me in mine, which proved instantly uncomfortable. We tried to find a position that worked for both of us to sit in one chair, but the chair insisted on its single-person capacity limit.

"Did the Mexicans think to add a couch in this building?" I asked.

"Wi-Fi's crappy everywhere else but this part of the building," she explained. *"Lo siento, mi amor."*

She climbed up on the table and crossed her legs, and leaned forward to me.

"Where have you been all my life, Cameron? We could have solved so many conspiracies together. All of these politicians would have no chance. We'd run them out of town," she said before refreshing the blogs again.

No stories. And these sites were supposed to be scrappy!

"You grew up in the wrong town that one day you couldn't wait to get out of," I explained. "You should have been in Lagrima all along."

I joined her up on the conference table and we lay down next to each other in a surprisingly comfortable position, given that we were on our backs, on a table. A wave of exhaustion hit us both as gravity guided more blood to our heads.

"Lagrima's not so bad, you know," I said, almost dozing off.

With my eyes closed, I grasped her hand and heard her light breathing.

The last thing I heard her say before falling asleep was "How could it be bad? Lagrima made *you*."

• • •

"Cameron! Cameron!" Lena was shaking me awake. "Story's online. The fart—it's out!"

I lurched upright and saw the wall clock indicated it was almost six a.m.

"Look!" She pointed at the screen as I got off the table and sat next to her to read the story.

HillZone had gotten to it first, with a 5:02 a.m. post time.

The first thing I saw was a grainy but unmistakable screenshot from the video. It was BIB, with a faint trace of a smile.

NEXT-IN-LINE SPEAKER ADMITS TO MURDER OF FORMER STAFFER? was the headline.

A less-reputable website touted *BIB'S FIB*.

The articles were scant and filled with caveats. But the video spoke for itself.

"No way," said Lena, who had popped open a laptop. "The *Washington Post*, the *New York Times*—they've picked up the story. And 'Congressman Billy Beck' is trending!"

All of the articles described the mysterious, overnight receipt of a video from "lasirenita." A couple noted the connection between the username and Ariel Lancaster. We scoured the Internet like seven-year-olds foraging for presents on Christmas morning, excitedly reading each article to each other.

A *ding* announced a text on the phone that Memo gave me. I picked it up to find a simple, grudging compliment:

Nice camera work, son.

Can't let you have all the fun, I responded. **Or the credit—don't want this to go to your head.**

Keep your eye on the news this morning was all he replied.

By ten a.m., a few blogs had declared Ariel's death a murder. One more identified the "accomplice" in the video as Chief of Staff Katie Campbell. They all called on local authorities to investigate the connection between the fatal accident and BIB. Nadia Zyne had released a strange denial of the seemingly undeniable evidence in the video. I was in the middle of reading HillZone's report on her claim, which was that the video was "fabricated." And then the page auto-refreshed and a new story claimed the top spot.

The headline screamed: *SENIOR CONGRESS-MAN ARRESTED FOR CONSPIRACY AND MURDER CHARGES*. Plus a picture of FBI agents escorting BIB from the Rayburn building, the congressman sporting the obligatory *this can all be explained* look.

Lena and I took turns reading particularly damning phrases from the article to each other. It was exciting and queasy all at once.

"'. . . but not the murder you're thinking about. Not the earlier allegations from this morning. This crime is six years old. . . .'"

"'. . . sufficient evidence that suggests Beck was behind the death of pharma king Wade Branson. Former Navy SEAL

Russell Meteer turned himself in to the FBI . . . ,'" read Lena. I scrolled down the page.

". . . even as authorities scramble to investigate a video that seems to show Beck's acknowledgment of a role in the death of Ariel Lancaster, former staffer of Beck's and daughter of fellow Congresswoman Nani Lancaster as well . . ." I couldn't believe the words I was reading. Rather, I couldn't believe that the words that had been in my head all summer were now on the screen. Shared with the world.

Lena started searching for related articles, which asserted: *PARTY SCRAMBLING TO IDENTIFY REPLACEMENT CANDIDATE FOR SPEAKER OF THE HOUSE AS ELECTION NEARS; WHO WAS WADE BRANSON?*; and, already, an op-ed about violence-prone Navy SEAL veterans.

Then, Lena found a statement from Nani Lancaster. *BEREAVED MOTHER AND BETRAYED COLLEAGUE REACTS TO BECK NEWS*, the headline announced.

A spokesperson for Lancaster had released the message: "Congresswoman Lancaster is troubled by the allegations against her colleague and friend Congressman Beck. She trusts that the justice system will accurately identify his innocence or guilt. She hopes the country will not allow one man's tragic indiscretions to distract from the critical work she was elected to do. She vows to do her part to unite the party and provide continuity in this time of transition."

"She knew," I said. "She basically said it to my face. She looked the other way because BIB was helping her out. Because they were political friends."

"What a loyal friend," she observed. "'One man's tragic indiscretions.' She might as well be condemning the guy. The only winner in this thing is her."

The last bombshell of the day was Katie Campbell, who turned herself in to the same police department BIB once claimed to "own." She copped to conspiracy for Ariel's murder and was apparently hashing out some deal for minimal prosecution in exchange for her unique POV on BIB's maneuverings over the past several years.

"I guess allegiance has its bounds," I said.

"I guess you're going to need a new mentor," commented Lena. She added, "Do you think it's safe for you to walk the streets again?"

"As long as you promise 'lasirenita' is going to remain anonymous."

"I learned all my tricks from our IT guy. It's watertight," she claimed.

"Continental socialite *and* competent hacker," I said. I wondered what else Lena was capable of.

"More than competent, my friend. But don't worry—I only use my powers for good," she replied with a mischievous smirk. "And don't call me a socialite."

"Well, then I guess I will be able to leave this building." I brushed some dried mud off my pants and added, "I should really get home and clean up. There is this party at Tortilla Coast tonight, though. End-of-summer thing. Wanna come?"

"Nothing like good-bad Mexican food to celebrate a fallen politician," she said.

We kissed good-bye, and I headed out of the embassy. I took a few steps toward my place and then stopped in my tracks; there was somewhere else I had to go first.

28

A metro ride to the Smithsonian stop got me within walking distance of the most upstaged monument in the city. I jogged toward the Jefferson Memorial, which nearly blinded me with its brightness in the morning light. The temple-like structure appeared bigger and more regal as I neared it.

A closer examination revealed a less exalted reality, however. There was a thick coating of dirt and trash around the rim of the monument. A custodian dutifully cleaned up the empty bottles and wrappers people had left behind the night before. He scraped away at persistent pieces of dried gum. But the coating of grime remained. The closer I looked, the filthier it got. When I wiped the outside wall with my hand, a brown-gray dust covered my fingers. I stepped back to look up at Mr. Jefferson himself. I wondered who his Katie Campbell was.

And if there were any Russell Meteers in his life—fighting and killing to protect his reputation.

No offense, Mr. Jefferson, but if you had the summer I've had, you would be asking the same questions.

I stepped down from the Jefferson Monument and across the parking area that led down to Second George. He was, predictably, all alone.

I sat next to him, dwarfed by his larger than life dimensions. Five minutes of silence passed before I noticed the note. It was lodged in the pages of the iron book Mr. Mason held ajar with his right index finger. I almost said *Excuse me* as I lifted the neatly folded piece of paper out from the book.

I recognized Katie's handwriting immediately.

C,

I figured you might stop by here.

I hated you for what you found this summer. You found the worst of me. You found the truth when it was too late for me.

But I mean it when I say that I found the best in you. And it reminded me why I started. And how far I've strayed.

Truth is, I'm tired of protecting, covering, hiding. . . . You spend enough time around darkness and it gets to you. In you.

So by the time you read this message, I'll be tearing down a man whom I have focused on building up for the past eight years.

And then I'll see if I can build up myself for a while.

That's part of the deal. I cooperate. Then I disappear.

I'm sorry. Your turn. Do it right.

To the Second Georges,

K

I sat there with Second George for almost an hour—thinking about this city that had built up many and destroyed others. And the countless, nameless people in the background who really made things happen—and didn't even get a second-rate monument to show for it.

I pulled out my wallet and held the tiny picture of my mom in my hand. Dad said it was one of her favorite pictures of herself, so she'd had some extra prints made. She was just a few years older in it than I was now.

"I think it's because her smile looks so real—that's just how she was," he would say.

But I knew better.

It was because this city would always be a part of her, and keeping those small government ID pictures was a way of reminding her of that. A reminder of her pre-Lagrima life. What she was truly capable of. What just might have been again in the future.

And even though she never returned to DC, I felt like I had been there that summer for both of us. Finishing what she started, making a difference. Even if it was in the last way I had expected.

I held the weathered, faded photo between my clasped hands and then slipped it down into the crack of Second George's book, replacing Katie's note. It was my monument now. Because even if there would be no official statue for my mom, Second George seemed like the kind of guy who would share the spotlight.

As I started to walk away from the statue, I called my dad. In the background, I heard the grainy, bass-less strains of Los Lonely Boys blasting from the blown-out car speakers. I've always hated "Heaven," but somehow the song sounded less offensive, even comforting in that moment.

"Cam, I see your boss got into a little bit of trouble!" he said. "Everything okay? Are they going to let you come home?"

"Yes," I answered. "Yes, I'm coming home."

"What are you up to?" he asked.

"Just checking in with some old friends before I leave," I responded, turning to look at Second George's face—and his new bookmark—one last time.

"Well, speaking of old friends, I convinced Berto to pick you up at the airport, even though he says you are . . . what was it he said?" My dad paused.

"A douchebag!" barked Rogelito from the background.

I guess the word was out.

"Well, after hearing how you've basically ignored your best friend, I might say you're more of a dick," said my dad.

"Dad! You're my dad. You can't call me that."

"I'm going to be calling you a lot worse for a while—get used to it," shouted Berto.

"Okay, okay, I've got some catching up to do," I admitted to my dad. "You know, remember where you came from but take the best of where you've been."

"Cameron, where did you hear that before?" he asked with a sudden, serious intent.

"I don't know, just came to my mind," I explained. "Why?"

"That's exactly what your mother said when she moved out west with me. 'Take the best of where you've been.'"

Like mother, like son.

29

Though everyone was talking about the BIB scandal at Tortilla
Coast the following Friday evening, there was no question why
they had assembled there: the big reveal of HillZone.com's
Fifty Hottest Staffers on Capitol Hill.

Though the inescapable business casual apparel made
the room look like Brooks Brothers goes to Acapulco, it was
a decent party. I looked around the restaurant and recognized
many of the faces from metro rides and hallways on the Hill.

"Look, it's no big deal, but the IT guy's roommate works at
HillZone, and he told me I'm on the list," said Hillary, literally
behind the backside of her hand and into Lena's ear. Lena
and I had been talking about her upcoming Princeton class
schedule when Hillary had appeared and spoken what were
her first words to Lena.

"Marielena Cruz," she said and extended her hand to Hillary.

Hillary leaned forward for an elaborate triple-cheek-kiss routine that was clearly foreign to Lena.

"Oh, I know who you are. I'm Hillary Wallace," she responded. "Cameron and I go way back, don't we, Cam? You snagged yourself one of the good ones, *chica*! And so did I. Zeph? Zeph!" She released her inner Lagriman with a hearty, ranch-hand shout and scanned the inside of the increasingly packed restaurant. "Anyway, awful day at the office. Investigators are still questioning half the staff. But Zeph and I got off easy. I mean, seriously, how is an intern going to stir up any trouble in one teensy summer?"

"Good question," I said as Lena did a knowing squeeze of my hand.

"Anyway, I'm sick of talking about it," Hillary continued. Then, back to Lena, "So I hear you're from Mexico. I love Mexico. Have you ever been to Mazatlan?"

She incorrectly invented a dramatic emphasis on the second syllable of the city name.

"I can't say that I have," replied Lena with another tight squeeze of my hand, which seemed to say *WTF?*

Hillary's eyes grew at the prospect of being able to tell someone about her family's cruise to Mazatlán during spring break of her senior year of high school. A server brought us a bowl of chips and salsa and took our drink orders. Hillary proceeded with arduous detail about her family's trip. Including the obligatory selfie of her with cornrowed hair, still saved to her phone.

"I look hideous, don't I?" Her affected pronunciation of the adjective rhymed with "Amadeus." "But it's secretly cute, right?" she pestered a decreasingly interested but graciously engaged Lena.

"Those are cornrows!" Lena opted for stating a fact.

"I know, it's crazy," she replied, as Zeph mercifully appeared to dilute the Hillary-ness of the conversation. "I'm so glad you like them. Zephaniah, Marielena likes my cornrow picture!"

"You can call me Lena," she said as she reached out to shake Zeph's hand.

"You can call me Zeph," he answered. "Apologies that we seem to be a little excited about this Top 50 thing. Ever since those investigators finally let us go this afternoon, it's all we've been talking about. By the way, they never asked for you, Cameron. Full-on roll call of the whole office, but they didn't ask for you. . . ."

I tensed up as Zeph started a conversation I didn't want to have. Hillary changed the subject, her interruption welcome for once. "Pictures of all fifty staffers will appear on the TV screens. And then the full article shows up online."

At that point, we saw Marcus parting the increasingly cramped crowds to reach our corner of the restaurant.

"Marcus," said Hillary as she looked him up and down. "What are you doing here?" Because Marcus doesn't belong at a 50 Hottest Staffers on Capitol Hill party, obviously.

"Just wanted to say good-bye to you guys," he answered. "And get out of the office. Weird day. Weird summer."

"How is everyone doing?" I asked.

"Refreshing their résumés," said Marcus. "But I was pretty much on my way out of there anyway."

"Just couldn't find a way to finish that literacy report?" I teased.

"Shut up," he said. "No, I've got a friend on the subcommittee on fisheries and wildlife, and there's a spot there, so I'm feeling pretty good about it."

"*That's* where the real power is," said Hillary with her particular brand of tactless sarcasm. No one responded.

"And you heard about Jigar?" Marcus inquired.

We hadn't.

He explained, "Went into this new fancy manicure bar for men yesterday. Get your barf bags out, because the place is called MAN-icure. Anyway, he got the whole deal, whatever they do in those places. And then when they gave him the bill, he told them that he works for the next Speaker of the House. The owner was not impressed. Word got back to Nadia, and now she's not giving him any references for a new job. I heard him talking to a state government on the phone today. A *state government.*"

"I can think of nothing worse," said Hillary. Followed by, "What about Nadia?"

"Nadia is now working for a fashion industry lobbyist firm on K Street. She left the office for lunch and then never came back. We saw the update on her LinkedIn profile a couple hours ago."

"That woman is invincible. A goddess," mused Hillary. "What's the name of the firm?" Always thinking about the next internship. . . .

"And Katie!" said Marcus. "Didn't see that coming. Evil henchman disguised as awkward, bossy, mean, but kind of cute—okay, beautiful eyes—and—"

"You had a thing for her," I said. "I knew it!"

"My mom always says I'm attracted to the bad girls," he mused as Hillary snort-laughed in judgment.

"Pretty good girl," I corrected him. "Bad situation."

"OMG," said Hillary, dramatic emphasis on each letter. "You're defending her! Did you have a thing for her too? When you have Salma Hayek's hot younger sister right here by your side?"

"Why is Salma Hayek the only attractive Mexican anyone can think of?" was Lena's reaction, before covering her mouth and apologizing with a quick "Sorry."

"She looked out for me," I answered Hillary. "Just a shame she didn't do the same for herself."

Suddenly, the multiple four-foot TV screens in the restaurant lit up with fifty thumbnail photos of that summer's chosen few. All eyes scanned the rows of pictures and eruptions of laughter and cheers ensued.

I noticed Hillary's squinty, stressed eyes searching through the pictures as Lena said, "You still need to pack. Are you ready to get out of here?"

"Yes," I answered as Zeph pulled me closer to him and pointed at the TV.

"Third row, second from left," he said.

"I know, I know. Congratulations, Hillary," I told him.

"No, buddy," he said. "It's *you*."

"Don't be ridicu . . . ," I said as I looked up at the screen and saw the picture from my ID badge, nestled between a couple glamour shots of fellow staffers. "What?"

"You have got to be kidding me," said Hillary, coming to the conclusion that this was not her year on the Top 50 list. "Who nominated you? A full-time staffer has to nominate an intern. How did this happen?"

"Let's be happy for Cam and his accomplishment," said Zeph.

The restaurant buzzed as everyone celebrated and debated that summer's picks. Marcus pulled up the list online and read the text for my entry to us. "First time on the list, intern Cameron Carter has shown promise not just for his looks, but also for his insatiable curiosity and proactive work ethic this summer. Don't let this country kid fool you. He enjoys edamame and a good '90s cover band at Kramerbooks. Favorite monument? The Washington Monument observation deck, preferably after dark. Just don't ask for his ID."

My face flushed red as Marcus finished the paragraph. I looked to Lena, who innocently stared straight ahead, a sly smile creeping up on her face. Claiming a "jalapeño emergency," a teary-eyed Hillary led Zeph to the bathroom. Marcus lied that he'd "be right back," leaving Lena and me in the middle of the boisterous crowd.

"Congratulations," she said, as we clinked Diet Cokes.

"How did you . . . ," I asked.

"Stop asking questions." She smiled. "I know people. Haven't you figured that out yet?"

"But . . . ," I replied, incredulous and a little embarrassed at the dubious honor.

"Shut up. You earned it."

I motioned toward the door with my eyes and she followed me out. A couple of staffers held up a friend, who whined, "Oh no, I'm gonna barf, and this is my mom's St. John suit."

"Romantic place for a good-bye," Lena said to me.

"What?" I asked. "I'm not going to see you again before

I leave?" I felt that preemptive homesick feeling as I realized this was not how I had envisioned saying good-bye.

"Some immigration conference in San Diego that I need to help my dad with. Remember? I have a day job too!"

"But I'm supposed to surprise you by taking you back to the Washington Monument after hours! And then to all these places we need to go together—Eastern Market breakfast, U Street jazz clubs, that other Smithsonian museum by the airport . . . I was supposed to be giving you a half dozen Baked and Wired cupcakes. They say they're much better than the ones at Georgetown Cupcakes. . . ."

She was the kind of girl for whom dinner and a movie just wouldn't do. The kind of girl who made me want to do more, see more. The kind of girl who made me see more in myself. And I was beginning to mourn all the cool dates we would never be able to go on. And the country that would soon separate us.

"I guess you've been doing all kinds of research since you arrived. You're sounding like a local. I *have* always wanted to go to the other air and space museum," she admitted. "But the summer's over, Cam."

"Don't say that," I said, reaching for her hand. *"Don't say that.* This isn't how I thought we'd say good-bye. There was a time when I just wanted the summer to be over. And now I don't want it to end. I don't want you and me to end."

"Same place, next summer?" She smiled, trying to soften the blow of our approaching separation.

"Just watch out for guys with nice watches at Princeton," I teased. "Your Cartier Kryptonite . . ."

"You and that watch. . . ." She laughed. "If you didn't look so cute, I'd hit you right now. Okay, I'll hit you anyway."

She did. A pretty formidable punch, actually, which I answered with a bear hug.

"I think you've ruined me for Princeton guys, Cameron Carter. You've made quite an impression. On me and this town."

"You mean you aren't going to be able to find another guy who brought down a ranking congressman in two and a half months?"

"Don't go talking like you did it alone," she replied and kissed me. As I kissed back, headlights started to flash at us. It was Oscar, parked across the street and waiting to pick her up. She shot a look of annoyance, amusement, and rage his way, and the flashing stopped.

"That's my . . ." She started to explain.

". . . your ride," I said. "I don't think those Princeton guys are going to appreciate this chaperone of yours everywhere."

"Oh, don't worry, he's not coming with me." She laughed. "I'll just be a normal girl there."

She stepped toward the car and then darted back at me for

a last, quick kiss. Oscar honked the horn. We both laughed, and she crossed the street.

As she closed the car door, I shouted, "Lena!"

She rolled down the window and looked back at me, trying to inconspicuously wipe away a tear. Oscar started to ease the hulking black SUV down the street.

"I'm sorry, but that's not going to happen," I told her. "You'll never be a normal girl."

30

Zeph and Hillary were still asleep when I left the apartment for the last time. Given the Top 50 controversy, I thought it best to give Hillary some breathing room and not wake them up to say good-bye. We could reunite in the Bay Area sometime.

My rolling suitcase banged down each step of the building, and I helped the driver lift it into the deep trunk of the taxi. During the forty-five-minute drive to Dulles, an anxious man and domineering woman went at each other on the radio. They were speculating about the BIB scandal—what it meant for the party, the country, the world. The woman suggested that there could be more deaths. The man wondered if there were other accomplices beyond a penitent hitman. And who was this "lasirenita"?

"Radio okay with you?" asked the driver as we drove across the Potomac River.

"Sure," I instinctively said. The couple went on about poor Nani Lancaster—betrayed by her mentor just after her daughter dies.

"Look for Lancaster to really step up after the elections. Her future as a leader in the party is in the bag," the woman declared.

"Actually," I told the driver, "can you just turn it off?" He obliged, and all we heard was an occasional quick ripple of the tires rolling over cracks in the road. As we headed north on the George Washington Memorial Parkway, I looked back. The Lincoln and Washington memorials gleamed white against the mostly green and leafy landscape of the city. I thought about the grime that was hidden in the cracks of those structures. I thought about the buses of tourists who emptied out into the Capitol building and the Smithsonians. They'd take their pictures and see Ford's Theater and maybe even meet a photogenic congressman—and then go home humming the national anthem under their breath. I envied them. I thought about Katie and where they'd taken her—where she'd end up.

And I felt lucky to be getting out of the city alive.

But mostly and oddly, I thought about Lagrima, and how good it would feel to mow a lawn again. Back and forth, back and forth. Until the patch of grass was done, and I could call it a day.

• • •

I saw my dad before he saw me. He was wearing a jean jacket, hands in pockets. Berto stood at his side, texting on his phone. But my dad looked attentive, restless. The same way he would look when I got off the bus from summer camp—waiting to see me and confirm that I was safe. I was the only immediate family he had. How could it be any other way?

They stood at the bottom of a long escalator in the arrivals area of the Oakland airport. The instant he saw me, his face changed from anxious to Sunday-morning chill. Like he didn't want me to know he was worried. Like he'd known I was going to be fine all along.

"Welcome home, son," he said as we shook hands. After a summer of too-smooth and aggressive handshakes, his craggy hands and just-firm-enough grip felt like, well, home.

"So one of us has to fly three thousand miles just to have a conversation?" chided Berto.

"I guess so, you idiot." Our cupped hands made a popping noise as we gave each other a quick hug. "And I know, I suck."

"What was that? I didn't hear you," Berto taunted.

"I suck," I said a little louder.

"Oh yes, okay. And just so we're clear—tell me why you suck?" He assumed the tone of a TV interviewer interrogating a disgraced celebrity.

I played along. "Because I moved to a big city and it kind of took over my life, even though I didn't really have a choice."

"Continue . . . ," said Berto after a pause, taking pleasure in my contrition.

"Dude, are we really doing this?" I said.

"Yes, we are," he said calmly.

"Okay." I cleared my throat. "And I forgot everyone and everything that's really important to me . . . especially my dearest pal Humberto, who for the record did something strikingly similar to me on the night of junior prom when he said I couldn't join the twelve-couple cool-kid group date he was a part of, and the only reason he was invited was because that cheerleader found that wrestler cheating on her with a flag girl, so she needed someone at the last minute. What was her name anyway . . . Paisley?"

"Kayzlee," said Berto under his breath. "And you're slightly off topic."

"Kayzlee," I repeated loudly as I nodded my head. I noticed my dad look at his watch as we continued the playful dive back into the ruts of an old fight renewed. "You could easily have fit two more people in that Hummer limo."

"It was a fire code thing," said Berto. "And anyway—your counterpoint is noted, and your apology is accepted."

"And your brush with high school elites nearly destroyed you and everything you cherished," I said, trying not to break a smile.

"How was your flight?" my dad interrupted. He led us toward the baggage claim with a comfortably mundane change of conversation.

Berto revealed that his mother was making a welcome lunch for us the next day, and I said, "You have no idea how good that sounds."

As we neared the conveyor belt of the baggage claim, I thought I saw Lena sitting nearby. In one of her signature long dresses, cinched at the waist with a broad brown belt. The look-alike then stood up and walked toward us, wheeling a tiny suitcase behind her. She looked a lot like Lena because she was Lena. Standing in front of me. In the Oakland airport.

"Can I hitch a ride to Lagrima?" she asked. "Someone once told me it's a very nice place."

"What are you doing here?" I asked as my dad and Berto tried to contain their smiles. "How did you get here?"

"I got in a couple hours ago. San Diego conference is on autopilot, and I had a few days to kill. I've never been to Lagrima before, so I thought to myself, *Why not fly up there?* And your friend Humberto proved very helpful with the timing and logistics," she said as Berto savored my complete surprise.

I laughed in amazement. "You what?" I looked at Berto.

"You have a troubling pattern of underestimating my ability to find people and make things happen," said Lena. "But I guess that's all I can expect from one of the Fifty Hottest Staffers on Capitol Hill. . . ."

"Excuse me?" asked my dad.

"You mean, he didn't tell you? Cameron was selected as . . . ," Lena gladly began to explain.

"No, no, no. Stop there," I said. My dad would not appreciate the frivolous honor, and Berto already had enough to tease me about. "Let's get a snack before we hit the road?"

We drove to a sports bar near the airport, with Barry Manilow's "Looks Like We Made It" serenading us the whole way there. We entered the bar to find that someone had turned the channel to a news network. Images of Capitol Hill corridors flashed across the screen—familiar and yet somehow a universe away.

As we ordered food from the server, Lena asked if there was any edamame on the menu.

In response, my dad, Berto, and the server said, "What's that now?" "Excuse me?" and "Eda-what?" respectively.

"It's Cameron's favorite," replied Lena.

Acknowledging the less-informed taste buds in our presence, I looked at Lena and said, "See, it's not just me."

My dad shrugged his shoulders and went on. "Well, you guys can order anything you want. Actually, order three servings of anything you want. Lunch is on me."

"Dad, you don't have to . . . ," I said. Our family went Dutch at restaurants. When my dad took me to restaurants at all.

"I *could* handle three Philly cheesesteaks," said Berto.

"No, I insist," he said. "I was waiting to tell you in person, Cameron . . ."

And then it hit me: *The CVSU contract.*

"You remember that college job I lost a while ago?" he asked.

"Yes," I said, trying my best to seem surprised.

"Well, I got a call yesterday, and they want me to do it. We got the CVSU contract, buddy. We got it."

Memo did it.

"Congratulations," said Lena.

"Dad, that's incredible! There's no one who would do a better job. I'm really proud of you."

"Couldn't have done it without your help," he said.

That's one way of putting it, I thought. Though I didn't plan to tell Dad about my extra nudge from across the country that summer.

"Okay, so are we still getting three of everything?" asked Berto.

I heard a familiar voice behind me on TV. It was Nani Lancaster—her voice a little bolder, more upbeat than when we'd last spoken. Perhaps just less drunk. But it was terrifying, all the same. I turned to look at her on TV. I was the only person in the restaurant watching. The ticker at the bottom of the screen read, "Rep Lancaster speaks out as former colleague Rep Beck resigns from Congress."

She looked confident, intense, and sharp. Ready. "My fellow Americans, only our judicial system and the Almighty will judge Congressman Beck. Thank you for your support and trust in these trying times for my family and our government. You have shown me that the American people care most about progress. We don't dwell on scandal. . . ."

Of course you don't want anyone to dwell on this scandal.

"We don't point fingers. We move forward together. And God willing, this November, we will—"

The channel abruptly changed to a football game, and multiple bar patrons erupted in cheers.

I heard a familiar dull *ding* in my backpack. It took me an extra second to realize that I still had the flip phone from Memo. It was the first time I realize he had not retrieved it from me before I'd left.

I unzipped my bag to see that there was a new message:

Hey, son. Could I interest you in another assignment?

I closed the phone and buried it deep within my backpack.

Lena asked intelligent questions about landscaping, and my dad was happy to talk with her about his favorite subject.

I smiled at her, and she held my hand. Berto's eyes were fixed on the football game.

I pulled my hand away from Lena to open my backpack again. I dug for the flip phone. The message was still there.

My fingers hovered over the keypad as I started to write back.

Epilogue

The man opens the door to a small room and sees the woman watching a big-screen TV. Nani Lancaster is talking about the Almighty and elections and partnering with America.

"Can you believe this?" she says to him, her open hand pointing at the TV. "Filling the vacuum. I called this one."

She sips piping-hot tea from a weathered UVA mug.

"You know she called Cameron into her office. Freaked him out good," he says.

"Well, she didn't scare him away completely," she says, picking up a picture frame of a young boy and holding it in her hand.

"He did a great job, you know," he says. "When you carried out a pedestrian hit-and-run in front of the Mexican embassy, it didn't hurt, but he did most of the work. You were right. He was perfect for the job. And I told him you'd be proud—just like you told me to."

"I'm good at making car accidents look real," she says. "And you're good at being Memo Adair."

They sit in silence as Lancaster reads an Abraham Lincoln quote. The woman opens a cabinet and pulls out a thick file with a sticker on it that reads, NANI LANCASTER.

"Does the secure mobile line still work?" she asks.

He activates the line and tells her she can text anything she wants. "But remember, he thinks it's me who's been on the other end all along. And you're going to have a tough time getting him back here. I think he wants to stay in Lagrima."

"I thought that too, once," she replies.

She hesitates for a minute and then types:

"Hey, son."

Her son.

"Could I interest you in another assignment?"

ACKNOWLEDGMENTS

First of all, thank you Neil Gaiman for this: "If you only write when you're inspired, you may be a fairly decent poet, but you'll never be a novelist because you're going to have to make your word count today and those words aren't going to wait for you whether you're inspired or not. . . . The process of writing can be magical. . . . Mostly it's a process of putting one word after another."

Fortunately, my sources of inspiration were never too faint or far away:

Thank you to Washington, DC, for being my first thrilling, sour, indelible, heady taste of life beyond the town I grew up in. This story might resemble a burn book, but I promise it is a love letter.

Thank you, Margaret Stohl, for the spark.

Much gratitude to the spectacular Richard Abate and Rachel Kim—and the whole 3 Arts team—for the motivating mix of candor and genuine care.

To everyone at Simon & Schuster, the customized attention and support I've felt from you completely belies what one might expect of a giant global publishing company. Thank you to my editor, David Gale; Amanda Ramirez; Justin Chanda;

ACKNOWLEDGMENTS

Katrina Groover; Greg Stadnyk; Lauren Hoffman; Chrissy
Noh; Lisa Moraleda; Anna Jarzab; and Michelle Leo.

Many thanks for perfectly timed insights and encourage-
ment from Julie Scheina, Jared Stone, Morgan James, Jessica
Kantor, Sarah Burnes, and Sarah Stevenson Johnson.

Thank you to the English and Government public school
teachers from whom I had the great fortune of learning: Miriam
Frye, Ellen Klopf, Linda Chrabas, Barbara McBride, Ronna
Rutishauser, Ken Adair, and Chris Walker. There's really
no adequate way to acknowledge your generous lifetimes of
investment in others, but this former student did listen to a
thing or two you said.

Thank you, Tom and Diane Stone, for instilling in me
your love of storytelling in all forms—including the singular
story of your own lives.

Finally and fundamentally: Karissa, you are my best
friend, my first reader, the inspiration for all of the grace and
love in anything I write, and the real reason anyone is holding
this book in their hands.